SEARCHING DRAGON

DRAGON RISING SERIES, BOOK 2

TRUDI JAYE

WWW.TRUDIJAYEWRITES.COM

Hi! My name is Trudi Jaye, and I've got a secret.

A secret society, that is.

Especially designed for people like you who love reading my books, the Trudi Jaye Secret Society is a place filled with magic and laughter, and most of all... free stories.

Everyone who joins the society is given access to an ancient tome full of the stories, novellas, bonus epilogues, and deleted scenes from all the different Trudi Jaye series.

Called **The Shadow Archives,** you can access it by heading to my website and joining the secret society...

Join my Secret Society today... if you dare!

Searching Dragon (Dragon Rising Series, book 2)

Published 25 November 2016 by Star Media Ltd

Copyright © Star Media Ltd, 2016

Cover design: PCTC Design

With love to Peter and Zoey for making the journey such a delight...

1

W e've been driving for hours.

The only reason I know this is because last time I was awake it was light, and now it's dark outside the little blue van that my father—or more likely Si —organized for us.

My dreams confuse me; full of flashes of light and people chasing me, so at first, I'm relieved I've woken up.

Then it's like a tidal wave of memories washes over me and I close my eyes again, trying not to drown in them.

I'm the last of the dragons.

On the run from powerful enemies.

And I have no idea if I can survive the change on my own.

I take careful breaths, trying to stay calm. But I'm lying here half slumped over at a weird angle. If I could feel more of my body, I'd probably have pins and needles in really uncomfortable places. Sleep is crusted at the corners of my eyes, and I have a pounding headache.

There's nothing I can do about any of these things.

As it is, I can barely open my eyelids.

Black dots appear in front of my eyes, and blood pounds in my ears.

I've never felt more vulnerable, not even when Vincent locked me at the bottom of a water chamber with no air and no way out.

Seth's in the driver's seat beside me, his eyes focused on the road like he's looking for treasure in the darkness.

Or maybe a needle in a haystack?

His hair is tousled, as if he's been running his hands through it, and when he glances down at me, his eyes are bloodshot.

He gives me a half smile. "You're awake. You okay?"

I try to move my mouth to say something, but all that comes out is a low moan.

I can't speak or move.

Despite the fact that my father assured me it's all part of the transformation process, I gasp in breaths like the air is about to run out.

I'm completely trapped.

No way to communicate, no way to save myself.

Seth looks between me and the road then back again. "Mei, it's okay. It's going to be okay. Just take a deep breath." He reaches out and grasps my hand in his.

His touch eases my panic, and I manage to take a few deep breaths.

I'm not completely helpless—Seth is here with me, and Si and my father will catch up to us soon. Together we'll be able to solve this mess.

I'm not alone any more.

My pulse returns to normal, and I manage to slow down the whirlwind of thoughts twisting through my head.

I blink twice.

"That's better. We're almost there." He turns back to the road, but his other hand clenches on the steering wheel.

My attempt to nod is a minuscule movement of my head.

I don't even know if Seth can tell I moved at all.

I look outside, realizing I can see better than usual in the dark night. I can tell it's night, but shapes and colors are still visible. Buildings and other cars flash by, and I notice every little detail.

"We're going to be fine. They didn't follow us." He hesitates and then glances at me again. "The coordinates your father gave us were wrong. They were in the sea."

He takes a deep breath. "You were asleep, so I decided to keep going and pick up the box from my brother. I figure it might have something that will help us."

I try to understand what he's telling me, but I feel like my brain is struggling to find purchase in a giant bowl of slippery goo.

Through sheer force of will, I stay composed, despite the thoughts raging through my head, crossing over each other and making me wish I could find an off-button. Everything has spiraled out of control so fast, I almost don't know which way is up.

Taking a deep breath, I force myself to concentrate on just one thing: the wooden box. Before we went to see my father, we mailed the box to Seth's brother. I'm not sure why we did it, other than instinct. We had a feeling that something might go wrong, and we didn't want the box to fall into the wrong hands.

Lucky we did, because it *would* have fallen into the wrong hands.

Going for the box makes sense; I need to find a dragon

nest, or I'm not going to survive the change. The box is the only other place that might have useful information.

But a nasty little voice of doubt rises in my head.

If the coordinates my father had were wrong, what chance is there that the box will tell us something more?

My breaths start coming short and sharp again, and I close my eyes, trying to ignore the terrible nagging fear.

I have to focus on what I can control.

Seth's right, we need the carved box that Jeff left me. I need to know more about being a dragon.

Emotion whirls through me, bright and glad and fearful all at once.

I'm a dragon.

When we looked through the box last time, I was pretty convinced I wasn't a dragon—or at least I didn't know—which made the information inside less valuable to me.

Right now? I wish I'd memorized every damn line of text inside that box.

I peer at Seth. Does he still have the ring? I didn't dare ask for it back after what I did last time I wore it. And I have no way of knowing if the Supernatural Intelligence Group took it off him when they captured us.

It's not like I can ask right now.

"We're almost at Newport News," Seth assures me. "But we can't just turn up in the middle of the night. My brother won't look kindly on us waking up his family. We'll have to wait in the van a while."

He's chatting at me, his words going a mile a minute. It's the most I've heard him say at one time. I probably look like hell; I guess he's scared I'm going to die.

Me too.

"My brother, he's pretty opinionated," Seth says. "We... uh... We don't always get along that well. I might have to leave you in the van, because I don't know how I'll explain you to him otherwise. I feel like I'm kidnapping you as it is." He glances over at me and makes a face. "How would the conversation go? 'Oh yeah, Mike, she's completely unable to move any part of her body. Why? Well, it's because she's about to turn into a dragon.' Not likely."

I wish I could speak, to tell him it's fine and that I don't mind.

To say anything at all.

He seems a little wild at the moment, like he's on the verge of falling apart, but he's holding it together by a hairsbreadth.

He hasn't told me much about his brother, other than that he works at the massive shipbuilding company that employs a large proportion of people in the city.

I'm beginning to think the mild disagreement I'd been imagining might be slightly less than the truth.

"I'll try to be fast. In and out. We don't have much time."

I nod again. At least in my head. My body doesn't actually move much.

We drive in silence for a while.

"You're going to be fine, Mei. We'll laugh about this when it's all over."

His eyes meet mine. The wildness is still there.

I want to lift my hand to cover his, to give him the comfort he's given me.

To let him know I'm here.

Nothing moves.

I can't help it—tears well in my eyes and a single drop falls over the edge and rolls down my cheek.

The salty water burns my skin as it travels down my face.

I've never experienced anything like this before in my life.

I'm here, I can see and understand what is going on, but I can't move a muscle.

I can't *participate.*

Seth reaches out and wipes away the tear. "Don't cry, Mei. You're going to be fine." He grasps my hand again.

My brain sends signals down to my hand, and I try to grip him a little tighter. I don't know if it works.

Now that I can't speak, the words I want to say are burning themselves into my brain. He's been there for me since he started. He followed me into every single place I dragged him.

We've known each other for less than a month, and I already can't imagine life without him.

I don't know what that means, but I know I'm glad he's the one who's here with me.

We're on the freeway, and signs of the city we're approaching are all around us. I try to ask how far it is, but nothing happens. Tears well again, but my pride won't let me actually cry again. I don't like the fact that I did it before.

I've never been to Newport News. It's the kind of place Jeff always avoided because of the huge human military presence. *You never know what they know and don't know about supers*, he always said.

Imagine what would happen if they discovered that dragons are real. I would be an amazing prize for them, I'm sure. What kind of things would the human military do with that information? Would they do tests on me? Keep me caged up like the Earthbound? Would they try to use me against other countries? I shudder at the thought. Maybe they'd just be afraid and try to kill me.

They would be just another group to add to the growing list of people who want me dead.

Seth gets off the freeway and takes the van on a twisting

route through the suburbs. Eventually he stops outside a brick-and-tile home on a street filled with similar houses.

He cuts the engine and just sits there, staring at the house.

"It's my family home. My dad travelled a bit, and my mom refused to join in, despite marrying into the military. So she stayed here, and my dad came back whenever he could. When he retired, they moved to Florida and gave the house to my brother."

This is where he grew up.

I look at the house through new eyes, greedily taking in the big oak tree in the front yard, the toys scattered around, and the swing set visible on one side.

This is what staying in one place looks like.

"We'll wait here until it's light enough to go in." Seth glances at his watch.

I would nod if I could, but I can't, so I just slump to one side and close my eyes.

I'm half asleep, dreaming of fire and death, when a loud thump makes the van shudder.

My eyes flick open, and adrenaline rushes through my body, even though I'm completely helpless.

Seth's door is yanked open. The overhead light goes on, blinding me momentarily.

A big, broad shape crowds the doorway, the spell web pulsing wildly over the outline. One enormous hand is holding a handgun pointed directly at Seth's chest.

Inside my head, I'm screaming.

2

"Who the hell are you, and why are you sitting outside my house?" a gravelly voice barks at us.

Seth has his hands in the air, palms out. "Dammit, Mike, it's me, Seth. We're just waiting for it to get light."

The handgun wavers and then lowers. "Fuck, bro. Tracey has been freaking out. She's convinced you're about to rob us." He checks me out, his sharp eyes taking in every detail. "Who's that? Why's she sitting funny?"

"Long story." Seth shrugs, as if that covers everything. "We've come to collect the box I mailed to you."

"What box?" Mike looks genuinely confused, and my heart sinks.

"Stop messing with me, Mike. I know it's here. We need it." Seth's voice is hard, and he is angrier than I've ever seen him. I watch his brother and eventually see it. A little spark tells me Seth is right. Mike's putting on a good act, but he has the box. Relief shivers through me.

"You coming in? Trace would never forgive you if you didn't say hi to her and the kids." He shifts back, and I get a better look at him. He's got short jet black hair and eyes so dark, they're almost black as well. Despite his broad shape, his features are angular, sharp...intelligent.

"We're in a hurry. I'll say hi, grab the box, and leave again."

Mike jerks the gun toward me. "What about her? You not going to bring your girlfriend in?"

Seth shakes his head. "She needs her rest. She's not feeling well, and can't walk very far. That's why I need to hurry."

His brother shakes his head right back at Seth. "You can't leave her in the car, man. That's just plain rude. And dangerous. You never know what kind of lowlifes are roaming the neighborhood, especially if she can't walk. I'll carry her in, if you're not strong enough to do it yourself."

I watch the emotions swim across Seth's face, fascinated by the way his brother is able to manipulate him so easily. I've never seen anything like it, even from Jeff.

"I'll carry her in," Seth relents, his voice terse. "But we can't stay long, Mike. And Mei isn't well. She can't speak or move, so don't expect anything of her."

Mike's eyes widen. "What the hell did you do to her, bro?"

"Nothing," Seth snaps, clearly at the end of his patience. "She's going to be fine. We just need that box, and we'll be on our way."

Seth comes around to the passenger seat and unclicks the seat belt. My whole body slides over, and my face crashes into Seth's shoulder. I'm completely unable to stop myself. I want to cry out, but no sound emerges from my frozen lips.

"I'm sorry, Mei," Seth murmurs in my ear. "He's like a dog with a bone. He won't let it go if I don't bring you in."

I hang limply in his arms, my head leaning against his chest. I want to say something, but nothing comes out, and Seth walks steadily toward the front door, following his brother's footsteps.

Inside, the house is friendly and cozy. Noisy too. Several children of varying sizes are running around, yelling and chasing each other. It takes me a few moments to work out how many there actually are—four. It seemed like double that number at first. I've never seen anything like it.

Seth places me carefully on a sofa in the lounge. He smooths one hand down the side of my cheek, a soft touch that I barely feel. I want to move closer, to get more of him.

"Stay here, don't move," he whispers with a wry smile, his hazel eyes staring intently into mine. They look more fiery today than usual.

My head lolls back on the sofa and I wish I could make a smart comment in reply. Or even just give him a slap. A glare would do.

He obviously sees something in my eyes, because he lets out a tiny snort of laughter, his eyes crinkling in the first sign of real amusement since I woke in the car.

"I know, I know. Terrible joke." He glances toward an arched doorway into what looks like the kitchen and then back at me. "I'll be quick. We'll be on the road again soon." He heads through the arch and out of sight.

A woman's loud screech is followed by a tumble of words so fast I can't make them out. I gather she's telling him off for parking outside, scaring her to death, not visiting more often, and in general not allowing her to bake him more cakes. His sister-in-law seems interesting.

"Now where's this girl Mike's been telling me about? Why didn't you bring her in here?"

"She wouldn't be able to sit up in here, Tracey. She's in the other room."

The sound of determined footsteps is the only warning I get before a curvy woman bursts into the lounge. She has curly blonde hair and a smiling face with unusual eyes. She stops short in front of me, and her eyes narrow. I look up at her and my heart falters for a moment. She's completely covered by the spell web, and it's glowing bright and strong. She's a not only a full super, she's also really powerful.

And not just any super. She's one of the sharp-eyed eagle shifters who often see more than they're supposed to. Jeff always swore when he recognized their distinctive features—golden-hazel eyes, a sharp nose, and slightly pointed ears. *They're more trouble than they're worth*, he always said.

This one seems like she's going to be trouble. She touches my cheek, turning my face so I'm looking directly into her eyes. "You're that girl they've been looking for, aren't you?"

Even if I'd been able to, I wouldn't have moved. Her eyes are mesmerizing. Their depths swirl in a constant motion that makes me want to tell her everything I know. It's lucky I can't talk.

I glance desperately to one side, trying to will Seth to come into the room with us.

I'd known his brother would have some supernatural powers, given Seth's patchy spell web covering. I'd been expecting something similarly patchy and vague. The fact that Mike's spell web glows strong and bright over his entire body is a surprise, but not unheard-of. That he's married to another full super? It indicates knowledge of the supernatural world that isn't helpful.

As far as the supernatural community is concerned, I'm

some kind of outlaw, a fugitive from justice. And there is nothing an eagle likes more than justice and truth. Suddenly the decision to come here seems stupid.

Where the hell is Seth?

The eagle—Tracey—leans in closer. "What's the matter with you?" she asks. "Why aren't you moving?"

I blink. It's all I'm capable of.

Seth bursts back into the room and glances from Tracey to me. "What's the matter?" he asks.

"What have you gotten yourself tangled up in, Seth?" Tracey asks, her arms crossed over her chest. At least she isn't focused on me anymore.

"What do you mean?"

"She's in trouble. And if you're with her, so are you."

Seth shakes his head. "It's not what you think."

"How do you know what I think?" She takes a step toward Seth. "Except for the fact that you've brought a dangerous criminal into my *home*, introduced her to my *kids*."

From her tone, Tracey thinks I'm worse than bringing home a serial killer.

"She's not dangerous, Tracey. And it's not as bad as you're making out."

"There have been reports all night, bulletins saying to lock our doors and not to let strangers come near us. Because of her." Tracey points one long, shaking finger at me. If I'd been able to move, I would have stood up right then and left. But this is Seth's family. He doesn't see that Tracey has already decided about me. He needs to explain what's happening to them, to make them understand.

"I wouldn't endanger the kids, Tracey. I would never do anything that might hurt the kids."

It's only then I notice that the sounds of the house, of

kids running and playing, have stopped. Mike seems to have disappeared as well, leaving Tracey to face Seth. The silence feels heavy, ominous, and I know something is wrong.

I try to move, to talk, to tell Seth that we're in trouble. But I can't. Nothing moves, no sound emerges. I start blinking, trying to get Seth to notice the flickering of my lashes. But his eyes are focused on Tracey. He's desperate to convince her.

I hear the cars before Seth does. The squealing tires as they turn the corner onto the street gives them away. The flashing lights draw his attention as they screech to a halt outside.

Seth turns toward the window and then back to Tracey. "What have you done?" he whispers, his face going pale.

"What's right," she answers staunchly.

"You have no idea what you've done. Those people out there will kill us. Kill me. They are not on our side, on the side of supernaturals." Seth rushes toward me and gathers me into his arms.

Behind him, Tracey stands motionless, hesitating for the first time.

"Get me the box, Tracey." Seth's voice is hard, uncompromising.

"I don't—"

"Get me the fucking box!" Seth's voice slices like a knife through the air.

Tracey jerks and runs back into the kitchen. At first I think she's gone for good, but she returns with the carved box in her hands.

"I'm going out through the tunnel. If you have any love for me left inside you, it will remain a family secret." Seth doesn't even glance at Tracey before storming toward the hallway stairs. I look back and see the shock on her face.

He pushes his way into the cupboard under the stairs, shutting the door firmly behind us. It's tight and awkward and musty-smelling. Outside I can hear sirens and more cars squealing to a halt on the road. My muscles twitch painfully as my body tries to react to my fear and adrenaline. Seth moves toward the back of the cupboard, accidentally knocking my head on a couple of coats and something harder that feels like it might be a hockey stick.

He faces the back wall, moving me around in his arms so he can use one hand. I can't see what he does with the handle, but a door clicks open, and seconds later we're in a dark tunnel heading down into the earth below us. It's even more musty smelling in here, the air so heavy and damp I can feel it on my skin. When he shuts the door, we're in complete darkness.

"I don't think she'll say anything. But just in case she does, we have to hurry," whispers Seth, his voice ragged. He's still really mad.

I blink, even though I know he can't see me. I hope he's right about his family not giving us away. I'm still trying to figure out where we're going and why there's a secret family tunnel.

Seth strides down the sloping tunnel like he can see in the pitch black. Maybe he can. This night has been so full of surprises about Seth and his family, I'm starting to realize I don't know anything about him. But then I hear him counting paces under his breath. It's not magic or special powers that's helping him down this tunnel so quickly, it's just math. Si would appreciate that.

At around fifteen paces, we come up against a wall. Seth turns confidently to the left and holds me tight against him as he clicks open another door. I take a deep breath and his spicy gunpowder scent fills my nostrils. My heart pounds in my chest, the beat echoing through my whole body. It's the only part of me still able to move.

Seth shifts sideways to get us both through the door and then closes it behind us. There's a small shelf on the wall, and he angles himself so he can grab a torch from it. "I hope they've been changing the batteries like they're supposed to," he growls.

I want to ask why on Earth his family has a series of hidden tunnels under their house and why he thinks Tracey won't tell our pursuers that we're down here, despite clearly having called them. I want to know what the hell's going on that I'm missing. I want to yell and scream and kick and punch.

But I just lie in his arms, more useless than I have ever been in my entire life.

3

———

At the end of the tunnel, a set of keys hangs on the wall—Seth grabs them awkwardly with one hand and pushes open the metal door with his shoulder. We emerge into a garage with three cars and a motorbike parked neatly inside.

Seth doesn't even hesitate, heading straight for the middle vehicle, a dark blue four-wheel drive. His hands are gentle as he carefully places me in the passenger seat.

He buckles up my seat belt and puts the wooden box at my feet. As he closes the door, I slowly slide to the side, ending up on a weird lean. No matter what I do, I can't move a muscle, or even tell Seth there's a problem. I try to scream in frustration—nothing but a low moan emerges from my mouth. It feels like there's a hole being burned inside my chest, and I don't know if it's part of changing into a dragon, or just my frustration and anger at not being able to do anything.

Seth climbs into the cab on the other side, pressing a button on the keys, before turning the ignition.

The garage door silently opens behind us.

I can't see what's outside, but we've walked a fair distance from the house. Still, I prepare myself for a speeding car chase in which I'll be knocked around like a child's doll. My breathing starts to get a little ragged as I imagine the sharp twists and turns and what it might do to my unresponsive lump of a body.

As we reverse out the driveway, I catch a glimpse of other houses, but no cars or sirens. We must have gone to the street *behind* the house somehow. Again, I wonder exactly why Seth and his family need a secret exit and getaway cars. It's a mystery I'm gonna be compelled to solve—once I can move again.

We're driving down a leafy suburban street and away from Seth's old family home. My heart is pumping in my chest, and sweat is dripping down my neck and back. It itches, little pin pricks of irritation that I can't touch no matter how much I desperately wish I could. He's driving like a grandmother, probably going exactly the speed limit.

The leather on the seat sticks to the skin on my arm and helps me to hold my position, half slumped next to Seth. I keep waiting for sirens to wail behind us and for Seth to slam his foot on the accelerator. He's concentrating on driving his eyes flicking to the rear vision mirror, like he's expecting a car chase any second as well.

Before long, we're cruising along the freeway. After a while, I let out a long breath. We seem to have escaped.

Seth glances over at me, his face serious. "I really thought it would be safe to go see them. I can't believe they called the SIG."

I blink twice to let him know it's fine, that he couldn't have known. Hell, *I* would have called the SIG for help a couple of weeks ago. Now the world has gone mad and they're hunting me down like I'm a killer.

Seth turns back to the road and keeps driving.

There's a clock on the dash, and I watch the glowing numbers click over from one number to the next for a long time. There's nothing else I can do. We've been driving for about an hour; the sun is shining through the windscreen directly into my eyes and the radio is driving me nuts with its super-happy DJs.

"We need to stop and look through the box," Seth says. "It might have a clue to where we're supposed to be going."

I blink my agreement.

"I think we have to find the nest," he says hesitantly.

I blink again. I know what he means. Without a nest, I don't think I can survive the change. My dad was pretty clear on that point.

The next visible lights at the side of the freeway turn out to be a cheap-looking motel, so Seth turns into the concrete forecourt. He parks outside the reception building, coming back with a set of keys and directions to our room.

It's down the far end of the two-story block of units, and I'm grateful. I don't want any witnesses to see how pathetic I am.

Once he's carried me inside the tiny room, he lays me down on the double bed, and I let out a sigh of relief. It's musty and weird-smelling and the bed squeaks a protest, but I don't care. This is the most comfortable I've been since we left the hotel with Si and my father.

Thinking of my father makes me wish he was here with us. He might have been a terrible dad, but he helped us escape the SIG when it counted, and he's been preparing for this situation for years.

He'll know how to figure this out, and he might even have an idea where another nest might be.

"I'll ring the others on the burner phone," Seth says,

pulling out the mobile phone we bought just before being found at the hotel by the SIG. He's just as anxious to meet back up with them as I am.

"Hi, Si? It's Seth."

There's silence as he listens to the reply.

"We're at a motel." His answer is short. I can hear someone talking on the other end, and it's not making Seth's face any less stressed.

"Is this line secure?" He pauses. "Okay. All right, yes. We're at the Happy Hibiscus Inn, about two hours from Newport News." I can tell he's reluctant to give the information.

"Okay. Okay. Yes, I'll tell her. See you soon."

Seth's expression is serious as he turns to face me. "That was Si. He's on his way."

For a second, I'm elated. Si's okay and he's going to be here soon. Then I realize he hasn't mentioned my father.

He sits down on the bed next to me and grabs my hand. My eyes widen as I wait for the bad news. What's happened? Is he dead? I search Seth's eyes, trying to figure out what he's going to say.

"Your father has been captured. The SIG gave him to the Earthbound."

A roaring sound emerges inside my head, making me feel like it's going to burst. I would put my hands to my head to try and control it, if I could move them.

"He's a smart man," Seth assures me. "He'll be fine."

I gaze at him, but his face is unreadable. I know he can't promise me anything like that. My father has been captured by the men he used to work for. What will they do with him? Why did they give him to the Earthbound?

Then it clicks into place.

They're using him as bait for me. I'm supposed to go

after my father and get captured, so they can use me to fix the spell web as they originally planned.

If I could move, I'd be pacing, railing against the world, yelling at Seth. Doing something at least. As it is, I can't even talk to Seth about it or ask him what he's thinking. A growl of frustration starts deep in my belly, but ends up as a low moan. The burning hole in my chest gets wider.

Seth is watching me closely, and his grip on my hand tightens when he hears the noise I'm making.

"We can check the box. Maybe it'll help," he says. Even though I know he's just trying to distract me, I blink my agreement. He gets the box from the small table and places it beside me on the bed. Opening the lock, he peers inside.

Hopefully it's as we left it. Who knows what his brother did with it.

He hesitates over the box and then pulls out his wallet, opening a tiny pocket on the inside and sliding out the ornate golden ring that caused so much trouble in the National Park. I feel like Gollum from *The Lord of the Rings*. All I want is for Seth to give me the ring, to feel the cool metal against my skin again. The need pulses off me in waves, and I desperately fight the desire to reach out and grab it from him. Another low moan escapes my lips.

Seth places it at the bottom of the box, and the attraction dies off somewhat. I can be sensible again. That ring is dangerous; I can't think properly around it. I need someone else to be in control of it. Luckily, Seth is around to be that person.

He flicks through the documents he pulls out. We've already searched through this box, trying to understand why it's all there, but this time it's different. This time all my doubts have been put to one side. I'm a dragon.

And I'm going to die if I can't find something in this box to tell us where to find a dragon's nest.

Seth starts reading through the book on dragons that talks about their habits in third person. There aren't many people left who actually lived in the time of dragons, three hundred years ago. All we know is that they were violent and destructive.

"Here we go, a section on Dragon Mating," Seth says, glancing at me with a grin. "'*Dragons mate with other supernaturals, never their own species. They don't like to spend time in each other's company and are likely to end up in battle if they meet.*' It goes on about how much they hate each other." Seth flips forward a few pages. "*Dragons give birth in human form. Once born, dragon babies are similar to other supernatural babies and need constant care and attention. When they reach the age of maturity, they must return to their nest to begin the final transformation into a full dragon. If they do not find a nest, their transformation becomes lethal.*"

I take a deep breath. Nothing we didn't already know. It's just scary to hear it laid out like that in black and white.

"*The nesting sites were hidden carefully by the dragon shifters, and it was the only time that a group of dragons could be together without destroying each other. Just before their 20th birthday, the parents would drop the young dragon, still in human form, inside the warmth of the nest. Ten days later, the parents would return for their young in dragon form.*" Seth looks up. "Ten days? That's a long time."

I blink my agreement. But I also figure that if I'd had a mommy dragon to drop me off, she probably would have done it a few days ago, before I became completely incapacitated.

"*There is little known about what happens during the nesting cycle. The mountain supers are closed-mouthed about it, in what could be considered an overly superstitious manner. As there are no dragons to consult with, this author can only guess at what might happen."* Seth harrumphs. "That's not much use to us." He glances down at me. His hazel eyes are fiery and bright in the morning sunshine. "We'll figure this out."

I blink.

"It says the young dragons have a connection to the nest. That they remember where it is for the rest of their lives."

I can't imagine being connected to a place like that. I've moved around all my life.

"Are you comfortable?" he asks.

I'm more comfortable than I've been since I lost the use of my body, but I have no way to tell him. He starts trying to change my pillows to a more comfortable position, pulling them out from under my head and puffing them up between his hands. I blink rapidly, trying to let him know that it's okay, that I'm okay. He finally notices the blinking and pulls back.

"Are you okay? Do you need something?"

I blink slowly once.

"No?"

I blink, very precisely, twice for yes.

"Yes? So once for no, and twice for yes?"

I blink twice again.

Seth grins and punches a fist in the air. "Yes! Houston we have contact."

I want to grin back at him, but nothing happens. I'm still trapped in this unmoving body, a hole burning in my chest, and no idea where to go to survive the next few days.

Inside my head, I scream in frustration.

4

A knock on the door jerks us both awake.

Seth jumps up from the bed, grabbing his gun from the nightstand. He stalks over to the door and looks through the hole. He relaxes slightly and takes the chain off the lock, opening the door. "What took you so long?" he says, only half joking.

Si steps into the room, his sharp eyes taking in the small space, landing on me last. A flare of panic flicks across his eyes, something I've never seen before. Si is always calm and collected; he never gets affected by what's happening around him. It's why he always wins in a fight; his clearheadedness beats passion and enthusiasm every time.

But he lost to the Earthbound at his retreat, I remind myself.

They killed Jeff and captured Si and handed him over to the SIG. And now they've got my father. My breath hitches in my chest, and I swallow hard.

Si comes over to crouch next to the bed and grasps my hand. "How are you?" he asks.

Seth comes up behind him. "She can't talk anymore. Can't do anything except blink."

I blink twice, agreeing with Seth.

"Once for no, twice for yes."

My gaze pushes into Si's, a question burning in my mind. I don't need to be able to speak; he knows what I'm asking.

His lips tighten. "The SIG captured your father and handed him over to the Earthbound before I could help him escape. He's okay as far as I can tell," he says. "They'll use him against you. Try to get you to give up, or come get him."

I blink twice. I figured out that much by myself.

"You can't do it. Your father wouldn't want you to." Si is adamant.

It's not like I can do much of anything at the moment, but I blink once. No, I'm not going to leave him there to rot in one of the Earthbound's cells. No, I'm not going to let Vincent test him in his water chamber or whatever other torture devices he's put together.

I haven't seen much of my father since he dumped me with Si and the other protectors as a baby. He made sure I had SIG agents as well, but he never bothered to visit himself. Then he double-crossed us when Seth and I went to him for help.

But he thought he was doing what was best for me. He assumed that I'd be protected by the SIG; and helped us escape as soon as he realized his mistake.

He saved me when it counted, and he kept me alive. If nothing else, I owe him for that.

All these thoughts are jumbled up in my head, like threads of yarn all snarled up together. I'm not sure what to think, what to feel.

"There's nothing we can do about that right now," Seth

says, interrupting my thoughts. "We have to get Mei to a nesting ground. There wasn't anything at the coordinates Damien gave us and there's nothing here that tells us where to go." Seth indicates the wooden box sitting on the side table.

Si walks over to the box and lifts the lid, shuffling through the papers. He pulls out the report that Jeff wrote all those years ago and flicks it open. "There are nesting grounds mentioned in this report."

"But none in the States. Nothing close."

I watch as Si thinks this through. "What if we look at the coordinates and figure out what they look like? It might give us an idea of the kind of place we're looking for? Maybe you just missed the nest?" he says.

"There was nothing there. At least, it was in the sea, deep underwater. I couldn't take Mei into the sea." Seth's hands are clenched, and he's struggling to keep himself calm. Si questioning his actions isn't helping. I desperately want to put my hand on his arm and tell him he's been doing a great job of looking after me. Instead, I just watch.

"How far away is it from here?"

"Not far. An hour maybe."

Si nods, his brain obviously sorting through the information. He taps his finger on the report. "What was the site you went to like? Did it have any large outcrops of volcanic rock? It says something about it here."

Seth stops a moment to consider. "There were big cliffs of white stone just down from where we were."

"Maybe the coordinates were slightly off?" Si raises his eyebrows, looking at Seth. He's really asking, not just being sarcastic.

I'm considering this possibility, wondering if we'll ever figure it out, when a wave of agonizing pain pushes its way down my body. A loud moaning fills the room, and I realize it's me. I'm able to move for the first time in almost twelve hours, but it's my back arching against the pain that's ricocheting through my body.

Si stands up, packing everything into the box. His expression is tense. "We have to get her to a nest. We're going back to the coordinates Damien gave you, and we're going to search every damn inch of that place."

It's hard to concentrate when it feels like knives are sticking into every part of your body, but I try to stay focused as Seth and Si bundle me and our belongings—which are negligible at this point—into our getaway SUV.

I can't see the car that Si arrived in, but I figure it must be there somewhere. Maybe it was stolen; that would explain why he's happy to leave it behind.

I slouch over again in the front seat, but this time Si puts his hand through from the back and holds me up. The pain is still simmering inside me, like I'm sitting inside a boiling pot. I'm burning up, but the discomfort is so much a part of me now, I can't differentiate it from anything else. I feel Si's hand on my arm, and he gives me a gentle squeeze, letting me know he's there.

I can't help it; I start to cry, silent, leaky tears that drip down my cheeks and onto my shirt.

It's a reminder of all that Si has ever done for me. He's been there from when I was a little kid, holding my hand, leading me along. Others left me, died because of me, but Si has made it this far.

Whatever happens, I'm glad he's here.

5

The car speeds along the freeway.

Seth's breaking about a dozen traffic laws, just to get back to the coordinates for the nesting ground in record time. I lie in a half-conscious state, not really paying much attention to anything, letting my mind wander, and trying to avoid thinking about the pain. I have to trust that Si and Seth will get me where I need to go.

Seth screeches to a halt at the parking lot of a beach access and gets out of the car. "Should we leave her here? Search the area ourselves?"

I can't see his face, but I assume Si nods, because they shut their doors and stride off in opposite directions. The leather of the car seat is sticky against my skin, and the salty freshness of the beach air comes in through the open window on Seth's side.

Is this the place I need to be? Will I recognize this place out of all others for the rest of my life? I gaze out at the white sand beach, the cliffs to one side and the water in the distance.

The waves are crashing on the beach, powerful examples of nature working its magic. I wouldn't mind if this was to be my place. It feels peaceful here, like nothing bad could ever happen.

Out of habit, I reach out along the spell web, trying to feel a connection, trying to find out more about this place.

Who lives here?

How has the nest remained hidden all these years?

As I open my mind to the spell web, something else slips inside my consciousness. A wisp of magic, an echo of something I recognize deep inside me. It's calling to me, pulling me away from this place. It's a feeling of home, of warmth and comfort, of knowing. I'm floating away from my body and toward the magic before I even realize what's happening. I look down and see the SUV below me and, through the back window, my dark hair over my slumped shoulders.

I feel a sudden sting of electricity, and then I'm back in my body. I gasp in a deep breath and then another. Was that my soul leaving my body? Did I almost die? I don't know, but fear is racing through my veins, and I can't think properly.

What I am sure of is that the nest isn't here.

It's down the coast a little way, hidden in plain sight. It may as well be a million miles away. There's no way for me to tell Seth or Si. Frustration builds inside me, almost overriding the pain still piercing my skin. To be so close, to have the knowledge and then to be unable to tell anyone; it's almost more than I can bear.

I try to move, this time using every single atom of magic inside me. For a second, it seems like it's going to work. I feel the magic coursing through my veins. And then it's as if I've been cut off. There's nothing left inside me. My body slumps to one side, and I knock my head on the drinks holder as I go down.

There's wetness on my cheek; for the third time in less than a day, I'm crying. I've never cried this much in my life. I'm a walking, talking crybaby, and I need to buck the hell up. What would Jeff say? He'd shake his head and tell me I'm giving up before it's over. *It's never over, not until you're dead.*

That thought stings a little, because Jeff died trying to protect me. But I'm still here, and if I'm going to live up to his memory, to be the person he trained me to be, then I need to fight.

I need to find a way out of this mess.

Looking up, I see a patch of blue sky outside the window, and it seems tantalizingly close. Maybe I can do that outside-my-body thing again?

I close my eyes and concentrate, moving past the physical pain and into my head. I feel the solid connection to the spell web and the strange nugget of new magic that has wedged itself inside my body.

And then suddenly, for a second time, I'm floating above the car and looking down at my physical body slumped over in the front seat.

Without thinking, I work my way along the spell web, similar to how I did it when I knocked out all of Vincent's soldiers, using it to find the others. Perhaps there's a way to communicate to Seth and Si through it?

Seth is climbing the cliff, his face a mask of determination. His patchy spell web is shivering in the early morning sunlight. I don't know how to speak words or make him understand I want to talk to him, but I push against the place where his spell web is strongest, over his heart.

Seth jerks back.

One hand loses its hold on the rocky cliff and a foot slips from the ledge. He leans forward, trying desperately to keep his other hand attached to the rock, the fingers going white with effort. Small stones drop down the cliff, bouncing to the bottom and smashing into tiny pieces.

He pulls his arm back up and grasps hold of the ledge again, gasping for breath. He looks around him, as if trying to see what pushed him.

I'm too afraid to do it again, so I hover there, waiting until he reaches the ledge he's obviously been aiming for. There's nothing up there. I can tell immediately, but he can't use the spell web like I can.

When he's finally sitting on the ledge, one elbow around his upraised knee, breathing hard, I push at him again through his spell web. This time he looks down, and then around. "Who's there? Who's doing that?"

I try to send soothing messages through the spell web to tell him it's just me.

"Mei?"

I want to jump and shout. *Yes, it's me.*

"How are you doing that?"

I can't send words, but I try to pull him back to the car, to tell him where we need to go.

Where *I* need to go, if I'm going to survive the change.

"You want me back at the car? Are you okay?" He's already standing up, preparing to go back down over the side of the cliff he's just climbed. I send reassuring messages and try to make sure he goes slowly and carefully down the ledge, but it's hard. I want him to hurry, just as much as he does.

He gets back to the car and opens the door, finding me slumped over to one side. "Oh jeez. Is that why you wanted me to come back? Are you okay?"

Si comes up behind him. "Did you find anything?"

Seth shakes his head. "No. But Mei did something. She called me back here."

Now that they're both here beside me, I use the spell web again. I push the picture I have in my head of where we need to go into both their heads through the spell web. I've never attempted to use it like this, and I'm kind of surprised when it works.

Seth looks down at me. "Is that you, Mei?"

I blink twice.

"Is that where the nest is?"

I blink twice again.

And then we're off.

6

The car is screaming down the road. Again.

Seth has his foot jammed firmly against the accelerator, but I'm floating away. I feel disconnected from what's happening around me.

All I know is that my nest is close, so close, and I don't know if I'm going to make it.

I can't move my body, although Si is holding me up from the backseat. Before, I could tell he was touching me, but now I can't feel it. My whole body is numb, like it's not connected to me anymore, and my vision is starting to fade.

Everything feels like it's closing down; my body is shutting itself off. We're so close, I can feel it calling to me.

But not close enough.

We screech to a halt on the road about half an hour from the original coordinates.

"Does that look like the mountain in the image she put in our heads?" Seth asks Si.

"Yes. That's it."

"But how do we get there?" asks Seth, his voice slightly panicked.

"We run."

As Seth pulls me out of the SUV, I catch a dim glimpse of a massive glowing area near the coastline. A series of tall rocky hills are coated in the glowing grid of the spell web, pulsing with energy. I don't understand how that can even be possible—I've never seen anything like it before.

Between the road and the glowing hills is rugged, rocky terrain with a thick forest coating any patches that would otherwise have been easygoing. It's not going to be an easy run, and they'll have to carry me the whole way.

Added to that is the fact that the sun is baking down on us.

But neither of them complain. Seth takes me up in his arms first, and my body flops against his chest, my head bumping in time to his steps. The scent of gunpowder and spice hit my senses, along with sweat and fear. I try to concentrate on where we're going, but my brain is getting foggy. My body feels like jello and I can barely keep my eyes open.

It might already be too late.

When I close my eyes, Seth jerks me awake again. "No sleeping now, Mei. You have to stay awake until we get there."

I blink twice, slowly and carefully. He's right; if I go to sleep now, it's the last of me gone. If I'm not in the nest at that point, I won't make it. I don't know why I'm so sure of this, but I am.

I manage to keep my eyes open and stay focused on the craggy peak ahead of us. When Seth starts running, my vision becomes blurry, the hills turning into green and grey blurs. Maybe Seth can feel the life seeping out of me, just like I can. Or maybe it's just intuition.

Whatever it is, I'm grateful. The edges of my mind are

becoming ragged, like something is eating at them. The world is swirling in front of me, my vision almost gone.

I feel every intake as Seth gasps for breath, his chest rising and falling against my body. I taste the salt on my lips from the tears that dried there earlier.

"Here, give me a turn," Si says gruffly from behind us.

Instead of arguing, Seth turns and hands me over. He's exhausted; he would never have stopped if he wasn't.

Si has a stronger grip, and he's a chameleon at the height of his powers. He takes off at a run, using his magic to keep us safe. I hear rather than see his chameleon skin come out over his body, the tiny scales making him stronger.

As Si's magic hums around us, it occurs to me that maybe I could do something with the spell web to help. I try to send my energy along the grid toward Si, like I did back at the beach, but nothing happens. I'm so weak, I can't even use the spell web.

Si jumps from one boulder to the next in a particularly difficult patch of terrain, and my head lolls to one side. I can see down my body, and for the first time I realize that my glowing section of grid has dimmed to almost nonexistent. My head lolls back again. I can't even work up the energy to be worried.

Up ahead, I see the large patch of rocky terrain covered in the spell web.

A painful yearning fills my body, and if I could have gasped at the sheer agony of it, I would have. Now that I'm within range, the nesting ground is somehow calling to me, trying to drag my soul toward it. I have a feeling of being in two places at once, and I start to tremble all over, my body reacting to the pull from the nest.

"I'll take over at the base of the mountain," Seth says.

I don't hear Si's answer; it's lost in the roaring sound that's rushing through my ears.

We're near the base of the ranges where the nest is hidden when my body starts to jerk and my mind is filled with painfully bright flashes of light.

Is this it? Are we too late?

One second, Seth's fierce hazel eyes are gazing down at me and I'm caught in their depths. Then next second, I don't know where I am. All I can see are fast-moving streaks of light, heat and pain. I can't feel my body, only a burning, blistering heat like the center of a fire.

Is this what it means to be a dragon?

Because so far, it feels like crap.

Then the tingling fear sets in. Have we made it close enough to the nest for me to change? Or will I die, just at the edges?

A gnawing pain fills me, and I don't know if it's my emotions, the fear and the terror so powerful they're climbing up out of my body like a physical thing, or if it's part of the transformation. My breaths are coming in tight, uneven gasps and I feel like I can't get enough air. Do dragons even breathe air?

Why did no one ever tell me what I was? Or prepare me for the nightmare of changing?

It's too much. I can't do it.

And then suddenly, we're there. At the nest. There's a bubbling, boiling, heat-filled connection that I feel immediately. Some tenuous connection back to the real world makes my eyes open. All around me I see flames, an enormous fire burning bright, licking at my body like a lover thought long lost.

One name fights to the top of my consciousness. *Seth.*

I look up and see him as he places me at the center of

the flames. His arms are blistering, his face is contorted in pain, but he's there with me. Behind him, I see Si pulling him backward out of the fire, Si's chameleon scales covering his whole body.

Then the world becomes nothing more than the flames and the heat. I'm part of the bright, burning fire, my whole being focused down into one speck. Power surrounds me, roaring and raging at my inability to understand what it's saying.

My own magic surges, like a tsunami of power determined to hit the shore, surely enough to take on this raging beast confronting me.

As the two powers strike, there's a terrible explosion, and I'm surrounded by white light and scalding pain. Fire and heat, burning up the air all around.

A tiny part of me wonders how Seth and Si could have survived it.

Another part knows there's no way they could have.

_____

7

I come back to consciousness slowly, my mind a blank slate.

There are no thoughts to distract me, no worries or concerns. I stretch out and am invaded by a feeling of strangeness. My body no longer feels like mine.

My eyes flash open.

The heat vision I had during the escape from the SIG headquarters is back in place.

Except here there's a lot more of the bright glowing red that indicates heat. The hottest place to be right now is right next to me; I'm glowing like a beacon, a burning red that's off the charts.

I blink once, then twice, trying to get rid of the heat vision.

It takes me a few attempts, but eventually my normal eyesight returns. It's a little blurry at first, but I'm lying in a large rock bowl at the top of the cliffs. There's no one else around, and I let out a breath.

But why isn't my vision as clear as it's always been? I

can't figure it out. It's like all my senses are pushing at me, helping me to define what I'm seeing, not just my eyes. The way everything smells around me, and how it would taste on my tongue are all informing what I can see.

Is it possible to see more by smelling what's around me?

There's even a sense of distance, of where everything is sitting in the air next to me that I've never felt before. I'm suddenly certain I know exactly where north and south are, without checking a compass.

It's like seeing in 5D, if there's such a thing.

And then I look down.

My body is no longer my own.

I'm enormous.

Red and gold scales create glittering patterns over my hide. Large hind legs are tucked under my body with huge black claws sitting against the smooth rock floor of the nest. My front legs are out in front of me as I try to make sense of my new body. Part of me is terrified, scared of this change. But what else did I expect?

I'm a *dragon* now.

I touch the scales with my hand—no wait, I think it's a paw—and feel the sensuously smooth way they join together. It's softer than a baby's skin and more beautiful than anything I've ever seen in my life. I lean down and take a sniff, trying to understand how this could be me. I smell the same as I always have, there's no new dragon scent to mark me. Just this crazy new skin I'm in.

I'm checking out the scales on the side of my new body when I notice I can see further around behind my head than I should be able to. My eyes must be in a different place. I put my paws—front legs?—up to my face and encounter a long nose and sharp teeth. I take in a surprised breath. This is going to take some getting used to.

Someone moans nearby, and I pull myself up, standing on my back legs.

Beside me is Seth, his body covered in ash and grime. He's unconscious, his breathing shallow.

I remember his face in the fire and his body burning as he placed me at the center of the flames in the large rocky nest. I lean in, suddenly concerned that he's in pain. Yet another person hurt looking out for me.

But on closer inspection, using my new eyesight with its super-effective smelling ability, he seems to be okay. The burns I thought I saw on his arms and face are just from the ash that's covering him, and I can't smell blood or anything else that would indicate he's injured.

As I watch him closely to make sure I haven't made some kind of mistake, something triggers in the back of my mind.

His spell web.

Instead of the patchy covering of the grid that he's always had up to now, Seth is now coated liberally in a strong glowing spell web, stronger than any other I've ever seen. He's gone from being weaker than anyone else I know to being stronger.

Once I notice it, I don't know how I could have missed it. I push at the spell web and experience a zing of energy as it pushes back.

I take a step backward and look around, my long neck able to turn my head in almost every direction without having to move my body. In the distance, I see Si, also unconscious.

He looks less fine.

He swirls in my vision, the smell of his pain rocking me back, the taste of his burns making me wish I'd been able to control the flames. His spell web is faint, and his whole body is flopped into the ground like he's become part of it.

I hear his breathing, shallow and ragged.

Without thinking, I take a step in his direction. My unfamiliar new body unbalances me, and I trip over my own feet and fall, landing heavily on my side and narrowly missing crushing Seth. I growl, letting out a puff of smoke in annoyance and then start coughing at the unfamiliar feel of smoke coming out my nose. It burns my throat and tastes of ash and coal. Beside me, Seth doesn't wake, although his eyes twitch under his closed lids.

I push myself up again, and this time take a careful step with one large hind leg. My foot is now three feet long with claws rather than toes and scales the color of blood. I put my arms out in front for balance and realize what I've been doing wrong. I'm supposed to walk on four paws, both my arms and legs now. My arms are front legs and need to be used differently in this form.

Slowly taking one step and then another, using all four legs, I eventually make my way over to Si. I put one paw out, trying to figure out what the exact problem is. His face is pale, and there are ragged patches of his chameleon skin over his body, the brown scales reflecting in the sunlight. He must have used his scales to protect himself from the fire, but in such a way that it depleted his energy. Or perhaps it just took too much of his magic?

My hand touches his forehead, and immediately I feel the blood pulsing through his veins and the magic in his body.

It's the strangest thing I've ever felt, and I'm suddenly convinced I could literally reach in and take these things for myself.

Without thinking, I give it a try. With no effort at all, Si's magic begins winding its way toward me like a sparkling mist, and he moans in pain.

I'm stealing Si's magic, and it's easier than taking candy from a baby.

8

I jerk back, gasping. The sparkling mist returns to Si's body, and he moans again, unconsciously moving away from me. His chameleon skin crackles as he moves.

I take another ragged breath. I just tried to steal Si's life essence, his magic, from him.

Even worse, I did it without even thinking about it, like it was as natural as eating or drinking.

Is this what being a dragon means?

I take a few steps back, still staring down at Si, unable to breathe. He's my only family left, and I almost killed him. More than any of the others, I would have been to blame for Si's death.

Is this what I amount to now? A vicious dragon who steals from others, who kills without thinking?

You are who you make yourself.

Jeff's stern voice is enough to break up the thoughts tangling my brain like cobwebs.

I don't have to do anything I don't want to. I am who I make myself.

But perhaps there's some way to use this new ability to give rather than to take? Turn the situation on its head, as Seth would say?

I lean down and put my front paw on Si's forehead again, making sure my black claws don't pierce his skin, and this time I attempt to push some of my own power into Si. It swarms in, too much, too fast, and Si's body jerks. I pull away, scared that I've hurt him. Leaning down, I sniff at his body. He seems okay—he's still unconscious, but not dead.

I softly replace my paw, this time rigidly controlling the power surge. I allow a tiny portion of my magic to enter Si's body, and give him back the energy he lost. The patchy chameleon scales melt away from his body and he returns to his full human form.

Si gasps in a breath and opens his eyes, his mouth gaping on the next breath and the next. He looks up at me, fear bright in his eyes and a tremor rolling over his body.

He's afraid of me.

I step back, holding up my front paws. "I'm sorry," I say, but the words don't come out, just a menacing growl that makes Si push himself further back against the edge of the rock.

I take another step back, and then trip over my own foot. I go rolling backward and only just manage to push myself away from landing on Seth in time, my legs flailing in the air for a couple of seconds.

I'm not exactly what you'd call a graceful dragon. If dragons could blush, I'd be tinged with pink right now. It takes a moment to get back to my feet, and as I dust myself off, I make a new discovery.

I have a tail.

I mean, of course I have a tail. All dragons have tails.

But I have an actual tail, with patterns of red and gold scales over it and a ridge of dark red-black horned bone going down the center that makes me smile.

I'm a beautiful dragon, if I do say so myself. It's as I'm trying to reach around and touch the scales on my tail that I make my most amazing discovery.

My wings.

They unfurl across my back, reaching up high into the sky behind me, a mixture of gossamer gold and red, with black ridges and claws. Once I know they're there, I find I can move them, and I lift them up and down. They catch a light breeze and hum in the air.

"Mei? Is that you?" The hesitant voice reminds me what I was doing. Si is standing nearby, his face looking up into mine.

Speaking in this form is obviously not something I can do, so I attempt to nod my head. It comes out in a jerky motion, and I almost knock my new dragon chin into my chest. But he understands.

He looks me over, but doesn't say a word about my transformation. "What happened to Seth?" is his only comment as he turns toward Seth's still unconscious form.

I'm not worried about Seth; his spell web is glowing like a damn beacon. He's just sleeping off whatever hit him. I edge closer, leaning over Si's shoulder as he checks Seth's body over.

I can smell the tiny cuts that are healing on Seth's body from the climb up the hill and the burnt skin he should have, but doesn't, plus a bitter scent I don't immediately recognize.

Somehow I can taste the metallic flavors of the healing that's going on inside Seth's body. My vision unexpectedly switches to heat, and I watch as colors swirl across his skin. He's lying perfectly still, his body outwardly calm, but inside it's working hard to finish whatever strange transformation is taking place. Si is still leaning over him, trying to wake him up, and can't see the swirling patterns I'm witnessing.

And then it stops. Just like that, Seth's system stills. I rapidly blink my eyes, trying to get back to my normal sight. When it finally comes to me, Seth is watching me with wide eyes, his whole body rigid with tension.

He's back.

Si helps him to sit up, and Seth takes a few breaths, nervously glancing from me to Si.

"Do you remember what happened?" Si asks, glancing over his shoulder at me as well. Neither of them seems happy about my current shape, but honestly, what were they expecting? The shimmering scales on my hind leg catch my eye, and I smile down at my new form. I kind of like it.

Seth shakes his head. "I remember running into the flames with Mei and you shouting at me." He puts one hand to his head, rubbing the skin on his forehead. "I think I remember you pulling me back, and then there was just this big explosion."

Si nods. "Last thing I remember is the explosion, coming directly from Mei."

I wince. Yet another case of me putting the people I love in harm's way.

"It can't have been that hot," Seth says, rubbing his arms.

I shake my head, wanting to tell him about the blisters I saw on his skin. I can't say the words, but I push the image at him along the spell web, watching his reaction carefully. He blinks a couple of times, then looks up at me closely. "Was that you?" he asks.

I nod my head. A puff of smoke escapes my nose. I cough.

"It was really hot in here. I only survived because of my chameleon genes." Si narrows his eyes at Seth, his body tightening into a defensive pose. "There's no way you should have survived. I think there's something you're not telling us."

9

———

Seth just shakes his head. "I don't know how I survived. Maybe Mei protected me somehow?" he says, glancing up at me again.

I blink, wondering if I could have done it without realizing.

I have no idea.

I put my head to one side, concentrating on what might have happened, and then almost topple over as my dragon nose becomes unbalanced. It's not as easy as you might imagine going from human to dragon form. I don't even know if I can change back, or if I'm stuck like this forever. Surely it must have said something in the book?

My panicked thoughts are dampened by logic.

My father didn't know my mother was a dragon at first. Dragons hide in human form.

Of course I'm going to be able to transform back.

If I can figure out how.

My thoughts distract me so much that I don't feel Seth's shape until he's almost touching me. When I do sense him, it's because I feel his form next to me through my scales. It's like my whole body is another sense that reaches out into the air around me.

I turn my head and look down at him.

He takes another step closer and lets out a breath. "I knew what you were. I thought I understood what it would mean. But I never really expected..." His eyes are glowing, and he reaches out with one hand to touch my side.

My haunches?

I don't even know what to call most of my new body parts.

Seth's fingers run along my new dragon skin, softly skimming the scales. I catch the familiar scent of gunpowder, plus a hint of smoky pine mixed with the blood, sweat and ash that cover his body.

I hear his breathing, the movement of his lungs, the soft exhale as he touches me. A golden shiver pushes itself along my skin, like a tidal wave of pleasure, shaking up my scales and making me close my eyes for a moment.

When I open them again, Seth is staring up at me, his eyes dilated, his expression wary, and I know he just experienced the same thing I did.

I don't know how, but the attraction I've been feeling for him has morphed into something that's raging inside me. I don't know what to do, or how to act. I'm a dragon, for crying out loud. I don't see how it can be a good thing, so I step back, away from him.

Si clears his throat. "So is there anything more to the process? Or is this you done?"

I shake my head. I don't know the answer to that. Am I done? It sounds like I'm a slab of meat on the grill.

I didn't even know I was a dragon until a couple of days ago. I don't know anything about the process other than I'm pretty sure I only just made it to the nest in time to survive the transformation. Wasn't the whole thing supposed to take ten days? What else is going to happen to me?

I blow out smoke through my nose, the wisps floating up into the air. Surely there must be someone who knows more about this than I do? What about Jeff's wooden box? There might be something in the book.

"We left the box in the car," Seth says, unconsciously answering my question.

I pull myself down to walk around the rock bowl on all fours, my wings jutting out behind me. There must be some kind of clue to what comes next in this place. Surely they would leave some kind of message or information for future dragons. The huge boulders are silent mocking reminders that I have no idea what I'm doing.

In the distance, waves crash on the beach, each one pounding the sand and changing the coastline. The water moves on without a care, not concerned that I've transformed into an extraordinary new form.

I sniff the air, and something tantalizing floats back to me.

I don't know what it is, but it has sweetness and warmth inside it. Saliva gathers inside my mouth, and I realize I'm hungry. No, that doesn't cover it: I'm starving, like I've never eaten properly in my life. I'm ravenous for sustenance, and I know without a doubt that the only thing that will stop my hunger is the source of the mouthwatering aroma that surrounds me like a haze.

Snapping at the air around me, I try to taste the smell. It dissipates into nothing, and my insides scream with frustration. But it slowly emerges again, winding itself around my body like a cloak, teasing and testing me at the same time.

I pace the edges of the bowl, sniffing the air, trying to locate the source of the smell. It clings to me, making it hard to decipher the direction, especially using my new senses. My nose is fifty times more powerful than it was before, and I'm picking up undertones of what can only be the wild-flowers down the mountain side and the salty taste of the seashells on the beach.

My stomach is growling at me, bubbling and roiling inside my body, telling me to hurry. It doesn't understand that I don't know anything about this new body, or how to find what I need. I spin this way and that, sniffing the air like the next breath might give me the clue I need. I don't even know what I'm looking for. I can't decipher the smell. What do dragons eat? The claws on my fore legs curl into a ball, their sharp tips piercing my new leathery dragon palms. It might be the dead bodies of one hundred sea lion pups for all I know. The thought sends a shudder down my hide, and I'm pretty certain it's not that after all.

What could it be? There's a metallic undertone that's potent and irresistible, but mostly it smells earthy and ancient. There's also a hint of what can only be fire. The desire to devour it fizzes inside me, scratching to get out. My breathing is ragged and my mouth dries out. I try to swallow, and it feels like I have sandpaper inside my neck. The smell is so close, but I can't get at it.

I pace up and down the side of the nest on all four legs, sniffing the air. The only thing I know for sure is that I have to find and eat whatever it is that I smell.

Seth steps in front of me, his arms held high. "Mei, what's the matter?"

I thud to a halt, almost crushing him. I twitch, feeling the sensation roll across my body, making my new scales click together, a sound so tiny I'm sure I'm the only one who hears it. I can't even answer him; I have no way to communicate what I'm feeling. How can I explain the smell in pictures inside his mind?

I shake my dragon head. My thoughts buzz in confusion and I struggle to focus on his form below me.

"Let us help you, Mei. What's the matter? Give me a clue, like last time."

He's so puny next to me, and I feel a rumble of annoyance deep down in my throat. He's trying to stop me from finding the source of the smell. Hunger is gnawing at my insides, making my stomach crawl and my skin tighten all over my body. My vision starts switching between heat sensing and normal vision, back and forth until my head is swirling.

Pushing him to one side, I continue pacing, my claws clicking on the rock bowl in a frantic staccato beat I can't control. The sound gives me an idea, and I halt my agitated movement. Leaning down, I dig at the rock beneath my feet with my front claws. Small stones crumble under my assault, but the hard rock underneath doesn't budge. I keep digging, scraping my new claws along the rocks, creating a discordant sound that disrupts the air around me. Underneath it all, I can still smell the ancient earthy tones of whatever it is I'm trying to find.

Seth appears beside me again, close to my side, but clear of my digging claws. I pause, distracted by his pine and gunpowder scent. He reaches up to put his hand on my body.

Without thinking, I swish my tail to keep him away, and it swipes his legs out from under his feet. He falls heavily onto his back, a huff of air making it obvious that I've knocked the wind out of him. He's dazed for a moment and shakes his head as if to clear it.

It just makes me angrier.

He should have known better than to come close to me, to touch me without permission. I don't have time for him to be inserting himself like that. I have to feed my hunger. My vision switches to heat, and it's like I'm blind. The only thing I can sense is the elusive ancient smell of earth and fire, driving my desire for food to a tipping point.

Smoke curls out of my nostrils, and my stomach rumbles and shakes. My vision is switching erratically back and forth, and I'm not entirely steady on my feet. The heat in my belly pushes its way upwards, burning and blistering my throat. I open my jaws, and instead of a roar, burning flames erupt out of my mouth.

It's not until my vision switches back to normal that I realize I've just blown a mouthful of dragon fire directly over Seth.

10

I stumble forward, but there's too much smoke to be able to see how what damage I've done. The smell of burning flesh assaults my nose, and if a dragon could gag, that's what I'd be doing.

Part of me wants to scream, but I can't make that noise either. I'm too afraid to open my mouth to roar, in case more fire comes out. The overwhelming hunger that was gnawing at me is momentarily replaced with the fear that I've killed Seth.

I've burned him. Badly. I know that much. Maybe so badly that there's nothing left of him but ash and coal. I take a step forward, afraid of what I might find through the smoke. Dragon fire isn't like normal fire. It's far more powerful and dangerous. No one could have survived. Not a second time in one day.

I take a sniff and the haunting aroma I was chasing drifts back into my awareness. My stomach rumbles, and the hunger resurfaces.

Ripples of emotion roll down my body, and my breath comes in gasps. Even now, knowing I've killed Seth, most of me just wants to turn around and keep digging at the rocks. Or pace along the sea wall to see if there's anything over that cliff. The hunger is like nothing else I've experienced in my life, and I don't think I can control it.

Is this what being a dragon is about? Hurting the people close to me and being out of control?

Will I always care for myself before others now that I'm a dragon? Will the sacrifices that everyone made for me be pointless?

Perhaps Vincent was right to lock me up. It's a fitting end for one such as me.

Don't let self-pity drive you. You're the one in control of your thoughts.

Jeff's words in my head halt me in my downward spiral. I take a gulping breath. Jeff was always the one who could break me out of the temptation to feel sorry for myself and the life I was living on the edges of society.

He brought the positivity into my life, despite the way it might have seemed to outsiders. His rough treatment of my feelings was the impetus I needed to work harder, stay stronger.

In this life, I'm going to need it. I push down the hunger for the moment, determined to help Seth. Until I know he's really dead, I can't do anything else. My vision has switched to heat sensing, and I can only see a blob of red in front of me, which could mean anything.

Instinct makes me reach for the spell web, the one thing I can be sure of not breaking, and I push healing energy along it toward Seth.

But instead of the pain and death I expect to find, Seth is there strong and clear. I pause, taking stock. Perhaps I didn't breathe fire? Maybe it wasn't that hot? I blink and switch to normal vision again. The smoke is dissipating and there's

Seth, singed and blistered, most of his shirt burned away, but still whole. His expression is a mix of shock and anger. He doesn't take his eyes off mine, but steps away from me, and one hand comes up, as if to fend me off.

I'm the enemy now, someone who has attacked and caused him pain. I can't explain that I didn't mean to do it, that I don't know how to control this new body and these overpowering emotions I'm feeling. I reach out, but he's backing away faster now, and my hand—dragon paw—reaches into thin air.

Perhaps it's better this way. Seth should get as far away from me as he can. The Earthbound will renew their efforts to find me now, and I'm pretty sure the SIG will be on my tail soon enough. Seth and Si could get hurt, and I don't want that for either of them. Better that they hate me.

I turn away, and the tentative control I had over my dragon emotions breaks away. Searing hot hunger burns its way through my stomach. I let out a screech, and dragon fire burns up into the air, and then I reel backward, almost falling over my tail.

I have to find food, and the only thing I know I can eat is whatever is letting off that smell. That delicious, warm, mossy smell that is somewhere close. If I can just find it, I won't have to deal with this misery any longer.

Ignoring Seth and Si, I stand tall on my hind legs, lift my nose up high and sniff the air around the nesting bowl. It smells like it's all around me, there's no direction for it, no one way to go. I lower myself again and stalk to the other side of the bowl and again lift my nose high. This side is near the ocean, and all I can smell here is the salty air and the water that overwhelms everything.

Turning, I'm about to try at the top of the nest, where a large rock overhang creates a natural shelter, when I notice that Seth and Si are already there, conferring in whispers. They're in my way. A growl rumbles from my throat as I stare at them through my dragon lens.

They're trying to keep me from my food. They don't want me to live. I bare my teeth at them, showing them I will fight for my food, wherever it may be. Until this moment, I haven't paid any attention to my large dragon teeth, but curling my lips up over my sharp incisors feels extremely satisfying.

Seth and Si look up, their faces stony. They move to one side, out of my way, and I let out a huff of smoke, my eyes following their every move. My stomach rumbles again, heat bubbling inside me, ready to come out. My head aches, like someone's been pounding on it with a hammer. I shake it slightly, but that only makes the pounding worse. I snarl again, this time aimed at no one, just at the world where I am in pain and unable to find the one thing I desire above all else.

I need to find where that smell is coming from. I push my nose into every corner of the overhang, looking for hidden entrances, or other clues to where I need to be going. There's nothing other than the smell and my increasing sense of desperation.

I'm standing under the ledge on the far side when I notice something out of the corner of my eye. I look over and see Seth standing in the center of the nest and the bottom of the bowl shape. He's making huge gestures at me, like he wants me to come toward him. My snarl still in place, I take a step toward him. He's the only one I can see, so my anger focuses on him.

He's like a fly, buzzing around in my space, trying to land on my foot. I have the urge to swat him, to show him I'm the one in charge.

I take a few slow steps in his direction, waiting for him to run like a scared rabbit.

My eyes flick from heat vision and back again, showing Seth burning brightly against the rest of the smooth rock nest. I rear back onto my hind legs and push my body up to its full height, my neck stretching my head up high.

Without thinking I spread my wings wide and feel them filling with wind behind me. I flap them experimentally, and for a second I'm lifted off the ground. My heart leaps in my throat and I let out a startled cry. The thought of flying is too much for me. I snap my wings closed and turn my attention back to Seth, who has run from the center of the nest back out to the edge.

I growl in triumph.

And then the rock beneath my feet disappears and I fall into darkness.

11

I plummet down, bashing my thick hide against the rocky sides of the hole I've fallen into, then land heavily on a rough rock floor. A rumbling noise fills the air, and the light above me disappears. I'm bruised from the abrupt tumble, shaky and breathless. My vision switches to heat, and I can't see a thing.

I blink, repeatedly, and manage to get it back to normal. It's pitch black, but I can sense the cavern around me. What just happened? I glance up, but whatever opening was once there is gone again. It's some kind of underground cell. It smells like an underground area that hasn't been open for many hundreds of years. Damp, mossy and dark. A scent tickles my nose, but I ignore it, too angry at being trapped down here.

My first thought is an overwhelming sense of betrayal. Seth and Si tricked me; they've locked me in this cage beneath the earth. I wonder whether they're going to call the Earthbound or the SIG to pick me up.

My head knows I can't blame Seth; I did just cover him

in dragon fire. He should be dead, and if he isn't, it's not because of me. I shake off my hurt feelings. I'm a dragon now. I'm going to have to get used to people treating me like this.

Right now, I have to figure out how to get out of here.

I walk toward the edge of the chamber, lifting my nose into the air and trying to sense another exit in the darkened room. Something makes my nose twitch again, and this time I stop in my tracks.

The most glorious scent slides into my nostrils, and along my taste buds. A shiver of excitement runs over my body. The scent I was searching for, the ancient smell that's been taunting me. It's all around me down here. I reach up and break off a rock formation hanging beside my head. I sniff it carefully to make sure and then stuff it inside my gaping dragon mouth.

The taste is divine.

It's more than anything I could have expected. Sensations explode in my mouth, fizzing and bursting with the flavors of everything I most desire. My eyesight goes to heat, and I can't see a thing, except sparkling stars all around me, bursting from the rocks and moving like a wave of fireflies through the darkness.

I break off more of the rock, and this time I can't contain the groan of pleasure as I devour it. This is what I was searching for, the only thing that could ease the raging hunger inside me.

Again and again, I break off pieces of the rocks, watching as the lights buzz around me, providing energy of a kind I've never experienced before. Soon I'm covered in them, a dusty glowing cloak that is beautiful in the pitch darkness. My dragon belly is rounded and full, and I've gorged myself on the rocks.

In the darkness of the cavern, I still don't entirely know what kind of rocks they are, but whatever minerals are inside them have filled me to the brim. The gnawing hunger is gone, replaced with the need to lose myself in the unconsciousness of sleep.

I stumble around the small chamber, searching for a good place. I trip over my legs, they're so heavy and awkward, but I soon discover an alcove that seems to be set up just for sleeping dragons.

At first I don't know how to lie down; I try to lie on my back like I would as a human, but my tail is in the way. I can't lie on my side, because it hurts my wings. Eventually I curl my dragon body up with my legs tucked under and my head on my front paws like a cat. The cavern is humming, and the minerals in the rocks around me echo the low noise. The tone seems designed to send me to sleep, and my eyes start to close.

As my lids droop down over my eyes, there's a noise at one side of the chamber. A dark shape is moving stealthily toward me. My eyes are too heavy to keep open, no matter how much I fight it, and suddenly I realize just how vulnerable I am.

Again.

I catch the glint of a sword being lifted high just as my eyes close and darkness falls around me. I attempt to stand, to move, to do anything, but my whole body feels leaden.

It's like I've turned to stone.

I growl, and the noise echoes around the room, but that's no defense against the intruder. With my eyes shut, I can't see who it is, and the overwhelming feeling of fullness and the desire for sleep are overtaking my other senses. All I can smell are the minerals around me; all I can hear is their humming. I'm full of the taste and the rocky touch of them.

A voice inside me is yelling, trying to get me to wake up, to fight off the intruder, whoever they may be.

But I can't keep myself awake, and darkness falls.

12

I wake slowly, my mind fuzzy.

When I try to move, I discover my front paws are tied together. I growl, lifting my head for the first time, and look around.

I'm still in the underground cavern, the rocks are still singing to me, but now the buzzing is less like a lullaby and more like a siren's call. I'm starving again.

Glancing down at my paws, I frown in confusion. Someone has used rope to tie me to an old metal ring placed in the wall. I give an experimental pull, and the ring falls away from the rock and clangs onto the ground.

I dip my head and bite at the rope, which falls away almost like it's embarrassed to be there.

Not much of a deterrent.

I growl again, but the need to eat is more powerful than the desire to find out who tied me up, and I stretch up into a standing position. Taking a few stiff steps, I have to remember how to walk as a dragon again. Hind legs are very different to human legs. I stumble in my eagerness to eat more of the rocks around me.

I reach up and pull off another piece, almost like I'm picking fruit from a tree. My sharp dragon teeth make short work of the rocks, and I wonder what else they could chew like it was butter. Probably a lot.

The sound of my dragon teeth munching on stone fills the small chamber, echoing around the room, and I almost miss the fact that someone is walking down the stairs just off to one side. Is it Seth or Si? Or someone else, the person who came into this area with a sword, just as I was falling asleep?

A rumble starts deep in my stomach, and I feel the heat of my flames readying to roar forth. This is the person who thought they could tie me up. My dragon gaze sharpens on the archway at the bottom of the stairs, and my lips form a snarl over my enormous teeth.

Whoever is there hesitates at the doorway. I hear them breathing, soft and measured. They're not afraid, simply cautious and aware of my skills.

I puff out a little smoke from my nostrils. They should be afraid.

"It's just me, Mei," says a familiar voice. *Seth.* My stomach flips over.

A rumbling growl forms deep in my chest.

"Are you feeling better? Put a picture in my head to let me know."

I send a picture of me eating him, piece by succulent piece.

There is silence. "We only tied you up because we weren't sure if you would still try to hurt us."

Hurt them? I shake my head.

"You burned me alive, Mei," Seth says quietly.

With that, my memories of the night before flood back, and I remember my desperation, my anger and frustration, and the overwhelming desire to eat. I remember burning Seth, and I don't know how he survived.

My anger disappears. My dragon instincts keep kicking in, making me do things I don't like. I stole Si's magic, and then I burned Seth, all without thinking it through. Even now, I want to stop eating the rocks, but I can't. It's like a powerful compulsion is pushing me in directions I don't want to go, and I don't know how to stop it.

If this is what it's going to be like as a dragon, I don't want it. To be constantly acting in a way that's against my better nature? No. I refuse. It was bad enough before, when people died because they were protecting me. Now people I love are going to die by my own hand. I don't know how Seth survived, but it's not something I can count on happening again.

I don't even know how to say I'm sorry. What is that in pictures?

I send Seth a picture of me begging for forgiveness.

He sighs. "I don't need you to say you're sorry, Mei. You were in the grip of some kind of frenzy. But you need to understand why we felt the need to tie you up. I can come in and untie the ropes if you like?"

I send him a picture of the ropes and the metal ring on the floor.

He pokes his head around the corner, eyes wide. "I guess we should have known that ropes wouldn't hold you," he says with a small smile. "While you were asleep, Si went back to the car for the box. We have the book here, and it has some information that's useful."

His face is familiar and his intense eyes are kind as they watch me. Just his presence down here calms me, and I'm able to think more logically. Reaching up, I pull off another piece of rock, chewing it thoughtfully. The book isn't enough. It doesn't tell me firsthand knowledge of being a dragon. It gives guesses and opinions from people who saw secondhand what it involved.

But it's the only guide I've got. I have to take what I can get.

"I'll bring it back down to show you," he says, then disappears back up the stairs.

I stare around the room, trying to analyse this whole mess. Am I going to feel this desperate need for food every time I get a little peckish? Surely there are clues down here? Something that says what being a dragon is all about?

No wonder the dragons killed each other off. They were probably just hungry all the time.

Wandering over to the walls, I touch the rough surface experimentally. The sensitive pads on my dragon paws feel the grooves and ridges of the rock, while my nose tells me it's more of the same rock I've been devouring. The scent is still irresistible to me, like eating golden sunlight mixed with fairy dust. It's somehow metallic and light-filled but magical at the same time. I walk along the edges of the wall, sniffing at the corners, trying to find a clue to guide me.

Just as I get back to the place I started, Seth clatters down the staircase again. I'm waiting by the stairs when he emerges, holding the box, with Si right behind him.

I bow to them both and try sending warm feelings in their direction through the spell web. They've stuck with me through an awful lot in the last few days, including me almost killing them. I'm not entirely sure what I've done to deserve that kind of loyalty, but I appreciate it.

They both stop in their tracks, and Seth's eyes widen. Si is harder to read, but I can tell they've both felt what I was sending.

"Did you do that?" Seth asks. He looks flustered. "I suddenly felt warm all over."

I shrug one shoulder. It doesn't work as well in dragon form as human, but he gets the idea.

"I would prefer if you didn't try to manipulate our feelings," Si says, his voice hard.

I blink at this unexpected reaction. I shake my head and send an image of me shaking his hand and thanking him.

"It feels more like you're overriding our emotions. Manipulate us."

I put my front paws up, palm up, in a gesture of apology. That hadn't been my intention at all. This is harder than I thought it would be, trying to communicate as a dragon. How do dragons talk to each other? Not that it matters; I'm the only one left.

I glance down at the box. The one thing I want to know is how to turn myself back to my human form. I'm sick of feeling out of control and too big for the space I'm in. I just want to be able to talk to Si and Seth normally.

I nudge Seth with my nose, indicating the box, and sending an image of me back to normal.

"You want to know how to turn back?" he says, smiling up at me.

I nod.

He opens the box, shuffles around inside, and then pulls out the book. He passes the box to Si and turns back to me. "Can you read in dragon form?"

I have no idea. I lean over, using my long neck, and peer at the book. The words look fuzzy and disjointed. My new senses can tell that a mountain supernatural held this book at some point in the past, and the feel of it is at least one hundred years old. But the words themselves are fuzzy and out of focus. I shake my head.

"I can read it out loud, and you two listen," says Seth. "There might be things that strike a chord with either of you that I won't pick up on."

I nod again and settle down more comfortably near Seth, who sits down with his back against the nearest wall. Si crouches nearby, keeping a wary eye on me while he listens.

The newly turned dragon will be ravenous, uncontrollably so. They must be fed immediately or they will hurt themselves and any others who might be unfortunate enough to be close by. The nesting ground will provide what you need. Seth pauses and looks up at me. "Is that what was happening up there?"

"It would have been nice if they'd said precisely what it was dragons ate and where to find it," Si mutters. "Or if we'd read that part before she changed."

I nod in reply to both comments.

A dragon must remain in their new dragon skin for the first ten days. They cannot change back, and they must remain close to their supply of food. If this is not followed correctly, it can harm the young dragon, causing problems and even death.

My death? Or the death of others? I feel strong and vital now, having eaten my fill, but perhaps the ravening hunger comes back every time I need to feed. The thought fills me with fear. I don't want to be susceptible to that kind of overwhelming emotion every time I'm hungry.

A young dragon must take wing within the first five days after changing. This will ensure their wings are strong and capable of flying.

The thought of flying makes me raise my head up. My wings move restlessly on my back, and I try to think about flying in the sky on my own. It seems too much, and I shake my head to get the images out.

The first change back to human form is unpleasant for the

young dragon. Their dragon body will refuse the transfer. It must be done early, before the first fifteen days is up, or the dragon side will rule forever. The young dragon may never be able to change back into a human form again."

I look up at the other two. How long have we been here? I don't want to miss that window. As much as I appreciate this new form, the thought of never returning to my normal human shape is disconcerting.

"So we wait here for at least ten days?" Si says. He's frowning, and I wonder what the problem is.

"Seems that way," Seth says.

"The Earthbound have Damien. If we're going to retrieve him," he glances at me and hesitates, "despite knowing it's probably a trap, we should do it soon." Si's words are blunt, but the emotion behind them is obvious to my new dragon senses. I can smell his fear and worry as if the words were written out in front of me.

I don't want to admit that I had completely forgotten about my father. Being a dragon has consumed everything else in my life.

I should be more worried about him. Better than anyone, I know what the Earthbound are capable of. But I have other things on my mind at the moment.

Like figuring out how to fly.

13

The view below is like a gaping wound on the side of the mountain. Nothing but air, cliffs and distant beaches below. I flap my wings experimentally, trying to test them without having to leap from the comfort of the nest.

If this doesn't work, it's going to hurt. Bad.

I take a big breath, unfold my wings and leap.

The wind catches the membranes between the bones on my wings, and I billow upward. But I have no control; the currents take me up and over the nest. I kick my legs in a frantic attempt to change my direction, but in the air my legs are useless.

I'm going backward, and I didn't even know that was possible. My enormous dragon heart is beating a mile a minute. I can't see where I'm going, and I tense up, expecting to hit some kind of rocky outcrop at any second. I try pushing my wings up and down, flapping them, to see if it has any effect.

My whole body is pushed even further up and I give a

squeak. Below me Seth and Si are yelling instructions I can't hear through the rushing wind.

The wind was supposed to give me a bit of extra push. That's why we decided I should give flying a go today. I didn't take into account the fast and furious nature of the erratic wind on the coast. The ocean air is a little crazy and unpredictable.

I flap my wings again, trying to control it, but the movement just pushes me higher, and further into the air currents. A new gust of wind catches my wings and pushes me toward the beach, away from the nest.

It's three days since I became a dragon, and the waiting has started to get to everyone. This is at least some form of action. Turns out, maybe it's the wrong kind of action.

The wind is carrying me off where it wants to take me, and I don't know how to stop it. My wings start to curl back into my side, an automatic shutdown mechanism. But this isn't the ground, and I can't just step out of the ring.

I start to fall, the air rushing past me, roaring in my ears. The beach is below me, but it's a long way down, getting closer by the second. I don't think I'd survive the landing, even in dragon form. Frantically I push my wings out wide, and they immediately catch the wind again.

Now I'm being blown out to sea, unable to control where I'm going.

I've always hated flying.

Jeff tried to take me on an airplane a couple times when I was younger, and it was always harrowing—for everyone. Being inside the small metal container, the feeling of flying itself, even just having to sit still in the same chair the whole time; it all made me too terrified to contain. I'd often end up screaming or crying hysterically, clutching the armrests and causing a huge scene.

After a couple of attempts, Jeff stopped booking us on flights. He said it was because the security was too tight, but we all knew it was because of me.

And now, here I am, up in the air again. Still unable to fly.

Push yourself, Mei. Nothing good comes from sitting on the fence.

The funny thing about Jeff speaking to me in my head is that, just like when he was alive, I listen to him. He trained me to think for myself on most occasions, but there's a line of thought locked into my brain that says if all else fails, listen to Jeff. He's the one who saved me when I was a kid, and he can do it again.

So I take a deep breath and get off the fence.

Not literally, of course.

I push my wings out even wider, locking the main stem into place and making the membrane stretch over the cobweb of bones that provide the structure of the wing. I try tipping to one side. My whole body dives down toward the ground, and it's like I'm speeding up the drop I took a moment before.

A scream launches from my mouth, but the noise is carried away on the wind behind me. I tip to the other side, trying to correct the moment, and arch my back. The movement pushes me up into the sky again, and I let out a relieved breath.

But then my wings catch an air current and I'm pushed to the left, further out over the glistening ocean. I wobble, fighting the current, still trying to figure out how to make this work. Why didn't I study flight or aerodynamics? Why didn't Jeff and Si make me learn all about birds when I was a kid? Or bats? Or any damn flying creature that might actually help me now?

I swivel my head and look back at the disappearing coastline. I don't know how to turn around. It should be easy, but it's not. It should be instinctual, but it's definitely not that either.

The only thing I can think of is to turn my body in the direction I want to go. But as soon as I try turning my long neck and shoulders the other way, I drop down in the air, fast, like I'm in a broken elevator. My wings have curled up, some kind of automatic reaction to the movement. I open them back up and straighten, taking giant, huffing breaths. Note to self: don't do that again.

Okay, so new plan.

Maybe I need to turn more gently, in a half circle. I lift one wing up and push the other down, attempting to bank to one side. It works, and I'm now facing the direction I came from. Experimentally, I try to flap my wings again. This time I'm more in control, I'm a bit more confident, and my wings are fully extended.

I'm flying.

I'm flying.

14

M y normal vision blinks out, turning into heat vision.

It freaks me out for a moment, and I drop. But then I notice I can see the air currents in front of me, designated by how hot or cold they are. After experimenting for a while, I discover the hot air currents take me higher, and the colder currents take me lower.

The muscles on my wings have started screaming in agony, and I figure it's like anything. You have to build the muscles up. I stop flapping and just glide along in the air back toward the nest.

It doesn't take me long, and I see Seth and Si standing on the edge, watching me with their arms raised to cover their eyes. The sun is beating down on us, making the scales on my body sparkle.

I grin. This is flying. Not sitting in a tin bucket. This is real, the way it's supposed to be done. No wonder I hated flying in airplanes.

I fly toward the basin, but at last minute, realize I don't know how to slow down or land. I'm coming in too fast, and if I let myself hit the ground, it will scrape off half my beautiful scales and probably crush Seth and Si in the process.

Banking, I push my wings to one side and swoop down low over the bowl of the nesting ground. The rush of air pushes the two men backward, and they struggle to stay standing.

I fly up again and head down to the beach this time. I think I need a runway to help me land for the first time. I don't know exactly how to slow down either. Every time I flap my wings it just takes me up higher and makes me go faster. Gliding is just as bad; the wind currents push me along like a steam train on wheels.

My wings ache badly now; I've done enough flying for the day. I look around for an idea, some way to help with my landing. My options seem to be the beach or the water.

Given that I barely know how to walk in dragon form, let alone swim, I aim for the beach. I come in low, flying over the sand, and put my legs down to catch myself against the rough surface. My back legs hit the ground, and I'm running for a moment, before stumbling, and then I'm going head over heels, crashing along the beach in an uncontrolled tumble.

Everything is getting hit, I feel my whole body being knocked by the hard sand, and I don't know how to stop.

I hear something tear, and pain shoots up my left wing. I scream and try to pull my wings in. My left wing stays where it is, but my momentum has died off. I crash up against the base of a rock cliff a few hundred yards from the section of beach below the nest.

I see two tiny spots racing down the side of the nest, along some path only they know about. The glowing spell web makes it easier to see them both, especially now Seth's is so much brighter. My wing is burning, and I turn my head to see what's happened. I immediately wish I hadn't looked. There's a gash in the main section of the wing membrane that looks bad. There's no blood, but the wing is hanging awkwardly around that area, and I think I've somehow managed to break it.

My first flight, and I'm already a lame dragon.

I manage to turn myself over and stand up, keeping the wing out to one side. It feels strangely numb, and I wobble a little on my feet. My sight switches to heat vision, and I look toward the cliffs to check on Si and Seth. They've made it onto the beach and seem to be sprinting toward me. My eyes close for a moment, and I let out a breath. It's good they're coming. I don't think I can stay awake any longer.

I'm half asleep, or perhaps in some kind of trance, when I feel myself leaving my body again. I'm suspended in the air above, watching my dragon form sleep on the beach. Seth and Si arrive moments later and rush over to my head. Seth yells my name, trying to shake me awake.

I feel the shuddering across my body, so I know I'm still connected. I don't *think* I'm dying.

There's a bright red stain across my wing where it's been hurt, and my focus narrows onto that. I move until I'm directly over the wound, and without thinking about it, I start to draw power from the spell web around me. Gathering as much of it as possible, I think push it into the wing. I'm excessively pleased when I can see it physically reforming in front of my eyes. It's almost healed when I look up and realize something is wrong.

Seth and Si have both collapsed onto the ground near my dragon form. The spell web is faint over their bodies and I'm not sure either of them is breathing.

I hear a *ping*, and then I'm flowing back into my dragon body. I blink my eyes open again and rise up onto my legs. I stretch my neck down to where the two men are lying prone and sniff their bodies. There's no blood or anything else that might indicate they were attacked. I look around, using all my new dragon senses, just to be sure. I smell only the usual beach smells, nothing strange or wrong.

I push at Seth with my front dragon paw, trying to get him to wake up. Could they be doing the same thing I was? An out of body experience, part of my healing?

My healing.

Suddenly I realize what's happened, and all feeling drains from my body. They're connected to the spell web. I just pulled enough power to heal my dragon body from the spell web around me. Where else would it get that energy from, than other supernaturals in the area?

My heart beating fast, I close my eyes and gather some of the energy in my own body and push it back through the spell web into both Seth and Si. I manage to control it, not letting it overwhelm their senses like the first time I attempted this on Si. I hold my breath, waiting anxious seconds for them to wake.

Seth opens his eyes first and stares up at me. Si isn't long after. They both look at me with wide eyes, and I know they can tell what happened. I sucked their life force out of them through the spell web and there was nothing they could do to stop it.

15

"We need to start planning," Si says, glancing over at me for the hundredth time.

I nod morosely, knowing what's coming next.

"You have to fly us there, Mei. We can't be sure we'll make it in time otherwise."

I shake my head. There's no way I'm taking either of them up into the air. I'd kill us all. I haven't been back into the skies since that first aborted flight. My wing is 100 percent better again, but both Seth and Si still have a gray tinge to their skin, even now, five days later.

The more I learn about my dragon-self and the powers I have, the more I think they were right to kill us all.

I can literally suck the life force out of a supernatural person connected to the spell web.

And if I'm in pain, or something is threatening me, I will do it instinctively, without thought and without being able to stop it.

My instinct to survive is greater than my own will. It

overrides my choices and ensures I endure whatever the costs.

It makes me feel sick inside, but there's nothing I can do about it.

But I do have some areas I can control, and I will do everything I can to protect Si and Seth, like they protected me.

And that means not taking them up in the sky where they could get hurt. I have no control over the flying, and I don't want to be responsible for causing either of them pain.

Well, more pain.

I push an image of all of us falling from the skies into Si's head.

He grunts and shakes his head. "That won't happen, especially if you practice now."

I push another image of my wing, broken and beaten.

"You're not much of a dragon if you won't fly," Si says, exasperation in his voice. "You have to put yourself out there, Mei. Lose the fear."

I shake my head. This isn't about fear. It's about protecting the people I love. From me.

"Do you think Jeff protected you all those years, just to see you cowering here on the cliff tops, too afraid to do anything?" Si stares at me intently.

I stand up, all four legs working together to move me back. I'm getting good at moving in this body now. I've figured out the way it's all supposed to work. The only thing I haven't figured out is flying.

"You're a dragon, Mei. It's who you are. You need to embrace it," Seth says from my other side. He's been quietly eating his breakfast of a muesli bar. I've been happily chowing down on the strange rocks below, but Seth and Si have been working on the weird collection of food that was stored in the boot of the car.

They're both wrong. I can't embrace being a dragon, because that would mean giving in to all the terrible urges I have. Stealing their power, and burning them when I can't get my way. That's what being a dragon means, and I don't want that. So I have to control it, push it down and make sure I don't let it come out in that same uncontrolled way it did when I first changed.

It means I'm only going to fly when I'm good and ready, and I'm damn well not going to carry passengers.

"Your father is still with the Earthbound. If we're going to rescue him, we have to leave here as soon as we can. We should probably even leave now," Si says.

I hesitate. I want to rescue my father, and Si's right, the longer we wait, the more damage they could be doing to him. And although the Earthbound are already expecting us, the longer we take, the more time they'll have to get settled in, to plan and prepare for us. I shiver, thinking of the small heated room Vincent locked me in last time. What else do they have hidden away for their prisoners?

Seth shakes his head. "I don't think that's wise. We should wait the full ten days, let Mei change back into her human form, and then leave. We don't know what it will be like."

I nod my head to agree. I don't want to go anywhere past this sanctuary in dragon form. If I dislike the fact I'm a dragon this much, imagine how other people will feel about it?

Si lets out a breath. "You need to practice flying, Mei. It's important. You need to build up your strength."

I let out a huff of breath, pushing the smell of my rocky breakfast into the air around me. I shake my head and move away from where they're sitting, to walk the edges of the nesting bowl. I pace along the ridge, looking out at the sea and trying to see as far as I can.

My vision has become stronger in the last few days, and I spot a school of fish way out in the ocean. It's more than just being able to see the colors; I can smell them and sense their shape as they push through the water, and I hear the sound of their scales rubbing against the water and their gills opening and shutting. It's a strange but exhilarating way to see the world.

I could love being a dragon, if it didn't mean death and destruction.

I'm so distracted by the fish that I'm not paying attention to where I'm walking, and my front foot slips on a loose piece of shale. With three other legs, this usually isn't a problem, but then my other front leg slides forward as well, and suddenly I'm sliding over the edge of the bowl and down the steep cliffs on the beach side of the nest.

Automatically I push out my wings, and the wind catches them, pushing me up and into the sky again.

At first I panic, my legs churning in the air, and my heart pounding.

But then something changes. Instead of falling and struggling to find my way in the air, I'm gliding. There's less wind today and it makes a huge difference. The air currents are softer, gentler, and I don't feel like I'm fighting to stay in control.

The wind caresses my face like a lover's hand, stroking my body. The air currents gently nudge me one way and then another, and soon I'm soaring out to sea, my wings strong and sure. It's a strange feeling, having wings holding me high.

I'm practicing banking and turning over the beach when

something catches my eye on the road behind the nest. A row of trucks, khaki green like the army uses, heading along the road toward us. I fly higher, watching. Could it be a coincidence?

The noise of a helicopter bursts into the air around me, and I turn, trying to locate the source. This isn't an accident. Somehow the Earthbound have found me, yet again.

I dive down toward the bowl, trying not to speed up too much. I manage to land on the edge and run my feet long the earth to slow myself down.

Seth and Si are both standing, hands covering their eyes and staring out toward the ocean. They've heard the chopper too. I make a noise of frustration, which comes out like a growl, and nod my head toward my back. They need to get on my back now.

There's no other option.

Seth climbs on first, grabbing hold of the bony ridges on my spine. Si only hesitates for a second, and then climbs up. As soon as they're on board, I leap off the edge. The extra weight throws me off immediately, and I end up diving down faster than I meant to. I wobble to one side and then the other, trying to find the right balance. I overcorrect a couple of times as we glide along the coastline. Eventually, I'm flying comfortably with both of them on my back. , I'm practically hugging the cliffs, but it's the only way I can think of to hide from the incoming helicopter.

But of course, it doesn't work. I turn my head, and behind us the helicopter is following our path along the cliffs.

Seth yells something, but the words are lost in the wind. I snatch the thought from his mind without thinking and nod. We need to think of a way to lose the helicopter, and flying up into the clouds might work.

I pump my wings, and we fly higher into the sky, fast and hard. We burst through the clouds and then up even further. Behind me the two men are clinging low to my back. I race higher and higher, desperate to lose them.

Up here the sky is perfect, the brightest of blues surrounded by a gentle light that makes me want to sigh and glide forever. It's only when I feel someone pounding on my back that I remember I'm carrying passengers and look back to check on them. Seth is fine; he's awake and glaring at me with his direct hazel eyes. But Si has slumped forward onto Seth's back, unconscious. I catch the words in Seth's head. I've flown too high and Si's unconscious because of the thin air.

Seth's trying to hold him safe with one hand and cling to my back with the other. I jerk in fright and catch the wind current I was following the wrong way.

My left wing dips, and suddenly I'm on my side, and Seth and Si are both toppling toward the earth.

16

I give a terrified roar and dive back around, using my wings instinctively to get me where I need to go. The two men are falling fast, and I don't have much time.

My wings are half tucked and I'm speeding faster than I've ever gone before. I'm diving down, my nose pointed straight to earth. The wind is hurtling past my face, and all I can hear is a roaring in my ears. I don't know if I'm going to make it in time.

And then suddenly I catch up to them. They're still together; Seth clutching onto Si, who is unconscious.

My moment of relief disappears when I realise I can't get them onto my back again. We're all falling toward the ground too fast. But if I don't do something right now, they're going to die.

The ground is looming, and in a panic, I make a grab for both of them with my front legs. Seth yells as one of my claws stabs him in the side, but I manage to hold onto them and swoop back up into the sky.

The monotonous sound of the chopper's rotors follows behind us. I turn my head and spot it further back. My flight up into the clouds has taken us ahead, but my stupidity in going too high almost cost us.

The blood is pumping frantically through my body; I'm trembling and lightheaded. I wonder how much excitement I can take. Perhaps dragons are like birds or mice—we die from too much shock. But then I remember the paintings of fighting dragons on Vincent's wall at the Earthbound compound. If it's true they loved to fight, then dragons can probably handle a whole lot more than this.

It's just me who's having trouble with it.

I concentrate on flying fast, carrying my passengers tucked close to my body and keeping just below the clouds. The red and gold of my scales isn't exactly discrete, but I figure speed is going to work in our favor. And I'm right. The sound of the chopper disappears, and soon it's just us flying along the coastline.

I'm still a day and a half from being able to transform from dragon to human form, and I have no idea where a dragon could hide in the meantime. We're speeding up the coastline, and before long, we've passed New York and Boston, which I only recognize because of the buildings in the distance. I'm flying further out to sea by this time and relying on the cloud cover to keep me hidden. Somehow I know I'm flying northeast, my new dragon senses letting me feel my direction in a whole new way. I can use the spell web to sense direction as well as other supernaturals now. Below us, fish leap, and a whale harmonizes with its brothers and sisters out to sea.

The land starts to change again, and soon I can see another landmass up ahead. My sketchy memory of the geography lessons Jeff used to give me comes in handy.

Nova Scotia.

Islands are visible along the coastline and I dip toward

the Earth again. The salty tang of the sea mixes with the fresh scent of grass and trees. The landscape is more natural up here, towns and villages separated by miles of emptiness. Perfect for a dragon who needs to land.

Up ahead is a small island, with low grass and a few trees that isn't ideal for protection, but ticks all the boxes for being isolated. I need to rest, and my hands feel like they're slipping in their hold of Seth and Si. I put the image of swooping over the beach into Seth's head, and then I tip my wings and head down. Si is still unconscious.

Swooping down over a small stretch of beach covered from view by thick trees, I fly as close to the ground as I can. Then I let go of Seth and Si.

They roll a couple of times, but I managed to get them pretty close to the sand, so they seem fine. It's me I'm concerned about. I don't know how to land, and it's harder than it looks. I did it back at the nest, but that's because I wasn't thinking about it. I try to remember what I did, but I was running on adrenaline. It's all a fog in my brain.

I have no choice. I just have to give it a go and hope for the best. I swoop around, angling down again. I try to keep my speed down, and head back in.

Seth has dragged Si's unconscious form to one side of the beach. I put out my hind legs, attempting to break my landing. As my feet hit the sand, I try running a little to ease the landing, but after two desperate steps, I trip and fall hard on my dragon chin, sliding along the sand and creating a rut through the middle of the beach.

"Smooth landing," Seth says from behind me. Despite the fact that he's teasing me, his voice is grim.

I put out my front paws and push myself up, shaking my head. It was a better landing than the first time I did one. Maybe Seth's thinking about how I almost killed them just after that landing. Si and Seth have definitely taken a beating since I turned into a dragon.

I stand up, and crane my neck to see how Si is doing. Seth is kneeling next to him, checking his vital signs.

"He's fine, just needs time to recover. It was oxygen deprivation, I think."

I nod. But if Si was knocked unconscious, why is Seth okay? I tip my head to one side.

"I know," Seth says, staring over at me, his eyes unusually dark. "I should be out as well. I don't know why I'm not." He's trying to hide it, but I can see his anger at me in the tense lines around his mouth, and the set of his jaw.

I slump down onto the sand. He's right to be angry; I'm out of control. I almost killed Si...again. It's getting ridiculous.

But his anger still hurts.

"He's coming to," Seth says.

I lift my head again and see Si moving his head from side to side. I move closer, trying to make sure he's okay. He sees me and his expression hardens for a second. Then it's gone, replaced by the blank look I recognise from the fighting ring. That's his game face. The expression he puts on when he doesn't want anyone to know what he's really thinking.

This is the same man who raised me, who took care of me and taught me how to defend myself. I spent hours with him in various training rings.

And now he's looking at me as if he doesn't know me. It's like a punch in the gut.

"How are you feeling, Si?" Seth asks.

"Like I just got hit by a truck," he says in a low voice. "You?"

Seth touches his side, and I notice the blood for the first

time. He's bleeding from where my claws punctured his side.

"I'm fine," he says shortly. He doesn't even look my way.

I want to say I'm sorry, to both of them, but I can't even do that. Si wasn't happy about me putting images inside his head last time. My only option is to stare at them both with remorse in my eyes and hope they understand.

"Did we lose all our supplies?" Si asks, ignoring my look.

I look to Seth for his answer as well. We had to leave the wooden box behind, that much I know. Both Seth and Si had a chance to go through it, but I've been in dragon form the whole time. I'd been planning to have another look through when the words didn't look like gobbledegook on a page.

"Not all of them." Seth pulls a few items out of his inside pocket. There's his penknife, and his wallet. I see a glint of gold; for some reason, he has the ring. He must have taken it out of the box.

I wait for the usual blast of longing, but I don't feel it. I frown. Could my dragon form be immune? Last, he grins and pulls out a few of the muesli bars they've been living off.

Si narrows his eyes and checks out the forest and rolling hills behind us thoughtfully. "I think I might prefer to try a little scavenging."

Seth lets out a bark of laughter, and I huff out a breath. I haven't been eating the muesli bars, but they don't look that appetizing.

"How'd they find us?" Seth asks.

Si shrugs. "They have access to the same information we do. Those reports were duplicates of the originals. They must have figured we'd need to find the nest."

"It took them a while."

"They've probably been swarming over those original coordinates we had."

There's a long pause and then Seth asks, "Did Damien —?" He stops and glances at me.

At first I don't understand what Seth's asking. Then it clicks. He thinks my father let us all go to the wrong coordinates on purpose. The idea would have been to throw off our pursuers, but it almost cost my life in the process. A low rumble starts in my stomach.

Si shakes his head. "I don't know. He's good, but is he that good?"

Good? Psychopathic more like. I let out a smoky huff of breath.

"How long do you think we've got before they catch up with us?" Seth asks.

Si looks back along the coastline. "Not long."

I point up to the trees on the edge of the beach.

"You want to hide in there?" asks Seth.

I nod.

Seth stares up at the forest, then at the coastline behind us. "I think it's a good idea. We need to be out of sight."

"We'll need to get rid of that," Si says, pointing to the long line of sand hollowed out from when I landed. I stand up and swish my tail along the ridgeline. It's not perfect, but it could pass for a natural line in the sand rather than a place a dragon landed.

We all trudge up to the trees. I struggle to find anywhere to enter at first, my huge body dwarfing the small gaps. I don't want to use my fire, because it'll be obvious to searchers. Even pushing over some of the trees isn't an option, because it's the kind of thing that would be visible overhead.

But eventually we find a small gully with fewer trees, and I squeeze my way through.

"We need to camouflage you," Seth says, following behind me. "Your scales reflect the sun and give you away too quickly."

We find a muddy patch near the stream and Seth grabs two handfuls of sludge; he begins slathering it over my golden red scales. Si joins in, and soon they're both smearing the thick mud over my body. By the expressions on their faces they're enjoying it far too much.

I have to work hard to not snarl at them; it's unpleasant having mud over my scales. It's thick and gluggy...and not very pretty. It's almost comical how difficult I find it; who knew I'd become so attached to my golden scales in such a short time?

But he's right, and I have to be sensible.

I'm just settling into the space they've created when the sound of an incoming chopper thunders through the air. Despite our preparations, I hadn't really expected them to follow us this far up.

I guess I underestimated their desire to find me.

Heart in my throat, I sit and watch the sky. Seth and Si crouch near me, their faces lifted toward the south. The sounds of the sea are drowned out by the rhythmic droning of the helicopter.

We watch as the helicopter flies overhead, but they don't stop. I let out a breath, and I feel the other two doing the same beside me.

"We stay hidden for the next two days," Si says.

I nod in agreement.

"Then we go to the Earthbound compound and get Damien out."

I'm not entirely convinced about this part of the plan—how are we going to fight all those Earthbound soldiers? I'm only one dragon, not ten.

But now that I've flown and carried them both while doing it, I can't use that as my objection any more. And I'm the one who insisted that we rescue my father, despite the odds. I haven't changed my mind.

I sigh. There's nothing I can do or say until I'm back in human form.

"I'm going to hunt, see what I can find," says Si. His expression is grim, and I feel like he just wants to get away from me. I don't really blame him.

Seth and I sit in our hiding place, the mud dripping

slowly down my side. We don't talk, and I don't know how to bridge the gap between us. I felt so close to him not so long ago. He looks like he's brooding, dark thoughts circling in his head.

I can guess what he's thinking. This whole mess has gotten out of hand. He turned up, all bright and shiny and new, for his first assignment as an SIG agent, and now he's sitting in the middle of nowhere, covered in mud and his own blood, a renegade agent being hunted down by people who wouldn't think twice about killing him.

I don't know how to apologise for that.

I touch his shoulder with my front paw. I push the image of me healing his wound into his head.

He shakes his head at first, but I won't let him say no.

Eventually he sighs and lifts up the side of his shirt. The wound is caked in blood and mud. It looks a little red, like it's on the verge of getting infected. I touch it gently and pulse a little of my magic toward him along the spell web.

It's as different to the healing I learned from Si as night and day. In my dragon form I can manipulate the power of the spell web, and use it to heal, the way I did for my wing. It feels easier, more innate, than Si's way of healing.

Seth lets out a sigh, and sits back against a boulder. He must have been in pain, because now his shoulders are much less tense, and he closes his eyes.

"Thanks," he says without opening them.

I shrug. I was the one who caused the wound, so I really can't take credit for healing him. I settle down in place beside Seth, and close my eyes as well.

There's still silence between us, but for some reason it feels...easier. After a while, Seth leans on my side, his breathing deep and even. He's fast asleep.

Si comes back an hour later with a couple rabbits for

dinner. It's gotten dark while he was gone, and our hiding spot is starting to feel less cosy and more cold.

"We'll wait until the helicopter flies back down the coastline," he says and sits down beside Seth. His muscles aren't as tense as they were before, and he seems to have his equilibrium back. At least he's lost his game face, and I can see his real expression again.

A little while later, the thumping of the helicopter blades tells us they've gone back down the coastline, and Si sets about lighting a fire and roasting the rabbits over the open flames. It's almost like we're camping—except I'm an enormous dragon.

Thankfully, I'm not hungry—my share of the rabbits wouldn't even fill one paw if I was—and the smell of the cooking meat doesn't attract me like it would have in human form.

I'm not sure how long I can go without eating the strange rocks, but I don't want to feel that same ravenous hunger again. A shiver goes down my side, flicking my scales over each other in a wave, and making a faint clicking sound. Mud is stuck between some of the scales, and it's hardening up, making me itch uncomfortably. I shake my whole body, trying to flick the mud away.

As Seth and Si eat the rabbits, I watch them closely, trying to figure out what they're each thinking. The flickering fire is reflected on their faces making them both look like avenging angels. They're focused on their first decent meal in a while, and after ten minutes of contemplation, I'm no nearer figuring either of them out.

"We can set up watch, one of us always needs to be awake just in case," says Si. "I'll go first watch."

After that, there's nothing to do but go to sleep.

For the next day and a half we wait in our hiding spot. Si

goes out to hunt, Seth explores further into the forest. I have to wait where I am, my body too big to go further into the forest, and my scales too shiny to risk going out into the open if I don't need to. Time passes slowly and I'm left alone with my thoughts. Despite the fact that I'm looking forward to switching back, I'm filled with a growing sense of dread. The book said it was an unpleasant process. Does that mean painful? Or just uncomfortable? I'm dealing with the unknown, and it's driving me insane.

On the morning designated for my return to human form, I wake to the sun shining through the trees, spreading a warm glow. Everything is peaceful on our island. Si and Seth have found plenty to eat, and I've remained completely full since the last time I ate.

I'm grateful the insatiable hunger hasn't returned. I have no idea how I'd find more of the special rock and there's no going back to the nest. I'm hoping it was just part of the changing process, but there's still a fear in the back of my mind that it will come back. The lack of control and the way I hurt my friends so easily keeps me awake at nights.

On the island, there's not much of a spell web. It's just me, Si, and Seth, whose bright glowing web is strangely hypnotic against the blues and yellows of the island.

"So, are you ready?" Seth asks. He's watching me carefully, and I know he's worried. In our rush to leave, we left the book back at the nesting ground, but we both remember clearly what it said about turning back to human form for the first time. It's going to be unpleasant. Whatever the hell that means.

Si stands next to Seth. He's looking grim as well, but there's something more than concern for me in that expression. I could be wrong, but my mentor appears to be having second thoughts about being around me at all. I can't blame him—since I've been in this form, I've almost killed him at least three times. It doesn't matter that it was accidental, done on instinct each time.

Part of me thinks he's right to be concerned.

Don't project or borrow trouble. It's never as bad as you think it is.

One of Jeff's favorite sayings. He was right most of the time.

I take a deep breath and nod. I'm tingling over most of my body, and I wonder if that's all it takes to start the change, a sense of being ready for it.

I wait for something to happen, but the tingling never moves on to anything else. I have to do this myself.

I close my eyes and concentrate on the energy inside me. There's a whole lot more buzzing around in there than I've ever felt before. Turning into my dragon shape has unleashed my full potential, although I've never really tested it. I'm too afraid of hurting Seth and Si.

But now I have no choice. I have to access that magic and try to turn back. For the first time, I realize I have no idea how to do it, and tremors rock my body, my scales clicking together noisily.

I take another breath, this time a little more panicky. Opening my eyes, I find Seth and Si still staring at me.

Seth takes a step forward and places one hand on my neck. It's the first time he's voluntarily touched me since the nest. "You've got this, Mei. You can do it. Just look inside yourself and figure out how."

I let out a breath and nod.

We're still hiding out in the forest, and I glance over to the open land next to the beach. For a start, I think I want to be out there, in the open. Changing will probably be a messy business, and I don't want to get my wings caught on a branch or find myself wedged between two pine trees. I push my way out of the hiding place, my mind already trying to decide how I'm going to do this.

I figure I need to picture my old shape, to be clear about what I want to go back to. It seems completely impossible that I could return to that tiny shape again after being a dragon now for ten days. But who said magic made sense?

Seth makes to follow me and I shake my head. I appreciate the thought, but I don't know how this works and I have a feeling it might involve fire again. I send an image of him and Si waiting in the trees, and he nods, stopping at the edge of the tree line, letting me go on alone.

I stop somewhere in the middle of the area, with the water to one side and the trees to the other. The picture of myself as Mei the supernatural is clear in my head, and I start to draw on the energy inside me to make the change.

I feel sparks straight away and a small rush of triumph spreads through my body. Perhaps this process is going to be easier than I thought.

Then the tiny sparks of energy turn into flaming balls of pain, and I know it's going to be just as bad as they said in the book.

If not worse.

18

Panicking, I try to stop the process, to take a breath and give myself a chance to begin again.

But it doesn't work. I've started off some kind of chain reaction, and there's no way to back out.

What started as pain along the outside of my body is now coursing through my veins, pushing agony into every little pore. It's like I'm burning up, and I seriously start to wonder if I'm going to survive. There's too much pain.

I'm standing on all fours, but even that is too much, and I slowly topple to one side, landing heavily.

My breathing is ragged and uneven, and my heart is pounding in my chest. For every heartbeat, there's a corresponding flare of pain through my body.

I've been holding back on screaming for fear of being discovered, but the noise comes up my throat anyway, a compulsion I can't control. The noise that erupts from my mouth is raw and guttural. It's like it belongs to someone else.

In the distance, I see Si holding onto Seth, who looks like he wants to run out and try to help me. I'm grateful that

Si is thinking sensibly. I'm as out of control now as I've ever been in this form, and there's no way I can stop whatever is going to happen. I could hurt Seth again, and not even be aware of it until it was too late.

My skin squeezes tight over my flesh, and I moan in pain. It feels like my body is being stretched, like that old-fashioned torture where they pulled all four limbs in opposite directions until the body wrenched apart. That's me. Right now.

Only no one else is doing this to me; I'm doing it to myself.

I cry out again, my keening dragon cry carrying across the landscape, scaring a flock of birds into flight. It echoes around me, and I lift my head, half expecting to see other dragons flying overhead. I suspect that's how this is supposed to be, with the support of other, wiser dragons around me, calming and comforting.

But I'm alone, except for two normal supers who don't understand what I'm going through any more than I do.

One big long burst of pain sizzles across my skin, coating my whole body in a layer of agony, and making my scales clatter together uncomfortably. The mud that's been caked to my hide for the last two days is starting to fall away, leaving gleaming gold and red patches. I close my eyes and start huffing breaths in and out, like women do in the movies when they're giving birth. I have no idea if it's going to help, but at this point, I'll take anything I can get.

I'm still breathing heavily, trying to focus on something else, when I realise the pain has stopped. I can't feel my body, but at least I'm not being ripped apart by pain.

Is that it? Am I...?

I open my eyes. Looking down, I still see my enormous

dragon body. I roll hesitantly to my feet, give myself a shake, and look around.

Did I fail? Or wait too long to change? Was the information in the book wrong?

Overhead, tall dark clouds have formed, like a strange monument the sky has made to celebrate my transformation. But nothing has happened, and I feel like a fraud. I don't know how to do this. There's no one to tell me what I'm supposed to be doing, and it's as frustrating as hell.

The earth beneath me starts to rumble, making rocks and pebbles rattle across the ground. I plant my feet wider on the ground to keep my balance. What's happening? Is this part of the transformation? Or something come to mess with me? Rain starts to fall from the dark clouds, pelting my whole body.

High above, a boom of thunder rolls across the sky, like the opening drumroll to a particularly loud rock song.

And then directly over me, the clouds part, and a blazing flash of white light blinds me from above. Searing heat fills my body, the feeling of being burned from the inside out.

Was I just hit by lightning?

I scream as the heat and pain flash through my body, finding every little crevice. I'm surrounded by an intense light, and there's no part of me that's free from the agony. I try to breathe and discover I can't, that I'm being held motionless in a moment in time where pain is everything and the rest of the world has disappeared. Fear and panic rule my thoughts, and I struggle against whatever is holding me.

It ends as suddenly as it began, and I gasp for breath, flinging my head back and forth, grateful I survived. I'm still in my dragon body, so whatever just happened wasn't enough to change me. I'm saturated now, the earth around me turning to mud under the onslaught of rain.

I see a flash of movement through the storm, and then Seth is beside me, his hands on my neck, murmuring words I can't understand.

Another bolt of lightning hits.

And another.

I scream, blinded by the light, unable to see Seth. Is he okay? Surely he couldn't survive a direct hit like that? It's one thing for a dragon to do it, another for an ordinary supernatural.

I can't lose Seth, not now, not like this.

Lightning hits again, and again, and this time I can't tell where the pain begins and ends. I'm desperate to know if Seth is okay, but I can't see enough to tell. The storm has darkened the sky, saturating everything around me.

At the same time, I'm starting to worry about myself. How much more can I take?

There's no gap between the bolts of lightning now.

It's just one long jagged line of energy connecting me to the clouds above. There's power and magic inside the lightning, and I wonder if I'm supposed to be feeding off it somehow. But all I can do is feel the pain and try not to die. Everything else is too much. I'm not strong enough to control it, or wield it. What would have happened if I'd had other dragons with me? Would it have been different? Would they have helped, or at least warned me of what was to come?

My life force is draining from me as each successive surge of lightning hits. It's too much, and I know it. I try to move, to roll out of the way of the storm, but my legs won't move. I desperately try to look around for Seth, but all my senses are overwhelmed.

Nothing but the pain is real to me.

I lie my head down on the ground. It's heavy, and my neck can no longer hold it up. My eyes search wildly around me, but there's nothing that can save me. This is it. Everything is draining from my body. I have nothing more to give.

If I wasn't so exhausted, I might cry.

My eyes close, and I lie there, waiting for death. It's the only thing that can happen now. There's no other possible place for me to go, and I weep inside for all the lost possibilities in my life. It's been so short, not enough time to do any of the things I wanted to do.

The storm rages overhead, and I feel my body melting into the earth, all the muscles relaxing as they stop their fight for life. Lightning hits my body again, but this time nothing jerks, nothing moves. I'm spent. There is nothing more for me here.

I let go of myself and start floating, up and away.

I look down from above and see two forms lying next to each other. Burned skin covers the bodies. One is completely naked but covered in mud; the other has patchy, half-burned clothing on his body. Neither is moving.

My body has changed.

Overhead the storm ends as quickly as it began. Something snaps inside my head, and I return to my body.

I'm human again.

19

M y eyes open and I immediately push myself up to sitting, searching for Seth. My arms feel small and weak, my body shattered. I see his body off to one side.

I crawl toward him on hands and knees. The earth is slick with mud, and I slip and slide over the surface before reaching him. He must have been thrown from my side when the lightning hit.

Pushing my ear into his chest, I listen for breathing. Nothing. I bang on his chest. "You can't die," I whisper. If I wasn't completely wiped out from changing back, I might have cried or perhaps yelled. But as it is, I can't work up the capacity to do anything so energetic.

Running footsteps behind me announce Si's arrival, and he eases me to one side before leaning in to inspect Seth's body. He grabs his wrist and checks for a pulse.

"He's alive. Barely."

I let out a sobbing breath. "I can't heal him. My magic's too weak."

"I'll see what I can do," says Si.

"Please save him," I say. My voice is rusty and broken.

Si turns back to Seth and puts both hands on Seth's chest. He closes his eyes and starts the delicate process of healing. I hold my breath beside him, trying not to interrupt. Healing isn't Si's first or greatest skill, and it's a difficult process at the best of times. I watch for what seems like hours as he slowly but surely pushes the right combination of magic into Seth's body, trying to soothe his soul and heal his body.

Eventually Si pulls back. "I've done my best. I've never felt anything like it before, the way his magic works inside his body."

I nod. I know exactly what Si means. I grasp one of Seth's hands and cling to it, willing him to be okay. It's not his turn to die, not today.

As I'm holding his hands, I notice his spell web for the first time. It's glowing even stronger now, but it's a different color. A golden white light is now shining along his grid, different to the red glowing lines I'm used to. I've never seen anything like it; what does it mean?

I'm not certain what kind of magic he has, or what the changes to his spell web might indicate... but his glowing spell web is beautiful.

Si glances back over at me and raises his eyebrows. "You might want to put this on," he says, shrugging out of his jacket.

I look down. I'm completely naked, albeit mud and ash covered. I take the jacket gratefully.

I'm staring down at Seth when I become aware of the sound of a helicopter in the distance. I glance up into the sky.

"They saw the storm," Si says, grappling with Seth's body.

I grab Seth's legs, and between the two of us, we run awkwardly back to the trees. I'm still getting used to being in human form again and stumble a couple of times. Who'd have thought I'd have trouble with only having two legs?

We make it to the forest, and now that I'm not an enormous dragon, it's easier to hide among the trees, but harder to carry Seth. We continue through the trees, running as fast as we can amid the low hanging branches and the logs and leaves.

"There's a cave up ahead. I saw it the other day," Si says. He leads the way through the trees, his feet pounding on the hard earth.

We emerge on another beach, and I glance frantically at the sky, trying to spot the incoming helicopter. "Where is it?"

Si ignores my words and keeps running, forcing me to follow as fast as I can. We come to the base of a small cliff face, with overgrown trees and vines running down from the top. He pushes aside the foliage and leads the way into the dark interior. "A rabbit disappeared in here yesterday."

It's dark, but my excellent dragon eyesight has followed me back into human form, and I can see the dim interior clearly. We head to the back of the cave and place Seth gently on the ground. He gasps in his sleep and thrashes his head back and forth.

"If they saw the storm, they'll probably get out and search," Si says.

I nod. "They'll find the place where I changed back." I hesitate. "Will they search the whole island?"

Si stares at me, his eyes intense. "You know the answer to that, as well as I do."

I swallow carefully. Of course I do. They'll search every damn square inch of this island to find me. They've been on our tail this whole time. Vincent is determined to have me any which way he can. "They might not find the cave," I say, although I know it's unlikely.

We sit in silence, waiting.

The thudding noise of the helicopter isn't as loud in here, and I'm not entirely sure when it stops, but the sound of men yelling and the silence of the animals and insects on the island lets us know when they start searching.

Seth is still unconscious, and I stare down at his face. What will happen if they find us? Will they even be concerned about Seth? Or Si?

They'll get thrown in the same cell that Seth occupied last time, with no chance of being let out. Now that we know what side the director of the SIG is on, the chances of getting out alive seem more remote.

But if I go now, if I give myself up, there's a chance.

I stand up. "You need to give me your trousers," I say. There's no way I'm giving myself up naked.

Si shakes his head. "Sit down. You're not going anywhere."

"We were going to the Earthbound anyway. This way, I'll just get there ahead of you."

"You don't know what they'll do to you."

"You just have to follow me there and then get me and my father out," I say, like it's the easiest thing in the world. I glance at Seth. "He needs time to recover. If we're all caught at the same time, there's no one else to get us out. We're stuck."

"No. I won't let you do it. Not after everything." Si's face is unreadable, but I catch a tiny muscle tic near one eye. He knows I'm right.

It doesn't matter what he says; I have to do this. It's the only way. "You don't have a choice. Now give me your damn pants," I say, holding out my hand.

20

S i stands up, glaring at me. "I've spent my whole life protecting you. If you think I'm going to let you give yourself up, you're mistaken."

"It's the only way, don't you see?" I take a step toward him, and he flinches. I stop, stunned. "You're afraid of me?"

Si lets out a breath of air and runs a hand through his short black hair. "Of course not. I know you, Mei, probably better than you know yourself. You're a good person." He hesitates. "But you've almost killed me several times since you became a dragon. I'm only here because of my chameleon scales and a healthy dose of luck." He rubs his hand down one arm, as if he can feel his scales even in human form.

"I would never—"

"Never on purpose," interrupts Si. He takes a breath and gestures toward Seth. "But I don't know how the hell he's even survived this long."

A flush works its way up my face. He's right, I'm a danger to my protectors. "Even more of a reason to let me go," I say bitterly.

Si shakes his head. "Don't be stupid. But Jeff's death? Lee's death? It's all a waste if you give up now."

"I'm not giving up. I'm making a strategic decision."

He shakes his head. "No. You're scared. You don't know what you're doing, and you're making a decision based on fear of being a dragon."

A tingle of fear shivers down my spine. He's right, I *am* afraid of my dragon side. Almost everything about it has been painful and unpleasant. I feel completely turned upside down and inside out. Briefly I consider just changing into a dragon, forcing them onto my back and flying away.

But I don't know if I can outrun the helicopter and the armed men again, and more importantly, I'm not entirely certain how to change back into a dragon.

How long does it take?

Will it hurt?

If it always involves the lightning, I think I might happily never do it again. All the more reason to give myself up, to make sure Si and Seth survive.

"I don't have enough information. I don't know how to be a dragon," I say desperately.

"Just be yourself. Being a dragon doesn't have to define who you are. We raised you to be a strong, independent woman. We raised you to make decisions."

I nod, listening to his advice, trying to work out where I stand on it. I take a step closer. "You're right," I say, looking into his deep brown eyes, mentally asking for his forgiveness.

I raise my hand, placing it on his arm. Then, faster than I've ever moved before, I step behind him, pull his arm back, and press my fingers into two very specific spots on his neck. His body goes limp, before he can even say a word. As I lower him to the ground beside Seth, there's a sick feeling in my stomach.

I've just used information that he gave me in confidence —a weak point on the chameleon body, in case I ever had to fight another chameleon. I should never have done that to him; it's a betrayal of the worst kind.

But I had to.

It was for his own good.

He's right, I've been raised to make decisions. And I'm going to start making them.

I pull off his khaki trousers, thankfully with a belt. He's wearing boxers underneath, so it's not as bad as it could have been. I wish I had a blanket or something I could put over him and Seth, but there's nothing.

I scramble into his pants, pulling the belt tight around my waist. My feet are still bare, and I look a little like a hobo, but it will have to do.

I'm suddenly overcome by the need to cry. A lump forms in my throat. Si's going to be angry with me when he wakes up. Really angry. I'm making the people close to me angry, and I'm handing myself in to people who want to imprison me and use my magic for themselves. All around, it feels like I'm choosing a bad bunch of options.

I don't know what I'm getting myself into, but I can't imagine it's going to be good. I stiffen my spine. At least this time I have more information. I know what I'm letting myself in for.

Climbing over the rocks, I stride back up the beach. If I act confident, maybe I'll feel it.

The Earthbound guards are stomping through the woods, making it easy for me to avoid them. I don't want them to find me anywhere near the others. I exit the woods and see the helicopter in the open area where the multiple strikes of lightning hit me.

Tremors rock my body. The memory of the change lingers in my mind, and it's difficult to concentrate on what I'm doing.

Shouts ring out. They've spotted me.

I manage to force my legs to move and I head toward the helicopter. They seem disorganized, and I briefly wonder if I shouldn't have just stolen the helicopter and used it to go pick up the others.

The one flaw in that plan is I have no idea how to fly a helicopter. If Seth were awake, that might have been more of an option.

I'm about halfway across the open area when hands grab me from behind. My reflexes kick into gear and I kick backward, before elbowing him in the face. The man falls back, his easy catch not quite as docile as he thought.

More soldiers swarm in my direction, and I try to calm my shaking hands. This is nothing worse than I've already been through. They want me alive, I know that. They might have a whole bunch of guns, but they're not allowed to use them on me.

My plan is to distract them so they forget to ask about the others and just force me into the helicopter and go.

All I can say is, my plan could have worked if they'd played by the rules. As it is, I feel the sting of the injection at my neck, and seconds later, I don't feel anything more.

21

My head is pounding like I drank a bottle of Jeff's favourite whiskey the night before. My whole body feels stiff, like I've been crammed into one position for a long time. Maybe I have. I crack open one eye, and see stone blocks and not much else. I'm in a cell with no windows and only the bed I'm on.

I assume I'm inside the Earthbound compound, but there's really nothing that makes me confident about it. I'm still covered in dirt and ash and only wearing Si's clothes. I pull the jacket closer around my body.

I don't know where they've taken me.

I don't know whether they found the others, or if I'm alone here.

I don't know anything, and it's terrifying.

My hands are shaking, and I cross my arms over my stomach, trying to stay calm.

Instead of being in control of this plan, I'm completely lost. I wish I was back in that cave with Seth and Si, holding my breath and hoping for the best.

Perhaps we could have stayed hidden. Perhaps they

wouldn't have stayed long. Perhaps we could have survived.

But probably not.

I sit myself up and shake out the cobwebs and self-doubt.

I made the best decision I could at the time. I made my choice, and now I'm going to live with it. I search the room, assessing what I have to work with and how I'm going to escape.

I did it once. I can do it again.

Just as I'm doing my third circle of the room, the door opens behind me. I turn, keeping the wall close at my back. Amos stands cautiously at the door, and I snarl. Last time I saw him, he held a gun on me.

His eyes narrow when he sees me at the back of the cell. He's lost that glowing innocence he used to have. Did I do that to him? Or was it his father?

"Hello, Mei."

I nod cautiously, not taking my eyes from him.

"I bet you thought you'd never find yourself back here again."

"No," I say, my voice rusty, still not used to speaking. I clear my throat.

"I told my father it was just a matter of time. That you would make a mistake eventually."

"Did he believe you?"

Amos hesitates. "Eventually."

"Was he angry?" I'm watching Amos's every move and tense for the possibility he might provide me with a way to escape. He's not exactly the world's greatest fighter.

But then movement behind him at the door indicates he's not alone. I see a guard in uniform and let out a frustrated breath.

His eyes flash at me. "That's none of your concern. What

you *should* worry about is what's going to happen now that your true nature has been revealed. You lied to me."

"About being a dragon? I didn't know. No one told me what I was."

Amos barks out a sharp laugh. "I don't believe you anymore, Mei. You showed me just how little you can be trusted."

"You were the one who gave me up to your father, not the other way around," I snap back, unable to help myself. Amos has somehow convinced himself he's the star in his own betrayal movie.

"For your own good!"

"No, for *your* own good. It's not good for me to be here, waiting to have my magic sucked out of me by your despotic father."

"If you'd come home with me, I could have protected you from him. It wouldn't have been like that." His features darken. "But not now. My father is determined to have your power for himself."

"Why? What does he need it for?"

"I told you already, to save the spell web. It's not strong enough anymore. We need the kind of power that only a dragon can create to keep it going."

"For the greater good, I suppose?" I ask, my voice heavy with sarcasm.

Amos frowns. "I understand why you're upset. No one wants to be the one who must be sacrificed."

"I'm not going to let you kill me so your father can keep his little power base. This is not a solution to the problem."

"It's the only solution. We've tried to fix it in other ways."

"What about my father? Why did you kidnap him? What did he ever do to the Earthbound?" I have to consciously force myself not to mention Seth and Si. If they don't have them here, then my talking about them will only put them in danger.

"Your father worked against the SIG and the Earthbound for many years, hiding you from us. He is a threat to our cause."

I clench my fists and feel rage building up inside me.

I take a step toward Amos. "He was hiding his *daughter* from certain death. Don't you think that's a good reason?"

Amos blinks and a furrow appears between his brows. "He... He had a responsibility." He doesn't sound so sure of his words now.

"What about the SIG director? He had Liling hidden all that time. Your father is still working with him."

Amos hesitates again. He's obviously not used to someone offering an opposite view to his father's. "My father would like to see you. I'm here to take you to him." He's trying to stand his ground with me, but it's a struggle. I can smell his fear.

My dragon is deep inside me now, but it's pushing to get out. I take a deep breath, trying to control the urge to change and breathe fire over Amos. The desire to kill him right here where he stands is almost overwhelming.

I can see that being a full dragon is going to make me a lot more bloodthirsty.

But changing isn't an option right now. I clench my fists. And if there's lightning and pain every time I do it, I don't want any part of it anyway. I grit my teeth and hold it in.

Amos sees something in my face. He takes a step back and glances toward the door.

I smile, and I know it's not a nice smile. "Sure, I'll go see your father," I say, slowly and carefully.

I want to teach that asshole a lesson in how to treat people.

mos practically skips back to the door, and I follow him out.

"You have to put on these handcuffs," he says, snatching them from one of the two guards standing at the door.

My eyes narrow, but I hold out my hands. Jeff taught me how to get out of handcuffs when I was twelve. The guard puts them on, sneering at me as he does it. He tightens them a bit too much, and the metal scrapes against my skin. A growl, from deep inside my chest, emerges from my mouth and the guard steps away quickly. I pull at the handcuffs, trying to loosen them, and the metal snaps in my hand. They fall to the ground as I look at them, stunned.

Amos moves away from me. "Hold her hands behind her back then," he says, his voice shaking.

I glare at the guards, daring them to come at me. I don't know what else I can do now that I'm a full dragon, but clearly I have more powers than I realized. Escaping might just be easier than I imagined.

There's a flurry of footsteps behind me, and I turn. A

contingent of five guards stands there, guns aimed at my chest. To the side is the mountain supernatural who tried to capture me when I was travelling with Amos and Seth. His face is impassive, but I notice his eye twitching minutely. I nod at him, but he doesn't return the gesture.

At the other side stands Liling, her expression fierce. "Please don't try anything, Mei. I don't want to have to kill you," she says quietly.

"What are you doing here, Liling? You're working for the Earthbound now?"

Liling shrugs. "My father is here. I'm helping him. It's the right thing to do."

I shake my head. "How come everyone around here thinks that killing me is the right thing to do?"

"I'm truly sorry for the necessity. But keeping the spell web in place is of prime importance if we are to maintain peace in our world. The only way to do that is to use your dragon powers."

"I'm sure there are a million other ways to do it, if anyone were to actually try to formulate another plan," I say, letting out a frustrated breath. "This is about Vincent gathering power and forcibly taking mine. I don't know why no one else can see that."

"You're wasting time arguing. It's been decided," Amos says. He nods at one of the guards and then toward me. I glare at the guard, and the man stays where he is.

"You need to come with us," Liling says. "Just talk to Vincent, hear him out."

I walk forward, keeping my focus on Liling. "If you had been the dragon, would you be so casual about being killed? The director thought you were the dragon all these years. He was grooming you for this."

Liling's face falls for a second, but her usual expression

returns so quickly that I almost think I imagined it. "I'm sorry, Mei. I really am." She motions for the mountain super to move forward, and he comes toward me, his eyes shining with an unnatural light.

"I don't know how much you know about being a dragon, but there are a race of mountain supernaturals who used to look after the nests," Liling says, watching his progress. "They had, as a necessity, immunity to certain dragon abilities."

I frown, not sure what she means. Given that I don't know half of the abilities I now have, it's not really a big deal. The mountain man comes up to me, his enormous body dwarfing mine. He looks down, and I see tears in his eyes.

"It's okay," I find myself saying. "I get this isn't your choice. Don't be upset." I put a hand on his arm, and it's solid muscle. He's like a damn rock. Like the last time I met him, a feeling of warmth and goodness flows out from him. I smile, I can't help it.

"There's a connection between us," he says softly. "We're part of the same whole, my species and yours. We work together to create harmony."

"There wasn't much harmony happening when the dragons were destroying the world," I say sarcastically.

He shakes his head. "There's so much you don't know. You were raised away from the rest of the world, by people who don't know your people or your history." He grasps my arm, and I'm forced to follow him.

"You're taking me to my death, so it doesn't really matter now, does it?"

He doesn't reply, just keeps walking me down the hallway. Behind us, Liling, Amos, and the guards follow cautiously.

"Do you remember what you did last time?" he says so low that it's almost under his breath. My new dragon hearing picks it up.

"Using the spell web?" I glance up at him, but his face is just as impassive as it was before. He's looking ahead, as if he's not talking to me at all.

He nods slightly. "Now that you're a full dragon, you can do something more. It's the spell web that binds me to Vincent. You can set me free."

I can't tell if he's messing with me, but I focus on the spell web, and the lightly glowing grid covering his body becomes more visible. I push out along the red lines, just like I did last time, and start to weave my magic through his spell web covering. It's like I'm dancing through his subconscious, feeling and hearing what he's feeling.

To one side, behind his head, I discover a dark patch. It's not glowing like the rest of the spell web, it's more like I imagine a black hole might look, an absence of light. I see the grid, but it's morphed into something dark and angry.

Tentatively, I push at the dark patch, and it gets smaller straight away. Without thinking about it too much, I push more of my magic along the spell web grid and over his body.

It streaks straight to the dark patch and attacks. Blinding light flashes behind my eyes. When I look again, the dark patch is gone and the mountain super's grid is glowing strong, much brighter than anyone else's—except for mine.

He grins, and for the first time, I see the full force of his personality. I can't help smiling back. "What's your name?" I ask.

"Carrick. You just saved me. So I will save you."

23

Everything around me blurs for a moment, and then Carrick moves, faster than I would have thought possible.

He takes out the first three guards with his massive fists before I even have a chance to do anything. But then I wade into the fray, kicking the gun out of the hands of the guard nearest me. I duck and swerve, then kick him low on the leg, breaking his knee. He falls with a scream, and I move on to the next man.

Gun shots go off, and I flick my attention back to Carrick, wondering if he's been hit. But I needn't have worried. The bullets flick off his skin like he really is made of rock.

"Don't hurt her," Amos yells. "We need her alive."

I turn my attention to him, narrowing my gaze. He's hiding at the back, yelling orders. How did I ever think he was a decent guy?

My attention moves to the guard in front of me.

He's holding his gun directed at my chest, but he's hesitating. They're not allowed to kill me. His loss. I move in low, kicking to the side in a fast move that he doesn't see until it hits his kidneys. Then I give him a sharp elbow to the face and a second blow to the neck. As he goes down, I grab his gun. It's not my first choice, but I'm going to use every weapon at my disposal.

Another guard goes down, and then I look up to see Liling standing in front of me, a gun held purposefully in her hands. She's not pointing at my heart, like the others. "I'm sorry, Mei. This isn't the way I would have chosen this to go," she says, before pulling the trigger.

The bullet hits my side like a freight train, and for a moment, it's like everything has frozen. Then the burning pain thrusts out through my body and I scream. I drop to my knees, clutching at my side, closing my eyes and trying to focus on something other than the bullet wound in my side.

This is the first time I've ever been shot, but not the first time I've been injured. I just have to control my breathing and concentrate on standing up again. I'm not going to give in this easily.

I take a deep breath and open my eyes. Amos is sprinting down the opposite hallway, and the guards are all lying on the floor in various states of consciousness. Liling is lying unconscious on the floor, downed by my massive defender.

It's already over.

Carrick takes one look at me and picks me up, carrying me in his arms, his long strides eating up the distance down the long hallway.

"Wait." I put my hand on his chest. "Did they capture Seth and Si as well?"

He shakes his head. "No."

A breath I didn't know I was holding whooshes out as

relief sinks its teeth into me. It was bothering me, the thought they might have been brought in for no better reason than that they were with me.

I let go and shift in and out of consciousness, only coming to fully when Carrick opens a door and the outside light shines over us, making me squint. We're in a high-walled courtyard with trees and plants all around.

I suddenly remember why I needed to come here in the first place. "Wait. We need to find my father. We have to save him."

Carrick shakes his head. "The cell where they're holding your father is too deep within the complex. I can't get you in and out of there, especially now you've been shot."

I push away from him, struggling to turn back, to go get my father. I'm not thinking clearly, and the sunlight is making my head swim.

"If you want to get out of here alive, you need to stay still," Carrick says harshly. The strong words break through my panic, and I quiet down.

Carrick is running now, each jarring movement causing jolts of pain to echo through my body. He's heading toward an outside door at the far end of the walled garden. As Carrick turns along a new path, he almost collides with an old man dressed in ancient-looking brown work clothes. Based on his appearance, he's a gardener, and he stares up at Carrick's face with a mixture of fear and awe.

"Don't say a word, old man," Carrick says, and carries on as if he threatens people every day.

I look back and see the gardener watching us, not moving.

"Do you know him?" I ask weakly.

"Yes. He will say nothing."

We're out the door and moving along the back of the

compound. It's a grass-covered open space with trees at the edges near the massive concrete wall that surrounds the whole compound.

I let out a breath, and gaze up at Carrick's stoic expression. There's something about him that gives me hope. It makes me feel like it might be possible to get out of this situation alive, that perhaps the Earthbound, despite their superior resources, might not win. I don't know if it's part of the mountain supernatural's connection to dragons, or if it's just his charismatic personality.

There's an old shed at the far end and Carrick seems to be heading for it. He runs to the back and pushes open the door. We enter the musty-smelling space, and I curl up my nose. Cobwebs brush my face and I wave a hand to get rid of them. I sneeze, and pain shoots up my entire body. I moan, unable to stop the sound.

"I'm going to heal you here before we go any further." Carrick places me gently on the ground.

"You're a healer?" I say.

He shakes his head. "It's part of our connection. I can do things for dragons that I cannot do for anyone else."

"Kind of a redundant talent, huh?" I say weakly.

A corner of his mouth tips up in a smile. "Not anymore."

"Thank you," I whisper. "For getting me out of there."

"Don't thank me until we're actually out. This isn't a done deal yet."

I nod and lie quietly as he places his hands over the bullet wound.

"I don't think it's serious," he says. "Just a flesh wound. Luckily, they were trying not to hurt you."

"So they could kill me later," I mutter.

Carrick pushes at my wound, suddenly and with such force that I scream. Blinding pain blazes out from the bullet hole on my side, and everything turns to a brilliant white light for what seems like a never-ending period of time.

And then I open my eyes. Carrick is kneeling in front of me, panting like he's just run a marathon. His eyes are bloodshot and blood is dripping from a new wound in his side.

"What did you do?" I ask, gazing at him in shock.

"I took on your pain," he says. "The wound is now mine."

"No," I say, horrified. "Undo it. You can't do that." This is worse than every other death on my hands.

It was my wound, and he's made it his own.

24

H e bats away my hands. "It's a flesh wound. I'm fine. But you will need all your strength if you're going to survive."

"You give it back to me, right now." Tears form in my eyes, and a drop forces its way out and down my cheek. I wipe it away angrily. I'm not usually a crier. At least, I never used to be.

Carrick eyes me compassionately. "Don't worry about the crying. It's a common aftereffect of the healing. You'll be fine in a minute." He takes a breath, and pushes himself to his feet. Blood is leaking from the wound onto his shirt, making the stain get wider even as I watch.

I shake my head at him. "You shouldn't have taken my wound. It's not right."

"I chose to do it. I had no means of escape, until you came along. He had my spell web firmly in his grasp. You set me free."

"Why did he want you?"

"Other than my charm?" Carrick shrugs. "He wanted a mountain supernatural because of our connection to dragons. He thought if he could control me, he could control you."

"He got that wrong."

"He did. Now I need you to stand up. We're not out of here yet."

I push myself to my feet and watch as Carrick takes a limping step toward the door. "Are you sure you're okay?" I ask as he winces and holds his side.

"Better than okay," he says with a lopsided grin. "I'm a free man again."

Despite his wound, he's still the one in charge of this escape, and I let him lead us out through the door and along a side path. It's got some cover due to a row of large old oak trees, and we run between each tree trunk, getting closer and closer to the massive wall surrounding the complex.

"How come we're not being attacked out here?" I ask, unable to believe we're still managing to avoid the guards.

"He doesn't believe anyone could escape to the outside wall, especially given the measures he put in place after Amos helped you."

I take this information in, thinking it over. "Are there other places where he's overconfident?"

Carrick grins. "Many."

We're close to the wall now, and I stare up, trying to figure out how he plans for us to climb over. It's enormous, made of smooth concrete with massive spikes at the top, so they've probably never worried about people scaling it.

"How are we supposed to get over the wall?" I ask. Last time I left, I'd been hiding in Amos's van and it hadn't been an issue.

Carrick grinned. "The trouble with having someone you think you will always be able to control, who then gets free, is that you've told them things, or had them use secret doors, that you can't just make them forget about."

I grin. "There's a secret exit?"

"You betcha."

We follow the line of the wall, keeping low and trying to stay hidden by the sparser foliage this far from the main buildings.

Carrick halts in front of me and pushes at a point on the wall that looks like every other part. Right next to us, a door swings open.

"I didn't even see it. There was no line at the hinge," I say.

"Magic."

"I thought they didn't like magic."

Carrick shrugs. "They'll use whatever works to achieve their goal."

I follow Carrick through the door. On the other side, the landscape changes. It's sparse and rocky, completely at odds with the lush and beautiful landscape inside the compound. For the first time, I understand how much has gone into creating the Earthbound sanctuary.

"What do we do now?" I ask.

"We walk," Carrick says. He points toward a scattering of trees in the distance, and I think I see the edges of a road. Carrick scans the horizon, as if waiting for an attack, and then takes off at a slow, awkward run.

There's no other option than to follow Carrick across the rocks. I watch him carefully, wincing whenever he stumbles. A couple of times, I try to help, but he gently pushes away any hand that I offer him. His hand is pressed against his wound, trying to stem the flow of blood, and his pale face is determined.

We're about halfway across when I hear the sound of a helicopter's rotors thumping through the sky.

Carrick looks backward, into the sky over the compound. "Dammit, he knows we're outside." He glances at me. "We must have tripped an alarm. It won't take them long to find us out here."

"Can we go back inside? Steal a car or something...?" My words trail off. I know what he's going to say.

He lets out a breath. "You need to change into your dragon form. It's the only way we'll beat the helicopter out of here." Carrick's voice is soft.

I halt beside him, my head already shaking vigorously. I'm terrified of changing back into a dragon—the lightning was enough to put me off forever. "No. I can't do that again." Glancing up into the sky, I try to spot the helicopter, but it's not visible yet. "We'll just have to run." But even as I say it, I know Carrick can't run anymore. We're also too out in the open here, there's nowhere to hide, nowhere to run *to*.

"I can't go back there, Mei. Not now," says Carrick urgently. "If you don't change and carry us away, that's where we'll both end up." His breath is rattling around in his chest, and blood is seeping out from the wound at his side, dripping onto the ground.

The wound he took on to help me escape.

"It hurts," I whisper, my body starting to shake. I don't want to go through that again. The lightning, the agony, the fear.

He shakes his head. "It gets easier every time. How many times have you changed so far?"

"Once," I say in a low voice.

Carrick nods. "There's some pain for the first few times, but nothing like you experienced before."

I stare up at him, trying to decide if I can trust this mountain man in front of me. The helicopter is only getting louder, and I know I have to act now.

"Just remember, whatever else happens, they need you alive," Carrick says, squinting in the direction of the helicopter.

"What about you?"

"I have my uses," he answers softly, his voice tinged with regret.

My fingers curl into fists. I'm not going to let them take us. I'm not going to let this big man become a slave again. I'll change into a dragon before I do that.

The image of my dragon form fills my head, the golden red scales, the leathery wings, and the sleek black claws emerging from my paws.

The magic inside me comes to life, and for a moment I feel a tingling sensation, like fireflies spinning in my stomach.

And then the stabbing pain hits me again, and I fall to the ground, clutching my stomach as I curl up into a small ball.

He lied to me.

This is just as bad at the first time.

25

I feel my wings pushing out from my back, the sharp bones puncturing my skin. My whole body stretches and expands, my skin dragged out and up. The points of my claws emerge from my hands and feet, and I scream.

"Hush, Mei. You mustn't lead them to us." Carrick is crouching nearby, his eyes intent on me. It occurs to me that he's probably never seen a dragon changing form in his lifetime. I glare up at him, raising my lips to show him my rows of sharp teeth.

He doesn't react, just waits for me to finish.

It only lasts for a few moments more. The pain dies down, and I stand, pushing my body up on my legs, glancing left and right, checking that my dragon shape is the same as last time.

Golden red scales cover my body, black ridge bones and claws. I give my wings an experimental flap, and they fill with air. I narrow my eyes at Carrick standing nearby; he seems puny in comparison to my dragon form. I let out a small puff of smoke through my nose and he grins at me.

Looking up into the air, I see the helicopter. They're heading in our direction. They must have seen us.

"I don't think I can climb on your back, you'll have to carry me," says Carrick.

I nod and grasp him with my paws, cradling him against my front. The smell of blood and basalt on him is much stronger in this form. There's also an underlying bitter smell that I think might be the beginning of an infection. I need to get Carrick out of here fast, so his wound can be healed.

My wound.

All of a sudden an area of the ground near us erupts like a volcano exploding, and I stumble to one side.

"They're shooting at us. Vincent won't be happy about that," mutters Carrick.

Growling, I resettle Carrick into my front arms. He's large, bigger than Seth and Si, but I manage to hold him without too much trouble. I leap into the air, and his extra weight unbalances me. I lean off to one side, almost crash landing down onto the rocks again, before correcting just in time. I pump my wings through the sky, easing us away from the compound.

Another rocket blasts the ground near where we were just standing, and I feel the rush of wind coming up from it. My wings dip to one side, but I find my equilibrium, and keep flying through the air away from the compound. It feels good to be airborne again, my powerful wings pushing us through the sky.

If I wasn't worried about being shot out of the sky by the helicopter behind us, I would be enjoying this more.

I dive from cloud to cloud, trying to use them as cover from the helicopter, and soon I'm well away from the compound. The beating drum of the helicopter's rotors fades into the background and I let out a smoky breath.

I shift my arms slightly to get a better grip on my passenger.

Carrick is not only bigger than Seth or Si, he's also much heavier than both of them put together. It's like carrying a sack of rocks in my arms and it's not long before I start to worry about dropping him. He seems to be fading in and out of consciousness. I start to wonder if he's even going to make it to a healer. My wound seems to be taking more out of him than he thought it would.

There are a few houses below us and I begin to circle downwards. I need to find somewhere to land that will keep us out of sight. I look briefly along the spell web to see if there are other supernaturals around. The only section of glowing red grid I can see is Carrick and myself.

When a couple of kids come out into a messy back yard and point up at us, I struggle against the urge to zoom back up into the clouds. There's nowhere for me to hide up here, and my gold and red scales catch the light. What do humans see when a dragon flies past? How does the spell web hide it from them? I can't even begin to imagine.

But I have to keep going.

We reach another road and I fly above it. My arms are tired, and my wings don't seem to be picking up the air currents as well as they did earlier. Changing from human to dragon form has used up a large chunk of my magic and I'm exhausted. I'm also not used to flying this far with a heavy load like Carrick. But I still can't find anywhere to land.

There's not much around; except for the occasional group of houses, it's mostly a barren, rocky landscape. I keep a nervous eye out for vehicles from the direction of the Earthbound compound, or helicopters swooping in to get us, but I think we've managed to lose them.

We've flown another few miles when I see a small town ahead. I'll need something to wear when I turn back to my human form—Si's oversized jacket and pants were destroyed when I changed—and stealing a few items seems my best option. We'll also need transportation of some kind —maybe I can find something there.

I push the image of me landing on the ground next to the road into Carrick's mind, and then slowly descend. I start running with my back legs as I get closer, trying to make sure I don't simply crash into the dirt. It's a little bumpy as I land, and Carrick grunts in pain, but I manage to get us both onto the ground with no further injuries.

I let out a tired huff of breath, and then place him gently on the ground.

"I won't make it far on foot," he says, squinting up at me. His face is pale, and sweat is making his skin glow.

I nod, and then help him to walk over and sit against a tree further back from the road. There are a couple of houses close by.

Leaning in, I place one paw against Carrick's side. Using the spell web, I gather some of my healing magic and push it into his wound. But I'm too tired, and there's not enough actual magic left. It doesn't heal up like I'd hoped it would.

"That's enough," says Carrick, pushing me away. "You need to save your strength." The wound is still there, but the tang of the infection is gone.

It'll have to be enough for now.

I don't want to run around naked, so I push the image of stealing clothes into his head.

He nods. "I'll wait here."

I leap into the air again, covering the short distance to the first house in a few seconds. I peer over the back fence, and give a dragon grin.

There's washing on the line just over the fence, and a couple of items in my size. I pluck a pair of shorts and a t-shirt off the line, and a little knot of guilt pushes its way into my stomach. I would feel better if there were some way I could pay for them. But with no money, and no other clothes, I don't have much option.

When I get back to Carrick he seems to be feeling better.

His colour is better, and he smiles at me as I make another awkward landing. I hide behind his tree and change back to human form, trying not to cry out as the stinging pain ravages my body again. When I'm fully human again, it feels like I've been hit by a bus, and I'm unsteady on my feet as I pull on my new clothes.

I hobble over to where Carrick is leaning against the tree and sit down next to him. "We're out," I say. I slump back against the hard bark of the tree and wish I could just go to sleep for a week.

He smiles down at me. "We are."

"What now?"

"We must keep moving. Vincent won't give up."

Resentment burns its way up my chest. "Why is he so focused on me?"

Carrick sighs. "To a man like Vincent, you are a unique prize. You represent power, control, and magic. He has become obsessed with you."

"Is there a way I can get Vincent off my back?"

Carrick shakes his head. "He thinks he can somehow take your power. He has been reading some of the old texts he's stolen from my people over the years. There are hints of it in there, although no one has ever tried to do it."

I sit up straighter, outraged. "He wants to become a dragon?"

Carrick lets out a faint huff of laughter at my reaction.

"He can never become a dragon himself, but he can steal your magic. He says he will use it to maintain the spell web."

"Anyone who believes that is a gullible fool," I say, thinking of Amos.

"Perhaps."

"How can I get him to stop?"

"I don't think you ever will."

I can't think of anything to say to that, and we lapse into silence. He'll always be on my tail? I'll always be looking over my shoulder, worrying that Vincent will find me?

But then, that's been my life so far.

Right now, I'm too tired to worry about Vincent or his obsession with me. I shuffle around until I find a more comfortable spot against the tree. My eyes drift close.

I'm almost asleep when the sound of a speeding vehicle breaks the peace.

I squint in the direction of the small township, and I see a car in the distance. It's hurtling toward the Earthbound sanctuary like it's a cat with a dog on its tail. My heart starts pounding and I glance up at Carrick. He's watching the car through narrowed eyes.

It's too much of a coincidence. It has to be one of Vincent's minions. We both shuffle to the side of the tree, but it's too late; if we move too much it'll be obvious.

We'll have more chance if we brazen it out and pretend we're just locals enjoying the shade.

I swallow hard and try to act like a human.

26

"It's not one of the Earthbound vehicles," says Carrick, still squinting in the direction of the car.

"How can you be sure?" I say, trying to use my dragon sight to discern the face of the driver. There's too much dust and debris being kicked up by the car to see more than an outline. I glance at Carrick. He's still holding his side, keeping the wound closed against the world.

He's not going to be able to fight.

When the car slows down, both Carrick and I pull ourselves to our feet. It screeches to a halt about ten yards from where we are, and the door opens. I'm tensed to make a move; ready to either fight or change into a dragon, whatever will work best. My whole body is exhausted, and I start to tremble. I don't know how we're going to survive another encounter. I should have kept flying.

A tall figure emerges from the car, bending his body out and up. A mop of brown hair, no longer regulation short, is matched with fiery hazel eyes.

Seth.

Before I know what I'm doing, I'm running. He's okay. He's alive.

I slam myself hard against his body, wrapping my arms around him, and consider never letting go. He feels so good, and his earthy pine and gunpowder smell, mixed with sweat and dirt, calms my nerves. There's also the usual smoky scent, but it's stronger now, more distinct.

I lean back and look at his spell web again. It's even stronger than last time, if that's possible.

"How did you find us?" I ask.

Seth shakes his head. "I didn't. I was heading toward the Earthbound compound to get you."

"And what would you have done when you got there?" My eyebrows are raised at him. He was just going to drive up in a car?

He shrugs. "I would have figured out a way in."

I roll my eyes. "That's officially the worst plan in the world."

He grins. "It worked out for me though, didn't it?"

"Where's Si?" I peer behind him into the car, but it's empty. There's a sinking feeling in my stomach.

Seth glances away. "He went to get help."

I watch Seth's face carefully. He's lying, I'm pretty sure of it. "From who?"

Seth shrugs. "I don't know. He said he'd call me."

Si's angry with me; I know that. I betrayed his confidence. I knocked him out. Even so, I'm hurt he didn't come with Seth to get me out. Surely he knew it was the best plan? Surely I mean enough to him that he would try to get me out of the compound?

I look around suddenly, remembering that we're not really safe yet. "We should go." I glance back at Carrick. "We need to get Carrick to a hospital."

Carrick shakes his head. "I just need to get to my people. They'll look after me."

We manage to get Carrick into the backseat of the car, squished up diagonally because of his height. He doesn't say a word, but he's obviously still in pain. I climb in the front next to Seth, and we make a U-turn and speed back down the road he just came along. I keep glancing back at Carrick to make sure he's alright.

We've been driving for a while, when something occurs to me. "Carrick, you know about dragons, right?" I say, turning to look at him again.

He nods slowly. "My people have kept records."

My heart starts thumping in my chest. "You need to tell me everything you know. I'm the only one left now. I need to know how it works."

Carrick frowns, his expression confused. "You're not the only dragon in the world," he says.

The words hit like a bombshell. My gut feels like I've just taken a physical punch from Carrick. For a moment, I don't know what to say. "Huh?"

"There are other dragons. Just none of recent birth, like you." Carrick's brown eyes have darkened to almost black.

"Vincent told me I was," I say. Carrick has turned my world upside down. I don't have to do this alone anymore? There are others who can help me understand what I am?

"Vincent doesn't know everything," says Carrick.

"You never told him?"

"He never asked." Carrick's voice holds a grim satisfaction.

"Where are they?" I demand. This changes everything.

"Mostly they went into hibernation when it became clear the Earthbound were going to defeat them all."

"How many dragons still live?"

Carrick shrugs. "I don't really know. Maybe five or six."

I let out a breath. That's still not many. Not enough to take on the whole Earthbound army and win.

"What else do you know about dragons?" I ask.

"What don't *you* know?"

"I don't know *anything*," I say, clutching the seat. "Give me the basic rundown."

Carrick sighs and settles back into his seat. He closes his eyes for a second, and when he opens them again, his eyes have changed. It's like a fire is burning inside them, with a black border the color of ash.

Then suddenly he's inside my head, and images are flashing past me. I see the nesting ground and other dragons helping the new dragons to change. I see other mountain supernaturals, just like Carrick, running around, assisting as well.

They lead the new dragon to the stones, and the dragons meekly eat them, with none of the ravening hunger that caused me so much pain.

I see the dragons take flight, beautiful and strong, into the sky. They float along the wind currents, then dive down to the earth, pulling up only at last minute, their control breathtaking. I see them land perfectly, their back legs coming down first, their wings bringing them close and placing them softly on the ground.

It all looks so much easier than I everything I've been through. And none of the dragons seem to dislike each other, or even fight in a pretend way. "They don't look like the dragons in the Earthbound tapestries," I say in a whisper.

"That's because they're not."

I nod, the awe for what I'm seeing soaking into every pore.

"But the Dragon Wars did happen," he says. "There were too many, just like the old stories say. They had terrible battles for territory, and they killed humans and other supernaturals in their paths. They made mistakes, just like anyone else."

I glance at him and see nothing but sadness on his face. "They didn't all hate each other, like Vincent said?"

"It probably seemed that way to the non-dragons who watched the wars. It was a terrible time. There was nothing good about it. But they didn't deserve to all be killed. They deserve a chance to right the wrongs."

I take a deep breath. "What happens when I change again?"

"It gets easier with time and practice."

Images of dragons shifting to human form and back, with nothing more than a few sparks, fill my head. My body goes slack with relief.

"What powers do I have?"

Carrick hesitates. "It's different for every dragon and every dragon species."

"Species?"

"There are different kinds of dragons. Water dragons have an affinity for water."

"That's me," I say positively.

"Your mother was a water dragon, so yes, you'd be one too," says Carrick, watching me closely. "There are also fire dragons, earth dragons, wind dragons. Many different kinds. They all start in the same place, and they all mate with a non-dragon supernatural."

My breath catches. "You knew my mother?"

"No, I'm sorry, I didn't know her. I simply know of her." His eyes are dark pools, and it feels like I could get lost inside them.

I nod, letting out a disappointed sigh.

We're both silent for a minute, but my curiosity gets the better of me. "Can two dragons mate?"

"They can be together, but they will never have children."

I nod carefully. This is more information than I've had on dragons since I found out I was one. I try to figure out what else I'll need to know. "What about flying?"

"You need to practice flying, to give your wings the muscle memory. Do it as much as you can early on." He winces and looks down at his wound.

Blood is still seeping out, the bright-red stain on his shirt increasing again.

"What else can you do, aside from taking my bullet wounds?" I'm talking to cover my anxiety. Sweat is breaking out again on his face, and he has dark shadows under his eyes. He looks bad.

"We just have a... connection. That's why I can take things from you, and you can do the same."

"I could take my wound back?" I say sharply.

He shakes his head. "No, it can't go back."

But I reach out along the spell web anyway. If nothing else, I can send him some energy to help him survive until we get to his people. I'm feeling stronger than I was earlier, so my magic should go further.

I frown when I realize how weak his spell web is; gaps are starting to appear in certain sections. Pushing my magic along it, I weave energy through the gaps, pulling it back together, and amping up the areas that don't feel as strong as they should.

When I pull away and look at him again, his color his back, and he looks much better. I let out a breath.

"Thank you," he says. "You're a fast learner."

I shrug. "I had to be. Jeff never gave me a chance to learn something a second time."

Seth glances at me, his eyebrows raised.

"In a good way," I add. "I'm not complaining."

"We'll be with my people in a couple of hours," Carrick says.

"So are there others? People I can learn from?" The idea of a group of people who can teach me how to be a dragon is exciting.

Carrick shakes his head. "You're not allowed to come with me into our stronghold. It's against the treaty."

My little dream bubble bursts. "Treaty?"

"The dragons signed a treaty with my people, agreeing that we would have a place where we could go to rest and live in peace should we choose it. The dragons loved us, but they could be demanding, sometimes asking for more than we could give without giving our lives."

My shoulders slump. "I wouldn't do that. I don't even know what to ask for."

"It doesn't matter. It's an old rule they won't break."

"So what should we do?" I ask, feeling lost. "We still have to get my father out."

Carrick leans forward. "You need to find other dragons."

"I thought they were hibernating?"

"You need to wake them up and learn from them. Convince them to fight the Earthbound with you."

The thought of other dragons makes me hesitate. "Won't they attack us?"

"You forget, that's part of the myth the Earthbound created around the dragons. Dragons might not always be friendly to each other, but they're intelligent and strong. They can be loving and giving, and certainly charismatic. You are among the last of your kind in the world. You need to find the others and bring them together if you are to defeat Vincent."

"Is that what I have to do? Defeat him? You don't think he'll grow tired of chasing me?"

Carrick shakes his head. "He will never stop, not until you're dead and he has your power. It's either you or him."

27

The landscape outside the car has gone from the barren desert-like expanse around the Earth-bound compound to lush mountain greenery. We're almost into the mountains where Carrick's people live.

Carrick is lying across the back seat, his eyes closed. His breathing is too ragged for him to be sleeping, but it's difficult for him to talk, so I let him rest.

I need to think about what he's told me, anyway. It's a lot to take in. The idea that the only way to be free is for Vincent to die sits uneasily on my shoulders.

Surely there's another way? Surely I could talk to him? Explain things? But as I go over what I know about Vincent, I know it's not possible.

If the only way for me to be safe is for Vincent to die, will I be the one to do it? To kill Vincent?

I stare out the window, wondering what I should do. We pass through some amazing landscapes, places I've never seen before. Big rocky mountains, the sun marking deep shadows on their craggy peaks. Rivers running wild through the canyons, taking a path only they understand. It's beautiful and wild and makes me want to disappear into the mountains and never come out again.

We stop for a break and to walk around. I head down to the river and wash off the ash and dirt that still cling to my skin from the first time I changed. The river runs fast, with clear mountain water, and I let out a sigh as I wash off the excess grime. As always, the water soothes my senses, and clears my head.

It reminds me of the waterfall near Si's home, and my chest tightens. I don't know if Si will ever forgive me; it hurts every time I think about him.

"Let's go," I say to the others as I stomp back up the path.

Carrick directs Seth along the winding mountain roads in his rumbling voice. He sounds exhausted now.

I push a little more energy his way through the spell web, but I think he needs more than my raw magic to help him heal. I let out a relieved breath of air when a sign for the small town we've been heading for appears in the distance.

Mountains loom behind the houses, white-capped peaks sitting prettily against a clear blue sky.

"This is it." Carrick's voice carries across the backseat.

Seth pulls the car over and parks near a tiny supermarket. People filter in and out of the automatic doors, and I watch them, wondering if their lives are as complicated as mine.

Do they have an enemy who will hunt them till they're dead?

Are they considering killing that same enemy?

I've killed people before. But it's always been a spur of the moment thing, mostly in self-defense. A me-or-them kind of situation.

This is premeditated. I would have to think about it, plan it.

"Will we see you again?" I ask Carrick, trying to squash down my thoughts.

"I don't know," he says. His color looks better, but he's still in pain, and his words are slow. "If the elders allow it."

"Where are these other dragons?"

"The only two I know of are here," he says, pulling out a piece of paper from an inside pocket on his shirt and holding it out. It's been folded several times and looks worn and old. I reach out and take it like it's a hand grenade.

"You had this for me?"

He nodded. "I hoped to see you again. It was dangerous, but I thought it a necessary risk."

"Because Vincent would have killed you?"

Carrick shook his head. "No, I was too valuable to him. Because he would hunt them down and kill them for his own benefit."

"Like he's planning to do with me?"

Carrick doesn't answer, just watches me with sad eyes. "I must go now. Keep going, don't stop here. You will be noticed. They watch us, trying to find a weakness to exploit, someone they can separate from the group."

"Is that what happened to you?"

Carrick's face darkens. "Something like that."

He climbs out of the car and slams the door shut, rattling the whole vehicle. Seth waits until he walks around and onto the footpath, and then he takes off, not even looking back. I turn to wave and watch Carrick getting smaller and smaller, until I can't see him anymore.

There was so much I needed to ask him. So much more I needed to know.

"What does the piece of paper say? Where are the dragons?" Seth asks.

I unfold paper and look blankly at the coordinates. "I don't know. We need to get to a computer so I can check, and maybe get a map."

"Did Carrick say how long you should go before turning back into a dragon?"

I shake my head. I hadn't even thought to ask.

"There might be a timeframe, like there was for flying."

Fear tightens around my chest, and for a moment I can't breathe. "I don't think so," I manage to say, despite having no idea if it's true or not. Carrick said it wouldn't hurt as much to change back, but the idea still makes me anxious.

Being a dragon is such a mystery to me, despite the answers Carrick was able to give. There's so much to learn. I'm not in control of it, and there's a large part of me that feels resentful because of that.

Not being able to keep the people around me safe, possibly hurting them myself because of desires and needs I don't fully understand...that's not who I want to be.

Seth watches me for a moment, then turns back to the road. He doesn't say anything, and I don't know if he's guessed any of what's going on in my head. I stubbornly keep my mouth shut, unable to speak the words to tell him what I'm feeling.

We drive for a couple of hours, listening to music and trying to figure out where the coordinates might be. I'm pretty sure they're somewhere outside of the US, but I can't tell more than that.

"I'll stop at the next library I see, and we can use their computers," Seth says.

I nod absently, gazing out the windshield, trying to decide if I'm more eager or fearful of meeting other dragons.

I thought I was the only one, and to find out there are others is big news. What will they be like?

I think of the tapestries at the Earthbound compound. Angry, violent, destructive. Tearing people apart with their teeth. That's what I've always been told dragons were like.

But Carrick's visions showed something different. Something beautiful and fierce. Excitement rises in my chest.

They'll be old; they'll remember the wars. Perhaps they'll want to hunt down and kill the people responsible for the deaths of all the other dragons in the world.

Perhaps they'll kill Vincent for me?

It's a tantalizing thought, but one I can't rely on.

Seth pulls into the parking lot in front of a small building. "According to the signs, this is the town library."

We sit and stare at the small white building in front of us. "We should go in," I say, not moving.

Seth turns to me, his hazel eyes serious. "If these coordinates are overseas, the only way for us to get there is for you to turn back into a dragon and fly us there," he says.

I nod. It's occurred to me already. I put my hands together in my lap, focusing on my ragged nails. "I'll do what has to be done," I say softly.

Seth reaches over and grabs my hand in both of his. His thumb rubs along the skin of my palm. "It's going to be okay, Mei. We'll get out of this mess," he says.

I'm not so convinced. I breathed dragon fire on Seth in a moment of anger, when my normal self wouldn't even have considered it. I remember the burns on Seth's arms, even if he seems to have forgotten it. "How did you survive all those times?" I ask finally. "The nesting flames, the dragon fire? The lightning when I changed? Most people would be dead."

My shaking has stopped, and I swallow, finally asking the question I've been needing to ask. "What are you, Seth?"

His eyes darken, and it's like I'm staring into a pool of water so deep, there's no bottom. "I... I don't know exactly. There... there are family rumors," he says in a low voice. He looks away out the car window.

I frown. "Rumors?"

"My brother, he's a supernatural, like the rest of my family."

I nod. His brother's spell web had been normal, just like any other super.

"But I've always been different. Not as strong. Something was off about my magic. I was an outsider in my own family. The rest of them are powerful supers."

"Why did you join the SIG?" The Supernatural Intelligence Group is an organization set up to monitor and keep the peace between humans and supernaturals. Mostly by being down on the supers. Agents tend to be humans like Jeff, with a natural immunity to the spell web that allows them to see supernaturals, or people with a weak supernatural ancestry that allows them to see past the spell web, but doesn't give them powers.

Usually stronger supernaturals steer clear.

"To piss off my dad, mainly," Seth says with a wry smile. "He's always been in the military, but not with any group who knew what he was. The SIG knew from the start where I came from. He hated that."

"Why try to piss him off?"

"He never said anything, but he was always disappointed in me. Growing up, he was so proud of my brother, talked to everyone about his achievements. How strong he was. He never talked about me."

"That must have hurt."

Seth shrugged. "I realize now how unimportant it was. But at the time, yeah, all I wanted was his approval. I did everything I could, excelled in school and sports, but it was never good enough. Because it wasn't *super* enough. I was competing against the humans and that didn't count."

I hesitate. "But now, something's changed?"

He nods. "Ever since I put you in that fire and got burned, something changed. It could be something to do with the dragon fire, perhaps that did something to me. But..."

"The rumors?"

"Yeah. The rumors. It goes back hundreds of genera-tions. My dad, he's always talked about it, but he said it only came out in the strongest members of the family. No one in his generation showed any signs of it. He used to say that if anyone was going to turn, it would be my brother. I was never in the running."

"What is it?" I whisper.

"I don't know for sure," he says, looking hesitant. "I could be wrong. Maybe it's something else."

"Tell me." Thousands of possibilities run through my brain, but I can't imagine what he's going to say.

What is he?

28

Seth takes a breath. Then hesitates. "It might not be true," he says.

I give him a look.

He stares out the window, as if he's looking for inspiration from the mountains in the distance. His hand is still locked in mine. "My ancestors were phoenixes. Rising from the ashes, born in fire, that kind of thing."

Of all the things I expected him to say— "But... do they even exist?"

"You're asking me that? After everything you've been through?"

I blink. He's right. "How can we find out if it's true?"

"I don't know. Dad didn't know anything more than that it was a possibility, a mutation in the family that sometimes threw itself up."

"How did your father know about it?"

"Family legend I guess. Passed down through the generations. It was a secret, something we weren't allowed to tell anyone outside the family. I don't know when the last time someone..."

"Turned into a phoenix?"

Seth nods. "My brother was always so strong, my dad convinced himself it meant something. He was gutted when Mike turned twenty and stayed an ordinary shifter."

"What kind of shifter is he?"

"My family are ravens, from a long and proud line." Seth sounds bitter.

"But wasn't Tracey an eagle?" I say curiously. Ravens tended to stay within their own clans, not marrying outsiders. They're almost fanatical about it.

"Mike and Tracey got married without my Dad's consent. It was a sore point. But they were in love. They were determined to make it work."

I nod, suddenly liking Mike a whole lot more. "What happened when you turned twenty?"

"Nothing. I never even gave it a thought." He hesitates. "It was only when I survived that blast of heat from the explosion in the nest that I started to wonder..."

The more I think about it, the more I think he could be right.

How else could he have survived being burned not just once, but three times? The lightning hit us directly. It would have killed anyone else. And his spell web has gone from strange and patchy to being brighter than anyone else's.

"What else does your family legend say about phoenixes?"

Seth shakes his head. "Nothing," he says, his frustration evident in his voice.

"So while we're trying to find out more about me, we also need to find out more about you?"

The corners of his mouth come up. "Something like that."

"Then let's get on with it. Let's find those coordinates and get going." I climb out of the car, gesturing that he follow me, and head determinedly toward the small building in front of us.

Inside, the library is small and quiet. The librarian buys our story of being new in town and shows us to the computer. Seth manages to be particularly charming, and she flutters her eyelashes at him as she leads us to the computer terminals. We promise to come back next time with proof of our new address in the small community, and she smiles and leaves us to it.

I see her in the distance, watching Seth with glowing eyes. I have to resist the urge to growl in her direction.

"Put the coordinates into here," Seth says, bringing up a website that turns latitude and longitude coordinates into positions on a map.

I nod absently, and type in the first lot of coordinates. I stare at the screen. "Ireland?"

Seth nods. "Yep. Ireland. County Kerry." He leans in closer. "A place called Puffin Island."

I shake my head. "I don't think I can fly all the way to Ireland. Not yet." I press print on the computer and a black and white map spits out of the small machine just down from us.

"Try the other one."

I put them into the computer, and another map pops up. "Russia?" It's closer, but hardly better.

"Northern Russia, a place called Severny Island." Seth rubs his face. "Have you ever been out of the country?"

I shake my head. No identity, no passport. Jeff always said we were safer hiding close to home, rather than in a strange land with strange customs. *That kind of thing makes you stick out like a sore thumb,* he'd say. "You?"

"Not to Russia. Or Ireland. I was hoping for something a little closer to home."

I nod. For all our joking about the places they could be, so was I. Canada would have been doable. Alaska. Hawaii. Did it really have to be in sodding Russia? "I guess we're going to Russia," I say softly.

We print out different versions of both maps, a world map for us to plan our route, plus some information on both sites that might help, and Seth puts them in his pocket. He looks at me properly for the first time and grimaces. "You need more clothes."

I look down. I'm still wearing my stolen shorts and t-shirt. "I'm going to change again soon. It won't matter." The thought sends a shiver through my body. What's going to happen this time? I take comfort in the fact that Carrick said it would be easier each time. But without the mountain super here to back up his claim, it starts to seem less likely. My fears start to widen, and I wonder how I'm going to push myself into changing again.

"Come on, Mei. Let's get out of here," Seth says, breaking into my panic attack. He grabs my hand, and pulls me in the direction of the exit.

I let him lead me out, numbly trying to convince myself it's going to be fine. His hand in mine is warm, sending tingles up my arm. Turning into a dragon again isn't going to make something bad happen, and Carrick said I'm not going to feel that same terrible hunger again. But what if I do something bad to Seth by accident?

Seth leads me into another store. It's full of secondhand clothes. He pulls a couple of notes out of his pocket. "I've got thirty dollars on me," he says. "That will have to buy you something to take with us. Then we need to park the car somewhere it won't be noticed and get on our way."

The look in his eyes tells me he knows I'm freaking out. But he's not going to let me stop and think too hard. I swallow down the bile trying to escape my throat and walk purposefully to a rack of jeans. I pull out a pair that looks vaguely the right size, along with a T-shirt and sweatshirt. I try them on in the small, musty changing room, the curtain only just providing enough protection from the rest of the store.

I walk out wearing my new clothes. "These will do." I hand a twenty-dollar bill to the woman behind the counter, who looks at it under the light, like she needs to check that it's not counterfeit. I want to roll my eyes, but manage to keep it inside as she hands me the change. "Thanks," I say. My whole outfit cost six dollars.

Seth comes up behind me. "This as well," he says, handing a small canvas backpack to the woman. It costs five dollars, but I can see Seth's point. I'll need something to carry my clothes about in while I'm a dragon. I'm waiting for the woman to ring up the bag when I see a red puffer jacket on a rack. I look at the price. It's fifteen dollars, but the Russian island we're heading for is close to the Arctic Circle.

"Here, Seth, try this on," I say, handing it to him.

He raises his eyebrows, but pulls it on. "It's warm," he says.

"You'll need it where we're going," I say, and hand it to the woman behind the counter.

We walk out the store, my stolen clothes rolled up under my arm.

"Now what?" I say, glancing around the small town street.

"I'll drive us somewhere secluded, and you can change."

I take a deep breath. "No time like the present."

"I have a feeling if I let you think about it too much, you'll actually implode."

My eyes dart to Seth, and he's got a small smile on his face.

"What makes you say that?"

"You're as tense as anything. And you keep giving me terrified looks whenever I talk about flying."

"What if it's the same as last time I flew with you?" I blurt out.

He shakes his head. "It's not going to be. Carrick showed you how to do it. You flew with him."

"He lied to me about it, just to convince me to change. He might have been lying about it again in the car. Once I've done it, I can't take it back."

"Why would he lie to you about that?" Seth asks, his voice filled with laughter. We're walking down the main street, back to where we parked the car. We're going past an appliance store when something flicks onto the multiple television screens in the display. My face, right next to Seth's.

I read the headline below. **Wanted in connection to the deaths of multiple victims. Armed and dangerous. Do not approach.**

I trip, only holding myself up by grabbing onto Seth's arm.

"Are you okay? What's the matter?" Seth looks down at me.

I can't speak. I just nod at the televisions.

Seth takes it all in with one glance, then puts his arm around me, and his head down. "Let's get out of here."

"We should have checked the news at the library," I say, my voice squeaking.

"I didn't think they'd put our faces out there," Seth mutters.

"They did it when they were chasing me last time and it worked. Ben gave us up," I remind him.

We run back to the car, and Seth quickly puts the town behind us.

"How are we going to find out what they're saying about us?" I ask.

"I don't want to use my phone. We don't have enough money for a hotel room and we can't go back to the library."

I pause for a moment. "It doesn't really matter does it? Whatever they're saying, we're wanted criminals. To both the humans and the supers."

Seth bangs his fist on the steering wheel. "This isn't right. He's turned both our lives upside down. We have to make sure he's stopped."

"We need to talk to the other dragons. Maybe they'll help us get my father and take on Vincent."

"Which means you have to change back into a dragon."

A thought occurs to me. "What about you? A phoenix should be able to fly, right?"

His expression falters for a moment. "I don't know." He starts looking as panicked as I feel.

29

Seth puts the car in neutral and pulls on the brake. "Are you sure it's okay?" he says for the third time.

"Of course. I was only joking about you flying," I say. He's going to have to figure it out at some point, but it doesn't have to be right now. We've got enough to deal with as it is.

We're parked at a rest stop, a few miles from town. In front of us is a scenic valley between two large mountains, with a river flowing through it.

"I mean, the rest of my family all fly," he says absently. "When they change. It's just that I've never been able to transform. I was never strong enough."

I put one hand on his arm. "Seth. It's okay. We've got time to figure this out. You don't have to fly."

There's a copse of trees to one side that seems like a good screen for me to make the transformation, and we walk over slowly, both lost in our thoughts.

"This is it," I say. "I can change here." I'm hidden from the road, and there's enough room for my dragon-self. My hands are clasped tightly in front of me to stop them from shaking.

He steps to one side. "I'll be just over there. Put your clothes in here," he says, handing me the small canvas bag.

I grab his hand and then decide it's not enough and pull him into a hug, the last I'll be able to have for a while. He's warm against me, and his hands come up to cradle my head against his chest. I feel the quick beat of his heart and close my eyes, savoring the sound, letting it ground me.

I take a deep breath, and his smoky scent fills my senses. I open my eyes and pull back. He's gazing down at me, his hazel eyes dark. He leans in and kisses me softly on the lips, taking his time. His hands are gentle on my neck, fingers curling into my hair as our kiss deepens. Warmth spreads through my body and I push my hands up under his shirt, feeling his bare skin against mine. He presses closer to me, and a rush of heat races across my skin. I just want to get closer to him, to taste him and feel him. His hazy aroma covers my body, pulsing through my veins and making me burn. It's exactly the kind of scent that affects a dragon. Smoke and fire working together.

When he pulls back, I let out a small whimper, but open my eyes and look up at him. He shakes his head. "Not here, not now, Mei," he says reluctantly. He traces my cheek with one finger.

I nod slowly, my brain coming back into focus. He's right. "It's time. If you could wait for me over there?" I whisper. The thought of him seeing me naked sends shivers down my spine, and I'm tempted to let him watch... But it would just mean more frustration for both of us. We need our minds on the mission.

Plus, I'm not entirely certain seeing me go from my

human form to a dragon will be anything other than freakish.

Quickly, I pull off my recently purchased clothes and fold them into the bag on top of Seth's new jacket. I put it to one side and go back to stand in the middle of the clearing. Taking a deep breath, I picture my dragon form, the red-gold scales over my body, the long tail, the wings stretched out high over my body. Almost as soon as I do it, the longing to be back in that form overcomes me. I ache for it and will it to be so fiercely, it takes my breath away. I feel my body moving, growing, becoming more. The pain makes me gasp. I feel like I'm being ripped apart. There's a cracking noise, and I'm in agony as everything expands and grows inside me.

I growl, trying to hold in the raw scream that wants to erupt from deep in my throat. I fall to my knees, or at least where my knees used to be, and hold my hands over my head. This transformation feels *worse* than when Carrick was with me, and panic rises up into my chest. Am I doing it wrong? What happens if the change doesn't go as it should? Will I end up half-human and half-dragon?

A sharp stinging pain hits my body, almost like an internal lightning strike. A tingling travels down my body, and sparks dance along my skin.

I open my eyes, and the last of my transformation is complete.

I'm back in dragon form, my scales glinting in the sunlight. My head swivels on my long neck as I look around, my vision more than simply sight. I feel everything around me in a different way, and it feels familiar and wonderful. I let out a roar of pleasure, forgetting for a moment where I am and what I'm doing.

Seth races around the corner, then skids to a halt. "That was fast."

I nod.

Lifting my front leg, I point to the bag at the side and then gesture toward my back. It's time to get out of here and start this mission.

Seth climbs on my back, the bag over his shoulder, his sunglasses on. He's clinging to my back ridges, ready to go, when it occurs to me that I have no real idea which way to go. I turn my head to look at Seth.

"Just head to the west," he says, as if he was thinking the same thing. "The direction of the setting sun."

I nod and leap into the sky, the way the dragons did in the images Carrick placed inside my head. This time, it feels easy and natural, like something I've done many times before and will do many times again. I shake my head. What did Carrick do to me? The images are more like memories inside my head that weren't there before.

It doesn't matter. As long as I can fly and move better than I did before, I'm happy. As long as I can get to Russia and talk to the dragon. Carrick said this dragon would help me, and I truly hope they will.

The sky welcomes me like an old friend.

This time the air currents are the path that I take to get to my destination, helping me through the wide blue wonder.

Somehow I know I'm heading west, my dragon senses filling in the compass points inside my head and laying them out across the landscape below us. I take deep dragon breaths and fill my lungs with the exotic scent of oxygen and the living air around me. I feel the heat of the sun and revel in the magical connection between the giant ball of fire and a creature like myself, based on the ground, but ruled by the same element.

I'm flying over the landscape like it's just a patterned quilt below us. I'm high enough that we can't be seen with the naked eye, but low enough that Seth can still breathe. Supernaturals can generally handle higher altitudes than humans, and he was fine at a higher altitude than Si. His possible status as a phoenix means he could potentially go even higher without a problem, but I'm not willing to test that theory, just in case.

Birds occasionally come into our flight path and fly beside me for a while. There's no fear in their manner, and they treat me like any other flying animal. I don't know why it feels strange; I suppose I've grown up with the idea that dragons were feared and hated throughout the world. No one told these birds they should hate someone like me.

The landscape changes again and again, mountains giving way to desert and then beaches and finally to ocean. I fly northwest once I reach the water, aiming for the landmass of Asia. My nose turns in the right direction like a magnet is pulling at me. If the stories I've been told are anything to go by, this is where I was born, my ancestral home.

The ocean fills my vision for what seems like forever. Fish make dark patches on the water, and a whale surfaces to blow water in my direction. I dive and dip, until Seth hits my back, and I remember I have a passenger.

Eventually I see land in the distance and circle down toward it. If the map in my head is right, this is one of the outlying islands of Japan, scarcely inhabited, and somewhere for a dragon like me to stop and rest. We've been flying for a long time now, and I can feel Seth's falling energy, as well as my own.

Again, the landing is as delicate and careful as those in the memories that Carrick has placed in my head, and I'm thankful he was able to help me that much. It's a rocky shoreline, but I can see fish jumping and shellfish on the rocks. We'll be able to find food and, hopefully, shelter here tonight.

Seth climbs down from my back, his whole body bent.

I turn to sniff at his body, and he gasps in pain before fainting right next to me onto the ground.

His body slides down the side of a rock and he's almost in the sea before I manage to grab him with my enormous dragon claws.

If I could speak, I would be yelling his name, maybe slapping his cheeks, trying to get him to wake up. As it is, I carry him carefully to the edge of a small sandy beach in between the rocks and lay him down.

I hesitate for a second, but there's really only one thing I can do.

I change back into human form. The pain hits me like a truck, and the cracking sound of bones transforming is loud in the silence of our isolated beach, but at least there's no lightning. In human form, my whole body aches. It feels like I've just run a marathon, and I stagger as I try to get up to go to Seth.

Instead of walking, I just crawl over and kneel next to him, naked as the day I was born. He comes back around, his eyes fluttering open. He gazes up into my eyes.

"What's happening? Are you okay?" I ask, holding his face in my hands.

"Something's wrong," he gasps, his eyes flashing orange and red. "I don't know what's happening. It *burns*."

30

I blink and look at him again with the spell web visible. It's doing strange things, swirling across his body in a pattern that is both mesmerizing and frightening at the same time. I don't know what it is, but he's right, something is happening.

Is this something to do with him being a phoenix?

I hold his hand, unable to help. His spell web continues to swirl, somehow breaking the familiar grid pattern. It's unlike anything I've ever seen, and I can't stop watching.

Seth lies on the sand, going in and out of consciousness for what seems like hours. He's burning up, sweat covering his body, and his eyes flutter even when he's unconscious. Power radiates off him, like he's at the center of a magical storm.

Eventually, he stays awake for more than five minutes, and the cold sand scratching at my knees convinces me I need to get dressed.

I pull my clothes out of the bag and put them on. Seth is breathing shallowly, his eyes closed, but conscious.

"How do you feel?" I ask tentatively. He's not technically sick, but I have no idea what's actually wrong.

"It hurts," he mutters in an undertone. I might not have heard if I didn't have dragon hearing.

I'm reluctant to try pushing my magic along his spell web to help with the pain. What if he really is changing into a phoenix? What if me interfering stops him being able to do some important part of it? I can't risk it.

Whatever it is, I don't want to mess it up. There's a natural progression to these things. The change into a phoenix is probably even more particular than a dragon's, and it's completely out of my experience.

Of all the supernaturals that live and hide in this world, I've never heard of, or believed in, the phoenix. Ordinary shifters, people able to use certain abilities to make themselves stronger and better, sure. Maybe a few with a bite that's worse than their bark.

But never a person who could burn and then rise again. A fucking flying legend, a myth that no one believes in.

No wonder their family had a secret entrance in their house. A getaway option. With a secret like that to protect, it must have seemed imperative.

It's a pity they focused on the wrong brother.

I run one hand over his forehead, trying to soothe him, doing my best to ease his pain. I'm not really sure what to do. We're on a barren island in the middle of nowhere, halfway through a mission that will see us land on a glacier island off the coast of Russia. I don't think I can keep going with him like this. But on the other hand, I can't take him back to the US where potentially we'll both be in danger.

Unable to make a choice, I stay where we landed.

When a growl of hunger disrupts my vigil next to Seth's

prone body, I find shellfish on the rocks, pulling them off with the help of a sharp stick. I make a pile next to Seth, keeping an eye on his spell web to make sure he's not getting worse. We'll need a fire to cook the shellfish and the fish I plan to catch next.

Collecting as much firewood as I can, I make a pile a small distance from Seth, then take off my clothes again. I need my dragon fire to start the campfire, but I also want to check out the surrounding area before starting it to make sure we're not going to draw unwanted attention to ourselves. I'm also thinking that my sharp dragon claws might make excellent fishing spears.

The change is getting faster, although it's still painful as my body stretches into my other much larger shape.

I leap off from the sand with barely a sound. Up in the air, I swoop and dive for a moment before remembering I need to be a little more circumspect.

I glide along the coastline searching the landscape for habitation. There's a village a few miles away, but far enough that I don't think we've attracted notice. I turn and glide back in the other direction and find nothing I deem dangerous.

Then I turn my attention to the sea just out from our little bay. A fish jumps in the water and I speed toward it, trying to grab it before it hits the water again. I'm too slow, missing it by an inch or two. I fly low over the same patch of water, looking down into the water below, searching for a school of fish just waiting to be caught. I don't know much about fish or how to catch them. I just know I have sharp claws and eyesight that's way better than the average person's.

Below the water, a shiver of silver catches my eye. A group of fish, swimming in formation, skittering back and forth under the water, probably trying to avoid my shadow in the sky. A thought occurs to me.

I fly up and then straight back down, hitting the water at high speed, the cool liquid caressing my dragon scales. It feels like I've come home, the water magic I've always had amplified one hundredfold.

It's my element, the place I've always felt at home, and now, in my dragon form, I feel like I could swim further and faster than ever before. I open my eyes and discover I have a waterproof membrane still covering them. I can see clearly under the sea without any problems.

Ahead of me is the school of fish, darting and diving away from me. I hold out my front paws, claws at the ready, and push through the water, the webbing on my back feet acting like flippers, my tail like a turbo button, making me even faster. I snatch several fish as I swoop past, and then push my way up and out of the water again.

I let out a roar of delight, unable to hold it in. I've discovered my place. All that water, it calls to me, and I can find a home there.

The wriggling fish in my hands brings me back to reality, and I dive back down to the small sandy beach where Seth is still unconscious. The pile of firewood looks small now, but I manage to breathe a small controlled amount of flames onto the wood and start a fire. Then I change back into my human form, put on my clothes, and attempt to put together some food.

It's not as easy as I had imagined. I've lived rough with Jeff and Si, but we had some basic implements. Even a knife would be good. As it is, I have to put each of the fish onto sticks whole and cook them over the fire. I pull the shellfish from their shells using a sharp stick and then manage to get them cooked in the embers at the bottom of the fire. I could eat them raw, but I don't know if Seth will be able to, and it's more for him that I'm cooking this meal.

I search around the edges of the beach and into the native forest that surrounds us, but I don't recognize a lot of the vegetation and don't want to take the risk of eating something poisonous.

Crouching down next to Seth, I touch his forehead, feeling the clammy sweat. I hold a piece of the fish up to his lips, and then discover it's impossible to make someone who's unconscious eat. If I could find some fresh water, that might help, but there doesn't seem to be any around.

I don't know what to do anymore. His spell web is still making strange patterns, and he's moaning like he's in pain.

Something is wrong.

I take a deep breath. The spell web has always been my friend, cloaking me in energy I can manipulate like another sense. Surely I can use it to help him?

Surely it wouldn't hurt?

Seth has been out for such a long time, it can't be right. I need to help him. Part of me is afraid of messing up his transformation, but the rest of me is worried that something is very wrong.

I have to help him.

I move closer and sit down, crossing my legs. Taking a deep breath, I cradle his hand in both of mine, and concentrate on his spell web. I start sending small pulses of my magic along the grid.

At first, when it hits Seth's patterns, nothing happens, but then the patterns start slowing down, merging into blocks of color. I keep sending my magic along the grid, hoping that something I'm doing is going to help him and not somehow cause a problem.

I keep it to low levels and focus on doing whatever it takes to stop him from hurting. That's all I want.

But every time my magic touches his, it creates a new block of color, until instead of a grid over everything, there's just one vast glowing layer.

I think I've made it worse, not better.

31

My hands are shaking and I pull back from Seth. The light from his grid glows too bright, and the heat is pulsing off his body in heavy waves.

I don't think I've helped him at all. In fact, I think I've made it worse.

Seth gasps for breath, and I grab hold of his hand again, trying not to freak out. What if I've messed up his transformation? I knew I shouldn't touch him, but I did it anyway, just because I was worried.

His grid begins to glow brighter and brighter, until I can't see Seth underneath it anymore. It's so bright, I can't watch. I avert my eyes and squeeze them closed. But I refuse to move from his side. I'm holding his hand, which still feels cool to my touch, despite the heat from the spell web.

Everything else around us is getting hotter and hotter. There's an underlying buzzing that's starting to hurt my ears, and along with being effectively blind because of the light, it makes me feel like I'm being attacked through my senses.

Seth's usual smoky gunpowder scent is amplified one hundredfold, and the smell clogs up my nostrils, making me cough. My eyes are running with moisture, and I can't breathe between hacking coughs.

In desperation, I do the only thing I can think of—I pull off my clothes and change into a dragon. The pain of it seems like nothing compared to my need to be with Seth.

As soon as I feel my dragon shape around me, it doesn't feel so hot, and I can see more easily. I'm not as affected by the smoke, and it mingles with my own sulphurous scent.

I put my long neck down so my face is next to Seth's and sniff. He's sweating and moaning softly to himself, but otherwise seems okay. This could be part of the change, perfectly natural.

Or it might be the result of my meddling where I shouldn't have.

At that moment, Seth lets out a blood-curdling scream that makes the scales along my back shudder. I can't do anything but sit beside him in dragon form, hoping that I haven't done something stupid.

His spell web is still a block of color, and heat is still burning off him. I glance around. If anyone came past in a boat about now, they'd be in for a shock.

It goes on for what seems like forever, but I continue to loom over him, uncertain what to do. I just know I'm not going anywhere.

Eventually the bright light of the spell web starts to fade. The heat subsides, and I let out a breath.

Seth's grid returns to normal, his face goes from flushed and sweating to pale and clammy, and he opens his eyes. There's a moment where I'm sure I see flames in his eyes, and then his usual hazel irises are gazing up at me.

"That was weird," he says.

I nod, unsure what else to do.

"I'm really hungry. Do we have any food?"

Our dinner is sitting to one side of the fire, long since off the heat. But I need to change back into human form to give it to him. I shrug; I'm going to have to get used to this kind of thing if I'm going to be changing into a dragon all the time.

I think about being human, and the painful process starts immediately. Bones snap, skin shrinks, and very soon I'm crouched on the sand, fully human and fully naked.

Seth's eyes widen, and he looks away as I scramble into my clothes again. When I'm dressed, I grab the flat stones I found for dinner plates and put some fish on them for him.

He takes it gratefully, shoveling the food into his mouth. "This tastes amazing. The best thing I've ever eaten."

Given that it's half burnt and half raw, I think this is either an exaggeration, or he's experiencing that same kind of burning hunger I had when I became a dragon. Except he's happy with anything, not some special kind of rock, thankfully.

I glance around, wondering what else a phoenix might want to eat. There's not much to choose from around here. I put some more of the fish onto his plate, this time with some of the shellfish.

He devours it all again, and I can't help smiling when he glances up at me with hopeful eyes. I hand the third fish to him; I can always get more.

He looks perfectly normal again, and I frown slightly. It's almost like I imagined it. Except I know I didn't. He's been changing for the last few hours, and now I'm pretty sure he's something different. Not the same kind of supernatural as he used to be.

"How will we find out more about you being a phoenix?" I ask.

He shrugs. "I'll probably have to ask my father. I think there might be family documents I can look at."

I hesitate. "Do you want to do that straight away?" I'd go with him right now if he needed to. But...

He looks up at me, surprised. "Of course not. We have to get to the Russian dragon."

I let out a breath. "Good."

"Are you rested enough? We could go soon, if you like." His bright hazel eyes are locked on my face. He does seem better than he has in days. What has his transformation done to him? How has it changed him?

His spell web is still vibrant, but it's tampered down now, so it just looks like he's sort of glowing with a white light around the edges. It's disconcerting, reminding me of when they portray angels on television.

"Let's go, then. Better to get this done as soon as we can." My fish-meal is flip-flopping around in my stomach like it's still alive at the thought of meeting this dragon. But I have no choice.

I need the help of other dragons if I'm going to get my father back and defeat Vincent.

32

S oon we're flying above the landscape again, high in the clouds. Seth feels better this time, his energy high, his grip firm. He even lets out a whoop of exhilaration as we climb over a mountain and swoop down the other side.

It's another few hours of flying before I start to see the kind of landscape we're expecting from this first set of coordinates. Up ahead is the island, a long archipelago, rocky and desolate. A cold, snowy environment with little habitation. The perfect place for a dragon to hibernate.

I fly in low, not too worried about being spotted. I can't see any sign of houses or villages for miles in any direction, just snow and a massive glacier flowing unhurriedly down a valley. I land carefully next to the edge of a large icy incline.

Seth jumps nimbly from my back, pulling the red puffer jacket closer around his body. "This is it. There must be a cave around here somewhere." He covers his eyes and gazes up into the sky.

The cliff face is high, and from here at the bottom, I can't see anything useful. Just in case, I walk carefully on all fours along the base of the cliff, sniffing and getting a feel for the environment.

Trying to smell another dragon.

Nothing. Seth is searching out wide in the other direction, across the rocky landscape, climbing up and over boulders and around scrappy bushes that are all that can survive between the snow and ice.

I look up again. The dragon has to be up in the cliff somewhere. There must be a cave I didn't notice on the way in. I glance over to Seth. He's fine searching this area.

I leap lightly off the ground and hover in front of the cliff, glancing up and along. I move backward, trying to get a wider view to see if I can spot a cave.

Wherever it is, it's well hidden. I fly up and down the cliff face, searching with my enhanced dragon vision, trying to see an entrance. It's got to be here. My breath puffs out as a white cloud in front of me. My thoughts go round and round inside my head.

I have to rescue my father.

I have to find out more about being a dragon.

I have to figure out how to defeat Vincent.

There must be a way.

I'm concentrating so hard on finding the cave that Seth's yell comes as a surprise. His shout is cut off abruptly, and I turn to see where he is. Perhaps he's fallen down some rocks? Knocked himself out?

Heart beating fast, I fly back to the last place I saw him. At first there's nothing on the icy tundra, just blue-white everywhere I look. I swing my head around, desperately trying to find him. Where could he have gone?

Then, out of the corner of my eye, I spot a dark patch. The opening to a cave. It's in a difficult portion of the terrain, not easily accessed by foot—unless you're a determined ex-SIG agent.

Cocking my wings, I dive down toward the hole and land neatly just outside. It's large enough for me to enter in dragon form, so I duck my head and cautiously walk inside. It's dark and cold, and it feels like I'm in one of those horror movies—where the girl goes down into the basement, and you know she really shouldn't be going into the basement.

But I have no choice. I have to find Seth.

My vision adjusts quickly, and I follow the large rocky hallway down into the earth. Rocks scatter underfoot, and the sound of dripping somewhere further into the cave gives me something to follow. The tunnel opens out into a larger open space. Rocks are scattered through the cavern and it seems empty at first. I can't understand where Seth has gone. Maybe I was wrong? Maybe he's still outside somewhere, stuck in a crevice?

Who's this then? Another sweet morsel for my dinner? A voice tumbles down into my head from above and I jerk back in surprise. I twist my head and look up.

An ice-blue dragon hangs from the ceiling, his tail wrapped around the rock formations like a possum, white-blue eyes swirling angrily, and his devilish teeth snarled in my direction. For a second I freeze, completely mesmerized by the sight of another dragon. He's the first of my kind I've ever seen. My heart thunders in my chest, and I struggle to breathe.

And then I see Seth, clutched in the dragon's claws, unconscious and dripping blood from a wound on his head.

A growl escapes my mouth with a puff of smoke. Fear for Seth pounds through my veins.

I move closer to where the new dragon is hanging. He looks old; a gray stringy beard is clinging to his enormous chin, and his teeth are yellowed and stained. His spell web is pulsing strangely, glowing brighter and then dimming, and brighter again.

Let him go, I say, instinctively talking into his head.

Or what? You'll kill me? He takes a few sniffs in the air around him. *You're a baby dragon, new out of your transformation. You couldn't fight a fruit bat, let alone me.*

We're not here to fight. I need your help, I think at him desperately. This form of communication is new to me, but it's second nature to the dragon above me.

What else do you have then, baby dragon? Did you bring me gifts or tokens of your respect? His scales shimmer even in the dull light of the cave; a mesmerizing mix of silvery white, bright blue, and the same aquatic green I just saw on the glacier we flew over.

I think of the rocks from the nesting ground. They

would have been perfect, if we hadn't been chased from there. *I bring my goodwill. The greetings from one of the last dragons to another.*

Is that all? He lets out a scornful huffing sound.

I stand up onto my hind legs and growl back. *I have nothing else, you greedy dragon. I'm the only dragon born in the last three hundred years, hunted by the Earthbound my whole life. I ask for your help.*

The white dragon growls back, and smoke emerges from his nostrils. *You're here to steal my powers.*

I hesitate, thinking how easy it was to take Si's magic through the spell web. *Steal your powers? I barely know how to use my own. That's why I need your help.*

And I think his spell web might actually electrocute me if I tried to access it.

Don't try to trick me, baby dragon. That's what all your kind want. The young are too impatient to become powerful. He sways from side to side, his nose still sniffing the air like he thinks he can smell the truth.

I frown up at the dragon. Something is off about him. His milky eyes are gazing off to one side, like he can't even be bothered looking at me, and his spell web is still pulsing, like it's a lamp about to blow. *I'm not like that. I just need your help. That's all.*

You'll only get my help if you let me eat him, the dragon replies, dangling a still-limp Seth over my head.

My heart is pounding hard in my chest. Seth looks so small and vulnerable. *I'm not going to let you eat him.* Another growl emerges from my mouth and I take a step closer.

Then I'm not going to help you. The dragon swings around on his tail, and he's suddenly airborne. *And I'm going to eat him anyway.*

He hovers for a moment near the roof of the cavern and then streaks toward the tunnel entrance.

A whoosh of air hits my face and I reach out to grab him, but he's past me before I even get my hand up. I spin and race after him, clambering awkwardly along the rock path on all four legs, a part of me admiring the way he flies in perfect motion.

I wish I could fly with such precision.

As it is, I'm clambering as fast as I can along the steep rocky pathway toward the light. He blocks it with his body for a moment, and then he's gone, up into the air.

Moments later, I emerge and leap into the air behind him, turning my head this way and that, trying to spot him in the sky. Fear for Seth is screaming through my body, making my scales shudder across my skin.

The dragon has disappeared as easily as if he were invisible. Against this icy landscape of white and pale blue, he may as well be.

I blink, and my heat vision comes into focus. There's nothing but cold and ice around me—except for a few hundred meters away. Even if the dragon doesn't show up, Seth does. His heat signature is like a beacon for the rest of the area to see by. At least for those with the ability to see heat.

I spin in the air and focus down toward the heat signature. Some latent instinct makes me blink out of heat vision, and I have to swerve dangerously to avoid hitting an old rocky outcrop directly in front of me.

Panting from the sudden rush of adrenaline, I keep my vision in normal mode, vowing to only flick into heat vision for seconds at a time.

Below me, the dragon is sitting on the edge of an ice

outcrop, looking back up into the sky. Beside him, Seth is lying across the ice, not moving.

The dragon still isn't looking directly at me, but he's grinning like a loon, and I start to wonder about his sanity. Why is he awake? Shouldn't he be hibernating? Did Seth wake him? I don't know the answer to any of these questions and it makes me nervous. He seems too alert to have only just come out of a deep sleep.

We're not here to hurt you. I'm still trying to reason with him. At the very least, it should distract him from Seth. *My name is Mei. What's yours?*

The dragon roars, and the sound thunders across the landscape. A flock of sea birds scatters, squawking into the air. Is there anyone else out here who can hear him? I recall seeing a small settlement at the bottom of this particular group of islands, but nothing up this way. Hopefully we'll be left alone.

I have to try and calm him down. He seems enraged by my request for his name. He's agitated, swinging his tail back and forth like an angry cat. I don't know anything about dragon etiquette or the way I should be acting toward him.

I'm the younger dragon; should I be more submissive? That doesn't seem to hold true to everything else I've been told. I think through the images Carrick put inside my head, but there's nothing helpful.

The ice-blue dragon swings his head from side to side, as if to some music only he can hear. Beside him, I see Seth stirring. I need to distract the dragon so he can escape.

I'm here to find out how to defeat the Earthbound, I say. I don't know why, but I can't do the same thing into Seth's head, at least not yet. Perhaps it's something that comes with age? The dragon's mind seems set up for it somehow. At a guess, I would say it's the main form of communication for dragons in this shape.

The dragon makes a sound like a coughing bark, and I realize that it's his version of a laugh. *You can't defeat them, baby dragon. There are too many of them, and they have their secret weapon.*

A chill runs along my scales. I don't want to ask, but I have to.

What kind of secret weapon?

34

The icy-blue dragon stands up to full height, like he's showing off his size and strength to some imaginary foe. *A machine that disables all our dragon abilities. Don't ask me how it works. I've seen it in action, and it's not something I plan to see again.*

Before he closes his mind off, I get a glimpse of a slaughter; many dragons, bathed in blood, lying dead on a battlefield. I shudder. The deaths of all those dragons means more to me now that I'm one of them.

You lose your magic for good? I've only just come into my powers; the thought of losing them makes my skin crawl.

Just while you're around the machine. But that's enough time for them to slaughter you.

I think of the tapestries in the Earthbound compound, with their lurid depictions of dragon deaths at the hands of noble Earthbound warriors. No sign of any machine in those images. I shake my head. *It's been a long time since they used that machine. I don't think they have it anymore.*

If they *do* have it, I don't think they know how to use it.

Vincent would have pulled it out and used it on me in a flash if he thought it would keep me docile. They like to imagine the Earthbound of old using their strength and power to defeat the dragons, instead of a machine that disabled them.

Even then, the answer is that you will never defeat them. You must hide, or you will die at their hands. A ripple goes over the ice-blue scales of the other dragon, as if he's remembering something he'd rather not.

I'm not going to hide away anymore. I've been doing that my whole life. I'm getting better at thinking into his head. *How long have you been down in that hole? You should be awake, living your life.*

The dragon hisses up at me, his teeth bared. *I've been awake for the last sixty years, and I don't like what I see. I'd rather be blissfully asleep than in this abominable world.*

I hesitate. *You've been awake for the last sixty years? Why?* For the first time, I notice a strange smell in the air, something bitter that makes my insides curl. I wonder if I really want to know the answer to my question.

The humans and their bombs.

Bombs?

The humans call them nu-cle-ar. They woke me up, made me sick. He looks in my direction, and I see his eyes, spinning strangely. They've stopped spinning fast, and now there's a lopsided pattern to them.

Something clicks in my head.

He's blind.

He's been using all his other dragon senses to get around, to fly and keep himself steady.

How did you survive? What other damage would a nuclear bomb cause a dragon? Perhaps it might make him a little unstable?

I hid in my cave, tending my wounds. Everything heals eventually.

But for sixty years? I'm horrified at the idea of sitting in a cave for that long. Or even near a cave—he clearly emerges from his hole sometimes.

It's nothing in dragon years, baby dragon. You think you know everything? Come back and talk to me once you've reached your first one hundred years—if you survive that long. He gives another of his barking laughs, the noise echoing across the landscape.

I swallow hard at the mention of living that long. All supers live longer than humans. But he's talking centuries. Hundreds and hundreds of years. *I need your help now.*

Out of the corner of my eye, I see Seth slowly edging away from the dragon. *You're just afraid,* I say, trying to distract him.

Afraid? Of course I'm afraid. The only reason I've survived is because I hid. All those brave dragons, the ones telling me I had to fight against the Earthbound, that we had to come together as a species and not give them the power? They all died.

His tail swishes agitatedly, and it sparkles in the cold sun. It's like he's covered in diamonds. *All dead. Gone. Every last one of them. They couldn't convince the other dragons to fight together, and then they came up against the machine. It killed them all, every last one of them. I only just escaped their fate. Only just.*

The words escape his mind in a jumbled way, like he's struggling to keep them in order. I have to concentrate really hard to understand him, it's so rushed. But I get the sense he's scared—really scared—of the Earthbound and what they're capable of.

What else do you know about them?

They're focused, merciless, and convinced of their own self-righteousness. To them, we're worse than the devil.

He's talking about the zealots from three centuries before, but I can't help thinking that Vincent might be a throwback to those times. Except he doesn't have the same experience dealing with dragons. I'm the only one he's ever met. *They're not like that anymore. At least not all of them.*

The dragon stands up on his hind legs and roars again. Seth's running now, away from the ice dragon, zigzagging through the rocks toward me. I can't tell if the other dragon has noticed or not. He's upset and agitated, but it's more from the memories that I'm forcing him to face than Seth's escape.

They'll always be like that. People never change. The dragon glances over to where Seth is climbing. *Even him. He's running because he thinks he has a chance against me. But he doesn't realize that he's going to die, like the others.*

He sends a mouthful of dragon fire toward Seth.

I leap forward, attempting to protect Seth from the flames, but I'm too far away. Thankfully they don't actually hit him, just heat up the air near his running form. Seth ignores the flames like they're nothing, not even flinching as he continues to climb toward me.

He's not human, says the ice dragon, his eyes on Seth. *Not so easy to barbeque a supernatural.*

I shake my head with relief. *He's not human. And I'm not going to let you eat him. You're old, tired, and scared. I have every advantage.* I try to give my voice the confidence I need to convince this dragon to stop chasing Seth and start paying attention to me.

He roars again, but this time it's in reply to another noise thundering across the barren landscape.

I look into the distance and see two tiny dots on the horizon, speeding toward us. Military jet fighters.

The stupid humans and their flying machines. The icy dragon's eyes are swirling, and he's swishing his tail in agitation.

35

The ice dragon howls, but moves quickly.

He scampers into the sky, following a low path almost up against the rocks. I leap into the air as well, grabbing Seth as I go. I follow the dragon as he skims the landscape, heading back to his hiding spot. As I land next to the entrance to the cave, I hesitate. We're sitting ducks inside this cave if they decide to bomb us.

"Come on, Mei. Inside. It's our only hope. You're too brightly colored."

I glance at Seth, sitting on my red and gold back. He's right, I'm not like the other dragon, whose scales blend with the landscape. I stand out.

It occurs to me that it's probably the main reason he survived. His camouflage is perfect, merging into the surrounding ice with no effort at all. It means that hiding isn't an option for me long term, unless I can find a suitable red-tented circus to cower inside.

Luckily, I'm not tempted by his talk of hibernation. But just because I won't hibernate, doesn't mean I won't hide from Russian fighter jets with who-knows-what kind of bombs in their arsenal. I run into the tunnel and down toward the cave.

Get out! Get out! You're not welcome here! The dragon screeches at me as I enter the cavern. He's hanging from the ceiling again, his head at a strange angle facing me. He's swinging in an agitated circle, his movements jerky.

I'll leave when they've gone. I'm trying to be calm, but he's getting frantic now, his eyes swirling in their uneven patterns. His scales are standing up like an angry cat's fur.

I didn't even know our scales could do that.

The milky clouds inside his eyes are mixing with the blue, and his claws are out for the first time. They look like icicles, a clear blue-green in color, with a wicked point on every single one. If it came to a fight, I'm pretty sure I'd lose.

You'll show them where I am. I won't be safe anymore.

I'll just stay down here until they've gone. Then I'll leave you in peace.

Peace? There's no such thing as peace for a dragon. There's only survival. And you're not going to last very long with your attitude, baby dragon. Just stay away from me. You and your fire creature.

He closes his eyes and curls upward toward the rocks at the top of the cave, wrapping his tail around the thickest stalactite. A low humming starts up, discordant and off-key, and I realize he's trying to block us out.

Overhead the fighter jets whizz past, the noise of their engines almost unbearable from directly underneath. I hold my breath, waiting for an explosion, and hoping a dragon can survive a bomb. I think of Seth. What about a phoenix?

Everything around us seems to shake for a few minutes; small rocks break off from the ceiling of the cave and rain down. For a moment I'm tempted to go back out the tunnel and launch myself into the sky. See what I can do to put a dent in those jet planes.

But I manage to hold myself in place and they pass over without launching anything. Everything settles down inside the cavern, except for a strange clicking noise. Narrowing my eyes up at the other dragon, I see his claws tapping together in an agitated rhythm.

I let out a breath and turn my neck to look up at Seth, still on my back. I raise my eyebrows.

"I don't know. He doesn't seem friendly. And I'm not keen on him eating me," he says.

They're gone, I say inside the other dragon's head.

He opens one eye. *That fire creature is dangerous to have around, baby dragon. A phoenix will burn you up as soon as look at you, you know.*

What do you mean?

They're about the only creature that can go hotter than a dragon. Burn themselves up and come back good as new, they can.

He's a friend.

He might seem like that now, but give him time. They all turn on you in the end. A phoenix can't be trusted. It's not in their nature to be loyal.

I glance back at Seth, who's staring up at the dragon in the ceiling. I can't imagine him betraying me. Not now.

I make an executive decision. The Russian dragon is a bust, not helpful at all. Possibly even a lunatic. We're going to try to find the other dragon in Ireland.

Lifting one ear, I try to decide if the fighter jets have definitely gone.

They'll do another pass, then disappear. The ice dragon opens one doleful eye. *You can leave as soon as that happens.*

Are you sure you won't change your mind? We could use your help.

I'm not leaving my home to fight a battle I know you're going to lose.

I sigh, not convinced he's wrong. But if I do nothing, I'll be on the run my whole life. The idea of living like this, hidden away in a cave, makes me shudder. This isn't a life. And this dragon isn't sane. He's holding on by the barest thread, and I don't want this shallow kind of existence.

At least tell me your name.

He tips his head to one side, and a shiver goes down his scales. *My name is Sergei. Now leave.* His blind eyes spin with glowing blue and white streaks in the darkness.

Thank you for talking to us, I say as I move cautiously toward the entrance. I can hear the fighter jets coming back now, doing their second predicted flight. Seth clings to my back, saying nothing. He hasn't been able to understand the exchanges I've been having with the Russian dragon, but he's trusting me to make the decisions.

Once I can't hear the jet planes any longer, or feel the rumbling in the sky, I poke my head out the tunnel and into the harsh light of the icy tundra wilderness where the Russian dragon lives.

While I trust Seth, I don't trust Sergei.

He seems like the dragons I would have expected before becoming one. Out for himself, aggressive, prone to angry outbursts, and liable to eat anyone not nailed down. I can't trust him any further than I can throw him.

I glance back into the cave for one last look at this strange creature who could be my only living kin, the first of my kind that I've ever met. It's too dark to see anything. His discordant humming wafts out from the ceiling where he's hiding, and it's my last impression of him. My heart contracts. It's such a lonely sound.

But I can't force him to come with me, or even help me.

I have to keep moving forward.

36

The smell of jet fuel lingers in the air, but the fighter jets have disappeared.

It seems to be clear.

The intrusion of the military aircraft into the sky above us has reminded me there could be more dangerous things in the air than birds and commercial aircraft. Countries like Russia and China have strong military air forces, with planes and other destructive weapons that could potentially take me out. I have to be careful out here.

I want to ask Seth precisely where the next set of coordinates is from here, but it would involve me turning back into my human form. It doesn't feel like a good idea right now. There's a lot of flying in between me and needing to know the exact location, so I just leap into the air and get going.

We fly southwest for several hours, my new sense of direction pushing us in the correct direction and my large wings beating hard, the air currents carrying us along.

We're moving fast, and we soon pass over water, and then land again. From this high up, I can see the outlines of three countries, like three fingers pointing down toward

Europe. Scandinavia. We're not far from Ireland and the next dragon. We're going to have to be more careful here. This area isn't so barren, and the Irish dragon won't have been able to find such an isolated spot to hide.

I hide out high in the clouds and listen hard for other flying craft. I manage to avoid a couple of commercial planes, but don't meet anything quite so sinister as the fighter jets again.

They're a reminder that humans have come a long way in the last three hundred years. It's no longer swords and shields against the might of dragons—it's nuclear bombs and chemical weapons against claws and teeth.

It makes dragons seem old fashioned.

I fly out over the ocean with the coastline of Ireland visible to the left. I know vaguely where I'm headed, but I'm going to have to land and turn back into my human form to talk to Seth so I can figure out exactly where the coordinates are.

I spot an island up ahead and aim for it, landing on the beach, just like last time. The air is fresher here; the lush smell of growing plants and the warmer coastal waters make me take some deep breaths to fill my lungs.

Seth climbs down and stretches his body, the creaks and cracks audible. He looks tired, his face lined and his eyes bloodshot when he takes off his sunglasses.

Nodding to the slightly charred backpack Seth is still wearing on his back, I indicate I want to change. Seth places the bag next to me, and then turns to face off down the beach, his back to me. It should be the last thing on my mind, worrying about getting changed in front of him, but I'm grateful for his thoughtfulness.

I take a breath, close my eyes, and think about being in my normal supernatural body again. Light flashes against my eyelids, I feel a sharp pain running along my body, like multiple needles pricking my skin, and I open my eyes to see the final changes taking place.

It's not just a physical change, although I can feel my bones shrinking and my skin molding to my smaller shape. It's also magical, taking place in a part of my brain that can't be seen, and using powers that are more than the physical laws humans believe in.

Once I'm fully transformed, the cold of the beach air hits my frail human skin, and I'm suddenly covered in goose pimples. I drag my clothes out and shove them on, shivering the whole time.

"Are you okay?" he asks, looking at me over his shoulder to check I'm dressed. "What happened back there?"

"Other than the Russian dragon wanting to eat you?"

He smiles, walking back toward me. "I'd be a tough snack."

"He wasn't entirely sane. And he refused to help." I rub my hands over my arms, trying to warm myself up.

Seth reaches up and lightly touches my cheek. "The other dragon will be happier to see us."

I raise one eyebrow. I'm not feeling nearly so optimistic. "Where are they in Ireland?" I ask.

"I don't know. We'll have to check the map." He holds his hand out to take the bag from me. I give it to him without a word.

He pulls our rough, folded-up Ireland map from the bag, and opens it out. "We're almost there," he says, pointing.

Taking a deep breath, I try to be excited about meeting another dragon. It doesn't work. "This time, I think we should go in with a plan. We can't risk being overwhelmed by another half-crazed dragon."

"I'm not sure how to plan for craziness," says Seth drily, his eyes flashing with amusement.

"Me either." I can't suppress a shiver, and Seth immediately steps closer and wraps me in his arms. His warmth seeps into me, and I let out the breath I didn't know I was holding. Closing my eyes, I let myself soak up the feeling of safety that being held this close to his heart brings me.

We stand like that for a while. I wish it could be longer. I wish it could all be different. But it's not.

I step away, pulling myself out of the security his arms. I want him to protest, to tell me to come back, but he doesn't. I look up into his face, and see the same determination I feel, reflected back at me in his flame-colored eyes.

We don't have time for the two of us. Not yet.

In the end, we decide to just land on the small island that matches the coordinates and see what happens. I'd like to have some way to tie up or otherwise incapacitate them, but we don't have anything with us that could work and we don't have time to fly around aimlessly searching. My father is still being held captive, and the Earthbound won't wait forever.

Instead, Seth agrees to stay close to me, so I can simply fly away if the next dragon tries anything.

As we fly in, I sense something different.

There's a sense of awareness in the air around us that wasn't present when we landed on the Russian island. The dragon here is much more a part of the environment, and it's like he's nurtured the very air around him.

I settle gently onto the ground and sniff. The island has a green lushness, despite the harsh surrounding landscape. There's definitely a dragon here, but he's sleeping. Hibernating.

Keeping my nose in the air, I walk on all fours swiftly

toward the far side of the island. There are two hills on the island, and it's the second one that's gathering my attention. I can see a vague covering of the spell web over it. The ground is slightly rockier on this side of the island. I step carefully, aware that I could come across another dragon at any second.

The ground under my feet shudders, a ripple rolling along the earth. If I didn't know better, I'd say it was a small earthquake or some other natural phenomenon. But it has to be the dragon waking up.

I'm halfway up the second hill when I see something gleaming up ahead. A small patch of earth has been knocked away, and the rocks beneath are glittering in the sun. It's an extraordinary shade of green, and it draws me closer. I reach out with my front paw and touch the stone. It moves under my hand. I jerk back and glance around. It's not rock. It's a dragon.

And I'm standing right on top of him.

37

I lift off from the ground straight away, looking for the contours of the dragon on the landscape.

He's molded himself into the ground so well that it's hard to see where he begins and the land ends. But his movement is becoming more pronounced, the shaking of the ground more visible.

He's waking up.

I glance at Seth, who is clinging to my bony back ridge, but he's watching the ground where the dragon is emerging. I hope this dragon is more coherent than the last one. Just in case, I stay in the air, not willing to land and put us in a weaker position. The green rolling grass beneath us cracks open, and I see the head of the dragon down by the sea. His head was inside a rocky cave, his wings curled on his back and his tail forming a ridge of rocks along a cliff face. His broad back was the second hill on the small island. Now that he's out of the earth, his spell web is glowing brightly over his body.

I wonder how often he's been awake in the last three

hundred years. Hopefully he's had more undisturbed sleep than the Russian dragon.

We watch as he unfurls himself from the land, the dirt and grass dripping from his body as he stands. He's bigger than the Russian dragon and almost double my size. From a distance, he's bright green with shimmering scales that seem to hum and dance together. But when I look closer, I realize his scales are a variety of greens, from deep forest colors to lighter more vibrant hues, all sparkling in the sunlight. He's somehow more majestic than Sergei, and the red and gold that I've been so proud of seems dull in comparison.

He looks up and sees me for the first time. His eyes swirl with dark menace. *Who are you to wake me?*

I swallow hard. This dragon definitely doesn't have the fluttering incoherence of the Russian dragon. *I need your help.*

You wake me for that? To help you? What is your task? To scare away villagers? Or perhaps to seek vengeance on a man who's done you wrong? Leave me. With that, he settles himself back down again, lowering his head.

No! Wait. You're one of the last dragons in the world. I'm the only new dragon to be born in three hundred years. I need your help to bring down the Earthbound. The words come rushing out of me like water from a burst dam.

His head rises back up. He looks at me like I'm an insect flying around his head. My instinct is to buzz out of the way, to avoid the possibility of one of his huge front legs swatting me out of the sky.

But I'm here on a mission. If this dragon won't help me, I'm screwed. Carrick only gave me two sets of coordinates. There might be more dragons in the world, but I don't know where they are.

The Earthbound? He glances around as if someone is going to pop out from behind a rock.

They have my father, and they're after me. They want to steal my magic to keep the spell web in place.

A ripple goes down the scaled hide of the dragon, and his spell web shudders. It's like he's trying to throw it off, to push it away, and for a moment it seems to lift up off his skin. And then it settles back down, and he lets out a huff of breath.

I had forgotten the shackles they threw over us. His head lowers, and his eyes half closed. He no longer looks proud, simply defeated. *We could not find a way to escape them. It is what defeated us in the end.*

The spell web? But it's not... I don't know how to explain the spell web and how it helps me. I've never seen it as chains binding me. *It's a tool, something you can use as well. It doesn't belong solely to the Earthbound.*

I send a pulse of magic along the spell web grid, attempting to show him.

He jerks back in surprise and then growls. *If you attack me again, little dragon, I will kill you.*

No! I wasn't attacking. Did it feel like an attack? I frown, confused by his reaction. I look closely at the grid over his body. It's jumping and fizzing along his skin, like there's an electric current woven into it. *Are you doing that to it?*

Doing what? He snarls at me, his dragon teeth visible at the side of his mouth.

Are you fighting it? As I say the words, I realize that's exactly what he's doing. Instead of working with the spell web, of treating it like another arm or leg, he sees it as an attack. *Stop fighting it. The spell web by itself can't hurt you. It can help you.*

The big green dragon shakes his head, as if to clear it,

and then eyes me as I hover over him. But he doesn't say a word.

Can you see the grid covering me? If seeing the grid is part of my dragon abilities, then he should be able to see it too. I send a pulse of magic along my web, allowing it to dance over my body, and into Seth. He glows brighter for a moment, and then I feel him sit up straighter. "What was that for?" he asks.

I turn and grin back up at him, my dragon teeth showing in amusement. I still can't talk to him in my dragon body, but he doesn't seem that bothered by the extra magic boost I've just given him.

How did you do that?

I turn back to the green dragon. *I used the spell web. It's not your enemy. You can use it to help you.*

The dragon shakes himself all over, and more of the dirt and grass from the island flicks into the air. I move to hover a little higher, out of range, watching him warily. He hasn't exactly been welcoming so far.

Come, follow me, little dragon. Let us talk. The green dragon takes off into the air, his huge wings creating a wall of wind that makes me lose my balance for a moment. I check on Seth, who's holding on tightly, and then follow him down the coastline.

Eventually we come to a small cottage, hidden in the lee of a hill, and he lands in a large courtyard.

Before our eyes, the green dragon changes, becoming a large, muscled—naked—man with such practiced ease that I blink to make sure I saw it properly.

He's already striding toward the door of the house, which unlocks as soon as he's close. I glimpse his muscled butt disappearing into the house before the shadows cover him.

38

I land softly in the courtyard and hesitate.

Seth climbs down from my back, and I look around at him. I don't know whether to change or not. I'm not entirely certain this dragon is friendly yet. He doesn't seem as crazy as the Russian dragon, and his presence on the island was more balanced and calm. Literally more grounded, given that he was hiding in plain sight.

"You may as well change," Seth says, as if he can read my thoughts. "You can always change back pretty quickly. And we need his help. Carrick was pretty adamant about that."

I nod slowly. Seth's right.

I take a breath and transform, the painful process stealing my breath. Seth is still standing in front of me, holding the backpack, looking down at the ground. He hands the bag to me, and I catch him looking at my body before he glances away. His ears go red, and I flush as well. I'm going to have to get used to being naked every time I change.

I hold the bag in front of me and quickly pull out my

jeans and shirt. Seth has his back to me now, and I yank on my clothes.

"Thanks," I say. "I'm dressed."

He turns back around, and our eyes catch for a moment. He's got a fiery tinge to his hazel eyes, and my dragon heart finds that compelling. He takes a step toward me, one hand raised to touch my shoulder, when a noise behind me draws our attention.

The green dragon.

I turn and find him still shirtless, but with a pair of loose trousers on. He's got long, shoulder-length hair, a wavy golden blond that shines in the sunlight. His skin is a swarthy brown, and he has muscles on his muscles. It's hard not to stare. He's moving around out front of the house, tidying up overturned pots, muttering to himself.

Beside me, I sense rather than see Seth stiffen.

"Uh, hi," I say. "Can we talk?"

He looks up from where he's crouched over an overgrown garden bed. "Go inside and make yourself at home," he says with a broad Irish accent. "I just have a few things I want to sort out." He strides off to a shed at one side of the house, rattling at the lock on the door before looking under a pot for the key.

I glance at Seth. "What do you think? Should we go inside?" All my instincts are screaming at me to stay right where we are. But I'm also having flashbacks to Seth's unmoving body on the rocks, so I think I might be over-reacting.

Seth sighs. "I guess we should." He takes off, leading the way into the small cottage.

Inside, it's dark and musty with cobwebs layered over the surfaces. Dust spills up into the air as we walk inside and I sneeze.

"I guess the family aren't as wealthy as they once were." The blond-haired man has come back in behind us, carrying logs for the fire, and a bulging canvas bag.

"Who?" I ask, frowning back at him.

"The family who owns this hunting lodge."

I glance around the small cottage. "How long since you were last here?"

"I'm not exactly sure. Maybe two hundred or so years ago? The last time I woke." He shrugs. "This cottage has been around for a very long time."

"So you haven't been asleep for the last three hundred years?" Seth asks.

"No, not the entire time. But the spell web always starts to itch and hurt too much, and so I return to sleep." He stares at me for a moment. "Until I saw you play with it like it was a child's toy."

I shrug. "It's not hard."

"No other dragon in all my years on this earth has been able to do what you do."

I open my mouth to reply, but realize I have nothing to say. I don't know why I can do it and no one else can. "I'm not special," I say eventually. "I'm pretty sure you can do the same thing."

"You must show me how." He comes to stand directly in front of me and holds one muscled arm out. "My name is Tarsal. I am the last of the green earth dragons."

"I'm Mei. I think I'm a water dragon, but I'm not entirely sure." The words are out of my mouth before I think about how silly I sound.

Tarsal nods regally at me over my hand like a courtier. The motion is natural and unforced, unlike the false old-fashioned manners Vincent has taken on. Tarsal's eyes are deep green with golden highlights that match his hair, and his hand is soft in mine.

Seth clears his throat and I step back hastily. This is certainly proof that dragons don't hate each other on sight. I certainly don't feel an automatic dislike for this dragon. When I think back to Sergei, it was the same—if he hadn't been trying to eat Seth, I wouldn't have felt the need to leave.

"I can help you with the spell web, if you help me." I look up into his green eyes, but find it too overwhelming, like he's sucking me into some kind of mesmerizing spell. As soon as I think it, I blink and snap out of whatever influence he had over me. "Stop that," I say.

He shrugs. "I had to try. It would be fun to have a little dragon at my beck and call."

Behind me I hear a rumbling noise and realize it's Seth. I turn my head; his eyes are full of fire, and he's clenching his fists.

"It's okay, Seth," I say, putting one hand on his arm. "I can handle this."

"I don't know if that's true," he mutters, his eyes never leaving Tarsal.

I turn back to Tarsal. "If Tarsal wants to learn to live in the real world with the spell web on him like a cloak rather than a chain, then he's going to have to listen to me."

"You can tell your little firebird to back down. He's no match for a dragon."

"I'd take you down in an instant, you arrogant fucking lizard," Seth says, his voice low and full of rage.

Tarsal takes a step toward Seth, who stands up to his full height. The two men tower over me uncomfortably.

"You can both take a step back," I say, pushing at both of

them. "This isn't the time or place. We have bigger problems than whatever is causing this pissing contest."

They both hold their position for a moment longer, and then Tarsal grins and steps back. "Never knew a phoenix who could control their anger. Firebird by name, firebird by nature."

"What do you know about phoenixes?" I ask, eager for information. Seth's never been prone to outbursts of anger before, but I glance at him now, and he's still glaring at Tarsal like he'd like to rip his throat out.

"Only what everyone knows," Tarsal says with a shrug.

"You might find that's more than the average person these days," I say wryly.

"Perhaps," he says. He waves a hand to the table and chairs that are placed next to an old Aga oven. "Come, let's sit and talk."

Gingerly, I head over to the table, trying to avoid the dust and keep spider webs out of my hair. I'm not squeamish precisely, we lived in some pretty dodgy places as I was growing up, but the fewer spiders in my life, the better.

I push out through the spell web and try something new, blowing a breath of air along it that will brush away all the dust and cobwebs in one hit.

Unlike my usual blunt force kind of approach, this is a subtle use of the spell web; it's like a tiny exhale of wind along the surfaces. I wouldn't usually think of things like this, but the obvious dislike Tarsal has for the spell web is making me want to show him how useful it can be.

I watch his reaction to what I'm doing, and the way he narrows his eyes. It convinces me he can see the spell web, just like I can. Seth can tell I've done something, but he doesn't see the glowing wave that spreads along the web, blowing the dust away.

Tarsal is still shirtless, and I can't help but stare as he sits down and the muscles in his chest flex. He's like a body-builder, only he's been asleep for hundreds of years. It's hard not to be impressed. I feel Seth shift beside me, and I look away from Tarsal's chest to his face. The older dragon is smirking at me; he saw me staring. I blush, trying to act like I do this all the time. It's not even like I'm particularly attracted to him; I'm just fascinated to be this close to another dragon.

"What do you want to know, little dragon?" he asks in a smooth voice.

"Everything," I say promptly. "I don't know anything about being a dragon. I changed two weeks ago."

His eyebrows lift, and he takes a closer look at my face. "You're that new? Who helped with the change?"

"Seth"—I glance his way with a smile—"and a protector named Si."

Tarsal's eyes widen. "No other dragons? None of the mountain supers helped you?"

I shake my head, his incredulousness making me nervous. "Just us. I was ravenous," I say apologetically. "But we found the rocks in the end."

"It's a miracle you're alive," he says, glancing at Seth. "And that your protectors weren't killed in the process. Baby dragons can be unreasonable creatures."

"I've been through worse," I say. And I have. The trans-formation was painful and strange, and the hunger almost drove me insane, but I've lost too many people in my life to consider simple pain and suffering the worst thing that could happen.

He looks into my eyes and seems to see something in them. He nods. "I will do what I can to help you, little dragon. You need mentors at a time like this."

I lean forward, excitement in my veins. "And will you help us defeat the Earthbound?"

He blinks, staring at my face for a moment. "Of course not. How do you think I survived this long?" he says before erupting into deep, genuinely amused, laughter.

39

"It's not funny," I say, my irritation rising as he continues to laugh. "I have to defeat them. It's my only choice, unless I want to..." I trail off, realizing I was about to disparage his life.

He's been hiding out, hibernating in the lush green hills of a tiny island for the last three hundred years. What does he think will happen? That someone else will wage the war for him, so he can simply rise up and return to his normal life?

He doesn't seem to notice my hesitation and continues to chuckle to himself, wiping away tears from laughing so hard.

But Seth has no such compunction. "Go on, say it, Mei. He's happy to hide away here, living a half-life. And you're not prepared to do that," he says.

The dragon looks up, surprise in his eyes. "Of course. What else does one do when faced with a superior force? Retreat to fight another day."

"They're not a superior force anymore. They've forgotten the tactics their ancestors learned fighting the dragons all those years ago. They don't have the machine that steals your power anymore. They just have the spell web, and even that is weakening. That's why they want me. Vincent, their leader, wants to take my power from me and use it for himself. He says it's for the spell web, but it's not. He's just power-hungry."

"People often are, little dragon. Do you know how the Dragon Wars started?"

"Overpopulation of dragons?"

He nods. "Yes, yes. There were too many of us. But it was more than that. Someone started whispering in the ears of the younger dragons, telling them that the only way they were going to survive was to take the power of their elders. It started slowly, one or two dragons disappearing, and no one knowing where they'd gone. But it soon developed into an outlandish kind of religion."

I lean forward, desperate to hear the real story of the destruction of the dragons.

"Dragons started fighting other dragons, and everyone became suspicious of each other. None of us could be in the same place for fear of the other dragon taking our power. Toward the end of the wars, we discovered the Earthbound were behind it. They'd used persuasion supers, those with mind powers, to convince the easily led younger dragons into the destruction of our entire species." His voice is bitter, and he looks at me with eyes that have seen too much pain.

"I'm not that easily led," I say fiercely.

"No, you don't seem to be." Tarsal is staring at me intently with his green and golden eyes.

I clench my fists in my lap and try to ignore him. "I have to go back, whatever happens. They have my father."

Tarsal leans back, the muscles on his chest clenching and unclenching. "You will regret that decision. The Earthbound do not play fair, they never have. It's a failing of the self-righteous. They think they can do anything, as long as they win."

I can tell he's not just talking about the Earthbound.

"What else can you tell me about them? The other dragon said there was a machine that took your powers?" I need to get some useful information out of Tarsal.

Tarsal's eyes sharpen on my face. "What other dragon?"

"We visited a Russian dragon hiding on an island. He's gone crazy."

"Ah, that sounds like Sergei."

I nod. "He tried to eat Seth."

Tarsal smiles and a dimple appears in his right cheek. "I've been told that a phoenix tastes divine, if you can pin them down."

"Do we do that? Eat meat?" I frown at him.

Tarsal shakes his head. "In dragon form, you need the minerals found in a very particular rock. The one you found underneath your nesting ground. We call it Dragon's Blood, but the human word for it is crocoite. Now you've tasted it, you'll be able to find it again."

"What if I can't find it?" Anxiety bubbles in my stomach at the thought of the unreasonable hunger I went through.

"You will be able to find some when you need it. The nesting grounds have it, if nowhere else."

"And in human form?"

"In human form, nothing changes. You are the same supernatural as you ever were."

"Except for the enhanced vision and hearing."

He nods. "Except for that. You'll also find you're stronger and can smell better. The change will come easier as time goes on as well." He leans back in his chair. "So tell me more about the spell web."

Fair's fair. I take a breath. "I was born with it on me, and I didn't realize that no one else could see it until I was about ten." I glance at Seth, who's watching me with his hazel eyes ringed with fire. "I can use it, manipulate it. I don't think the Earthbound know I can do that."

"They used it as a weapon. We always felt like we had to get it off us. It was like a blanket of chain mail, stealing our power and hampering us."

I shrug. "I don't see it like that. It's like another sense. I can use it to give me more awareness of what's happening around me. It saved us once or twice."

Seth leans toward me, his eyes bright. "Is that how you knocked out those soldiers on the mountain?"

I nod, flushing slightly. I feel bad that I never told Seth any of this.

But he doesn't seem concerned. "Can other people use it like that? Or just dragons?" he says.

"I don't know. I've never met anyone else who could see it." I glance at Tarsal. "You can see it as well, right?"

He hesitates, but then nods, a definite affirmative.

"Then it must be a dragon ability." I glance at Seth. "But just because you can't see it, doesn't mean you can't do anything else with it. We should test that out."

"How do you manipulate it, little dragon?" Tarsal is staring at me intently, like I hold the answers to the universe. Perhaps, to him, I do.

I try to gather my thoughts. It's just something I've always been able to do. I can't imagine it feeling like a burden or a straitjacket. It's always been my protection. "Imagine your magic travelling out along the spell web. Kind of like when you're changing and you imagine your other form."

He closes his eyes, and a little crease appears between

his eyebrows. I can feel him gathering his magic, and there's a ripple in the spell web, but nothing else happens. He lets out a frustrated breath and opens his eyes.

"I can't do it. Not like you can."

I frown. This is unexpected. I was sure working with the spell web was a dragon ability.

"You've been doing it a long time, right, Mei? Since you were little?" Seth says.

I nod, glancing at him, a question in my eyes.

"Then you've had years of practice. Maybe this isn't an innate talent, but a learned one. Something you have to do many times to be good at it."

It's possible, I suppose. "I was born with it on me."

"So it's something I'm going to have to work on?" Tarsal says, a twist to his mouth.

"Nothing is ever easy in this life," Seth answers.

Tarsal glares over at Seth, his eyes narrowed. "You are aware that you're not fully turned yet, phoenix? Mixing with a dragon has started the process, but your flames are not yet fully flaming."

Seth pales slightly. "What do you know of the process?"

"More than you. You must go through one more trial by fire. It used to be that it was a volcano, if I remember rightly." He stares more closely at Seth. "You'll be needing to do it soon, firebird. Otherwise you'll die before you can ever return."

"Are you sure?" I ask, glancing at Seth.

Tarsal barks out another laugh. "The most amusing thing about waking has been to find that my tormentors are so unaware of anything to do with their own powers. The world has changed in my absence."

Seth's face goes from pale to flushed in one quick moment. His eyes darken and the flames appear.

"Ah, there it is. The phoenix anger, so quick to ignite," Tarsal mocks.

I put a hand on Seth's arm and glare at Tarsal. "We're trying to help you, to help all the dragons. There's no need to be like that."

"You will never succeed in your aim. The Earthbound have self-righteousness on their side. Not to mention a few particularly nasty machines that can kill a dragon."

I shake my head. "You've been asleep for hundreds of years. The world is a different place. The Earthbound have lost that knowledge." I lean forward earnestly. "They're strong, but they're used to ordinary supernaturals and humans. They monitor and control the spell web. They can be beaten, especially with someone like you on our side."

But he shakes his head. "The only reason I've survived this long, little dragon, is that I'm willing to use whatever means I can to stay alive."

Even as he says the words, I feel a strange sensation inside my head, like a whirlwind is rushing in my mind, tugging at all the power, and pulling it away. I look up at Tarsal in shock. "Is that you?" I whisper. I know what he's doing. He's trying to take my power away from me. "You were one of the younger dragons the Earthbound convinced to take everyone's power, weren't you?"

Tarsal looks at me with hooded eyes. He doesn't answer, but I can see it in his face. I look over at Seth desperately, but he looks confused. He doesn't understand what's happening. "He's taking my power. He's trying to steal it for himself."

Seth jumps up, and the chair behind him is knocked back, falling over in a clatter. "Stop it," he says, looming over Tarsal.

Tarsal just laughs and sweeps one hand toward Seth.

Immediately Seth is knocked backward into the wall, his head hitting the stone. He falls to the floor, unconscious.

I turn back to Tarsal, anger flowing through me. But even as I try to stop him, I feel more of my power draining out of me, leaving patches inside me empty.

40

I launch to my feet and do the first thing that comes to mind.

I send out what power I have left over the spell web, pulsing it into Tarsal like an arrow. He reacts immediately, his face scrunched up in pain. The swirling whirlwind inside my head settles, and I'm able to push more energy out into the spell web, using it like the electric shock I gave Vincent's soldiers.

Tarsal cries out and falls backward, his expression one of startled fear.

Seth groans behind me, and I glance back to make sure he's okay.

In that moment, Tarsal leaps forward over the table, his huge fist raised to punch me in the face. Only years of training with Si allows me to leap to the side, pushing out a blocking hand and slamming into him, using both the spell web and my own body.

I take whatever energy I can from the spell web around me and blast it into Tarsal. Then I try something new. Tarsal hates the spell web, so I tighten it, making it push against him, restricting his movements.

He cries out in terror, falling to the floor, his hands curled up over his head and his knees crushed into his chest.

There's nothing good about his complete surrender. He's the only moderately sane dragon I've met. He's given us useful information, and I want to learn more from him. To do that, I need him on my side, not cowering at my feet.

I sigh and drag him up until he's sitting in one of the chairs, the one I've so recently vacated.

"What can I use to tie him up?" I mutter to myself.

But when I think about it, the only ties that will bind him successfully involve using the spell web. I push my magic out into the spell web again, testing my idea. I pull the strands tighter around his body, and Tarsal moans in distress. His eyes are glazed over, and he's twitching. Despite his size and overwhelming power, he's completely under my control.

"I will let the bindings go," I say carefully, "as long as you promise to never steal another dragon's power again."

He mumbles something under his breath.

"Promise me, or I will see to it that you end up at the bottom of the sea, wrapped up like a Christmas tree inside the spell web."

"Fine." He snaps the word out, glaring at me sideways.

"Say the words. Promise me."

"I promise to never steal another dragon's power again," he says sulkily.

I let go of the spell web binding him. He sags down into the seat, letting out a ragged breath. Once I'm certain he's not a threat, I race over to Seth.

Seth's breathing is shallow, but he's okay. I touch his

cheek, needing to make sure he's okay. I try to push some of my magic into him, to give him a boost, but he shakes his head. "No. You'll need it." He glances at Tarsal with a fiery expression, and clenches his fists like he's thinking about punching him.

I look back over my shoulder, following Seth's gaze. Tarsal looks defeated at the moment, but I have a feeling he won't stay like that for long. He comes from a generation who stole each other's magical essence to survive. I can't think of anything worse than stealing the magic from another person. It's kind of like stealing souls. I shudder. I don't understand how that could ever seem okay. It makes me wonder—yet again—if the Earthbound weren't in the right after all.

It was three hundred years ago; different times, I suppose. I don't know precisely what it was like for him and the other dragons. The world was overcrowded, with too many dragons vying for not enough space.

What would I have done to survive?

It's a tough question. I like to think I would have stuck to my morals and refused to steal. But if it was a question of survival, perhaps I wouldn't have had the luxury of being so high and mighty.

Turning back to Seth, I put a hand on his arm. "Can you stand?"

He nods cautiously and pushes himself against the wall. I help him to his feet. "We need to get back soon," I whisper in his ear. "We can't stay here forever."

He nods, his breath warm on my neck. Even now, tingles erupt over my skin from touching him, feeling him close, his breath near mine. Trying to push down my reaction to him, I put his arm around my shoulder and lead him over to the single bed in the room, helping him lie down. He closes his eyes and leans back into the dusty pillow. He's got black marks under his eyes, and deep lines around his mouth.

It's a mark of how tired and sore he really is that he's willing to close his eyes in front of Tarsal. I gently smooth his hair from his face and push gentle thoughts into his head. Within moments, he's asleep. I sit and watch him for a moment more, taking in his familiar features, running my hand softly down his cheek, the stubble from being on the run without supplies, rough under my palm.

I stand and turn to Tarsal. He's sitting up straighter now, his hair dangling around his face. His eyes are dark, and he's watching me warily.

"How did you do that?" he asks.

"I think I'm going to keep that to myself," I say.

His mouth thins, but he doesn't say a word.

"You think that's unfair?" I ask, taking an angry step toward him, my whole body stiff. "I would have *gladly* given you any information you wanted to know before you tried to steal my magic. Now you can go to hell. I don't want someone like you on my side." Inside, I wince at the words. I should be trying to convince him to come with us. But I can't fight alongside someone like him. He's only concerned about himself.

"It was different back then," he says softly. "You had to be hard to survive. If you didn't take their magic first, you were the weaker dragon and would end up a Shadow Dragon, able to remember the unfettered glory of being able to fly, but never able to transform ever again."

"It doesn't have to be like that," I insist, although I'm far from confident on that point.

Tarsal nods. "It's a hard habit to break. I'm sorry." He glances over at Seth. "I will find us something to eat."

I hesitate, considering stopping him. But what am I

going to do? Hold him tied up to the spell web the whole time we're here? Aside from anything else, it would drain too much of my magic.

He leaves the room, heading outside, without realizing my conflicting internal thoughts.

I watch out the window, wondering if he's really doing something so mundane as searching for food. He could leave us here, never to be seen again. I let out a breath. If he's not on our side, or willing to help us against the Earthbound, then it doesn't really matter if he decides to run. I wouldn't chase him. There would be no point.

But if he has something else in mind, some other plan to hurt or kill us... Well, I'll just have to keep a close eye on him. I look back over at Seth, but he's sleeping. I make a decision.

I'm going with Tarsal.

I step outside just as he's changing. It's magical to watch; the air sparkles with a radiance that I've never seen anywhere else. I was worried that it was somehow freakish, or that my bones could be seen awkwardly morphing into a dragon-sized body. But it's nothing like that at all. There's more magic in it than anything else. It's beautiful.

I stand there considering Tarsal's dragon form. If someone stole my essence, my magic, what would it feel like? I've only just gotten used to having it inside me. Someone taking it away would be devastating.

I step forward, pulling off my shirt and bra. My jeans follow, and I place them all neatly by the door. I stand in front of Tarsal, with not a stitch of clothing on, and he grins. Even though he's in dragon form, I get a sense of what he's thinking. My instinct is to cover myself, but I won't give him the satisfaction.

I think of my dragon shape, and instantly the change

starts to happen. It's much slower than Tarsal's, and the sparks that look beautiful on him seem blunt and bright during my change, hitting my body and making painful electricity spark along my skin.

But seconds later, I'm a dragon. *I'm coming with you.*

He raises his eyebrows. *I'm going to hunt for food.*

Where?

He glances down into the waves at the bottom of the cliff beside the house. *Fish seems the easiest.*

I nod, then follow him to the edge of the cliff. He leaps off, and I follow him down, watching how he manages the wind currents and keeps himself smooth in the sky. I'm much better than I was on my first flight, but nothing like the graceful elegance of Tarsal in the air.

He lands on a large rock, watching as I follow him down. I land next to him, his larger body dwarfing mine. *We wait here.* I look around, wondering what we're waiting for.

He's not a water dragon like me, so after waiting for whatever he's got planned for about five minutes, I get impatient. *I'm going in,* I say, grinning over at him. I leap up into the air, then dive straight into the water.

It's freezing cold, but I don't mind. My dragon body revels in the feeling of the icy waters along my scales. I take a few moments to swim through the murky darkness, letting my magic soar, and allowing the water to soothe my agitation.

I don't know what kind of fish are common in waters like this, but I see a few darting in and out of the rocks, so I guess it doesn't matter. I use my claws to stab a couple of them, and then resurface just a little away from the rocks where Tarsal still waits, my claws held up triumphantly

He snorts out a breath. *Figures.* He stands up to his full

height. *You can find more fish. I'll go harvest some herbs to go with it.*

I immediately disagree, but he shakes his head. *I'm not going to disappear. You have my word.*

I stare at him through narrowed eyes, bobbing in the waves. I hand the two fish up to him and nod. *Okay, fine. I'll find a few more fish and meet you back at the cottage. But don't try anything.* I don't know what he might do, but the instinct to warn him is too great for me to avoid it.

He flies like an arrow directly back up the cliff face and then disappears over.

I hesitate for a moment, wondering if I'm making a mistake.

Then I dive back under the water, hoping I'm not.

41

I land lightly in the courtyard, five more fish in my claws.

I'm not interested in eating fish as a dragon, but as soon as I change back into my human shape, I'm pretty sure I'm going to be starving. There's smoke drifting out the chimney and some interesting smells coming from inside. I change quickly, shaking off the excess water during the change, and then pull my clothes on. I'm going to have to find something easier to pull on and off than jeans. Something cotton, maybe the kind of wide pants that Si always used to wear. Or a nice summer dress. Not that practical for fighting, but a damn sight easier to get on and off than heavy jeans.

Opening the door, I get a burst of flavor in my nostrils and take a deep breath. It smells delicious, whatever it is. I don't know where he's gotten food from around here, but Tarsal sure knows how to cook.

"That smells good," I say with a smile. I glance over to the bed where Seth was sleeping, but it's empty. "Where's Seth?"

Tarsal looks up from the large metal pot he's stirring. "I thought he was with you. I came back and he wasn't here." He glances over to the bed, as if Seth is going to suddenly pop out from under it.

I frown and stride over to the bed. The backpack is sitting in the middle; the blanket is neatly folded. And Seth isn't hiding underneath. A flash of white draws my attention. A note. It's written roughly on paper in scrawling handwriting:

Mei,

    I need to finish my transformation. Don't follow me. I have to do this alone.

    Go save your father.

    Seth.

I turn abruptly. "Did you see him? Is this something to do with you?"

Tarsal looks up, confusion on his face. "What's the matter? Where has the firebird gone?"

"He's left. He says he has to finish his transformation." I search the room, half expecting to find Seth hiding in a dark corner and that it's all a joke.

"Clever lad. He hasn't got much time."

"He can't have gone far. I'm going to go catch him." He can't leave without me, I won't let him. I'm halfway to the door when Tarsal speaks.

"He's grown wings. He can fly. He'll be long gone if he left just after we did."

"Wings?" I sit down on a nearby chair. "I don't believe you."

"He hid them well. He would have grown them sometime in the last few days. There would have been a time when he was unconscious. I'm told it takes a while for the body to get it right."

I recall our experiences on the beach in Japan. He grew them then, and didn't tell me. My stomach clenches, and I feel like I'm going to throw up.

"If it's any consolation, he might not have realized what had happened at first. Phoenix wings aren't like ours. They're not a physical thing. They're made of air and fire, and take time after the initial change to actually start working properly. Given your terrible lack of knowledge, I'm assuming your friend probably didn't realize what was happening until very recently." He glances skyward, as if he can see through the cottage roof. "It might even be his first flight right now."

"Where would he be going?" I ask, although I have a pretty good idea.

"A volcano would be my guess. He needs to make the final transformation to phoenix."

I glare at Tarsal suspiciously. "Did you say anything to him while I was down in the water?"

Tarsal shakes his head. I narrow my eyes, but I can't see any indication that he's lying to me. My stomach knots up. I'm hurt that Seth would disappear like this without talking to me first. I just don't understand it, not after everything we've been through.

I wouldn't have stopped him, not if it meant his life. If anything, I could have helped him. I look down at the note still in my hand. *Go find your father.* Does that mean he's not coming back to help me save my father either? A small lump forms in my throat.

My father's gone, captured by the Earthbound. Si's disappeared, upset that I betrayed his confidence. Carrick took my wound and went home to his people. And now Seth, the one person I thought would never leave, has gone.

I stare morosely at Tarsal, who's still puttering around the Aga stovetop, stirring and adding spices. He's taken my pile of fish from the table where I placed it and is filleting them over a large bowl.

Even the dragons who were supposed to help me have turned out to be useless. Sergei was crazy as a loon, and Tarsal can't be trusted. He's given us some information, but he's also tried to steal my magic. I certainly don't want to go into battle with him. He could turn at any moment, swayed by God-knows-what bribery from Vincent.

My father is locked up in that place, and I have to get him out. But instead of gathering forces, finding people to stand at my side as I was supposed to do, I'm losing all my allies, one by one.

I glance over at the backpack.

Perhaps there's something in there, some clue as to where Seth's gone. I stride over and start rifling through, pulling everything out and putting it on the bed. There's a small pocket I've never noticed before on the inside, and I poke my hand into it. Something round and metallic hits my fingers. A shockwave goes through my body, and I slowly pull out the golden ring from Jeff's locked box.

Seth left it for me to find.

I hold the ring up in my hand, watching the way it shines in the dim light. I'm mesmerized by it almost immediately and don't notice at first that Tarsal has moved to stand at my side. He reaches out to grab the ring and I snatch my hand away. I turn and glare up at him, but he's not watching me. His whole focus is on the ring.

"Where did you get that?" he asks softly.

I shake my head. "I was given it. I don't know where it came from."

"It's a dangerous item for a little dragon like yourself to be carrying around. You shouldn't show it to anyone." With an effort, he steps back, away from the ring. I see it reflected in his eyes and hide it behind my back. As he turns away to deal with our dinner, I put the ring in my pocket. I don't like the way Tarsal was looking at it. I'm not going to let it out of my sight.

Tarsal sets two bowls for dinner and then places his delicious-smelling vegetable stew into the bowl, with the fried fish on top. I eat mechanically, knowing that I'm hungry and that I'll need all the energy that I can muster for what I'm now going to have to do by myself.

But the thought that Seth has deserted me turns everything to sawdust in my mouth. I could have helped him. I could have taken him to where he needed to go.

I thought we were a team.

Tarsal doesn't speak, and I appreciate that. I think he can see I'm upset over Seth's disappearance. "I'm going to head back to the States tomorrow," I say once I've finished my plate. "I have to rescue my father."

Tarsal nods. "I wish you luck in your journey."

"Thank you. I think I'll turn in now." I glance around. "Can I take the bed that Seth was in?"

"Sure. I'll sleep outside. I prefer it after all these years." Tarsal stands up, bowing one more time before he walks through the door.

I curl myself up in the bed, facing the door, wishing that Seth were here with me. We could have taken turns at keeping watch. I don't understand why Seth felt it was safe to leave me here by myself with Tarsal.

I don't trust Tarsal. He's already attacked once, and I don't think a promise means as much to him as it does to me.

For Tarsal, taking my magic will mean he can survive for another time. It seems the worst possible way to live to me, but perhaps to Tarsal, being alive is more important than living.

42

I wake and it's still dark.

For all that I didn't think I could or should sleep with Tarsal plotting outside, I must have dozed off. I can hear movement in the dim interior of the cottage, but my eyes haven't adjusted yet, so I can't see what it is.

I hold myself completely still, trying to figure out who it could be. Tarsal? Seth? Some other unnamed enemy? Surely the Earthbound couldn't have found me here.

The figure moves closer, and I recognize Tarsal's large shape.

He reaches slowly toward me, his hands going for the pocket of my jeans. The ring. He's after my ring. A surge of protectiveness rolls through me, and I have to fight the urge to immediately move and grab the ring for myself.

I hold still until the last possible moment, then kick out with my leg. It doesn't go quite as I planned because of the blanket covering me. Tarsal leaps back and manages to blunt my kick with one blocking arm. He snarls, a raw guttural sound that chills my blood. He's not the joking man from earlier; this is the real Tarsal.

"Give it to me," he snarls. "It's mine. I need it to go back into hibernation."

"The ring?"

"Yes, of course the ring."

"Why is it so important?"

He snarls again and makes a leap in my direction, planning to use his superior strength to overpower me. Again, I silently send thanks to Jeff and Si for teaching me how to beat opponents who are bigger and potentially better at fighting than me. By the time he makes his second attack, I've pulled the blanket away and manage to throw it over him as I roll in the opposite direction, down the bed.

He roars and lunges forward, but can't see with the blanket draped over his head and just gets empty bed. I crawl off the end and look for the closest thing I can find. I grab a chair and hold it over my head, bringing it down as hard as I can on Tarsal's head. The chair breaks apart but doesn't knock him out like I'd been hoping. He turns, ripping the blanket from over his head, and starts toward me.

"If you give it to me now, I'll spare your life. But if you fight me on this, I'm going to tear you apart, piece by tiny piece."

I back up. "Why do you need it so badly?"

"I can't get back into hibernation without more dragon magic. I've used up all my surplus. That's how it works. You need more magic than your own to lock yourself down into that kind of state. Now give it to me." He lunges forward again, but I'm expecting the move and step sideways, blocking his attack and pushing him toward the floor. He has superior strength and much better magic than me, but he's using traditional Western fighting skills, not the martial arts I've been trained in my entire life.

He stops for a moment, and that whirlwind effect starts inside my head again. He's trying to take my magic, to weaken me. It makes no sense, until I try to use the spell web against him again. He's been practicing, and the short burst of energy I send along the grid does nothing. He's able to keep attacking my magic, pulling on it like it's his for the taking. My secret weapon no longer works—I may as well have given him step-by-step instructions on how to defeat me.

As the whirlwind increases inside my head, I notice that Tarsal is standing stock still, his eyes closed. He needs to concentrate to make this work. My magic might be about to disappear from my body, but I still have all the usual tricks up my sleeve. After all, Si didn't like me using my magic in a fight.

I move forward, silent and deadly. I kick him three times in the knee before he opens his eyes, and then I punch him in the kidneys and around the side. He's too well muscled in the stomach for my punches to break through there. I side-step his lunging punch and then leap onto his back. The whirlwind inside my head has stopped, and the magic has settled back into the corners and crevices of my body.

But now he's fully focused on me again. I have my arms around his neck, trying to squeeze his windpipe, but Tarsal slams an elbow into my stomach, and I gasp out on nothing. I can't get another breath in; he's winded me and I drop my arms from around his neck.

He picks me up and throws me across the room, meaning for me to hit the hard concrete wall like Seth. But I've had better training, and I use the airtime to turn and roll, allowing my landing to become an escape from the room.

Once outside, I search for something in the dark to use

as a weapon and see an old spade hanging by the outhouse door.

I race toward the spade, but I'm too slow. Tarsal is right behind me and grabs my arm, pulling me back toward him. He wraps his arm around my neck from behind and tightens his grip. I kick out, aiming for his groin, but get his thigh, and he grunts, but doesn't let go. He punches me in the side with his other fist, and pain screams through my body.

"Give me the ring," he says through gritted teeth. "And I won't kill you here and now."

I keep struggling, even though I know it won't do anything.

He's too strong, and he's got me in a death grip. But I'm not going to give up without a fight. He can't just steal the ring and go back to hiding. I won't let him.

Tarsal tightens his grip around my neck. My breathing is labored, and my vision narrows.

The ring's in my back pocket, pressing against my skin through the material, its power pulsing in time with mine. My arms are free. It would be so easy to reach down, grab the ring, and put it on. My fingers itch to do it. Instead I kick out at Tarsal again, hitting him uselessly on his thigh. He grunts at the impact, but doesn't loosen his hold.

I still remember last time I wore the ring; the tidal wave of water rolling down the small forest stream, almost killing some innocent campers and Seth. I shudder at the memory of what I almost did.

I promised myself I'd never let the ring take over again, after last time.

But as my body weakens and my arms start to feel like they're made of lead instead of bone, I can only think of one thing: What if putting the ring back on is the only way to save myself?

drenaline rockets through my system, giving me strength I though I'd lost. I'm not ready to die just yet.

In one last desperate attempt, I grab Tarsal's arm with both of mine and lift my legs up and around his side.

It pulls on my neck painfully, but I manage two solid kicks to his side before he lets me go. Falling heavily to the ground, I manage to turn it into a half-roll, and then race to the spade and pick it up, wielding it in front of me like a spear.

"This is a mistake, little dragon. Now you're going to die slowly, instead of fast," Tarsal snarls at me, his eyes wild.

He's frantic to get back to his hibernation.

I don't understand it. "What does it achieve? Going back to sleep? It just prolongs the agony. Nothing will change until you do something to change it."

"I survived longer than the other dragons who made it their fight, didn't I?"

"But at what cost? What kind of life are you living?" I think of my mother who woke up and found love with my father. I hope she thought it was worth it. "You may as well be dead."

He growls and makes a leap at me, jumping back when I swing at him with the spade. It's heavy and unwieldy and won't give me much of an advantage for long. Tarsal stops moving, and I feel the whirlwind in my head again. I jab forward with the spade, and he leaps back again. The whirlwind stops.

"What do you hope to achieve, little dragon?" he says, and his voice has lost the frantic edge. He sounds more tired than anything else. "You're just one against the might of the Earthbound. They defeated the best of the dragon fighters in my time. What do you think you can do against them?"

"I have to at least *try*. I'm not going to sit back and watch them win again."

"You've lost the last of your friends, Mei," he says, calling me by my name for the first time. His eyes are serious, and he's stopped advancing. "You have no hope of winning against them now. Come into hibernation with me." He holds out one hand toward me.

I stare at it. All I have to do is reach out and take it.

The temptation to just go to sleep for a few years is overwhelming. My body could rest, instead of being sore all the time. No one would be chasing me, fighting me, trying to kill me. He's right, I've lost the last of my allies; everyone has deserted me.

Why should I care, if no one else does?

But my father is relying on me. He's stuck in some Earthbound cell, hoping someone cares enough to come for him. He may not be perfect, but he's the only family I have. If nothing else, I have to try to rescue him.

I shake my head at Tarsal and realize too late that he's used my moment of introspection to move to the side of me.

He leaps forward, grabs the spade by the handle, and pulls it from my hands. He's stronger than me, and it pulls away like he's taking candy from a baby. A stupid baby who wasn't paying attention.

He turns the spade and slams the handle into my forearm. I hear the bone breaking and can't help the scream of pain that is torn from my mouth.

"You should have just given me the ring, Mei. Now it's going to go badly for you." He's beside me now and wraps his arm around my neck a second time. He squeezes tight and punches my other side, causing radiating pain up my body. I can't even scream because he's blocking my windpipe with his muscled arm.

This is it. I have no choice. Through the haze that's starting to descend in my mind, I know I have one last chance to survive this. I distract him with an elbow to the chest and a backward kick to the groin, and then I reach into my pocket with my good arm, putting the ring on one-handed. I pull it out triumphantly and focus on the power in the ring.

This time I can tell who it belonged to. Another dragon.

Something happens to me, even as the haze grows darker over my eyes. A glow forms around my body and warmth spreads through every pore of my being. Tarsal drops me like I've suddenly become poisonous, and I fall to the ground in a heap. I gasp for breath, unable to pull myself up. My arm hangs uselessly at my side, pain still throbbing through it.

"What have you done? You put it on!" He's pulling his hair with both hands, almost like a cartoon character. I'm too busy breathing in as much air as I can to be worried about what he's doing.

"You won't be able to control it. Not yet. You're a baby dragon. You should have given it to me."

But the words are disappearing into the distance. I'm changing, breaking free of my human form, my clothes tearing from my body. There's a warm yellow glow all around me, helping me change and become my dragon-self.

Then I'm up in the air, flying with a grace and speed I haven't managed before today. I twist through the air, spiraling through the currents. I don't need my arm to fly, my wings are stronger and mightier than my puny arms. I glance back down at Tarsal. He's standing in the middle of the courtyard, watching me fly away. He doesn't even bother changing into his dragon shape.

A half-life isn't worth it, Tarsal. We're dragons—we're made to roar.

I let out a dragon snarl as I twist away in the sky. The wind on my face makes me feel alive, and I widen my jaws to roar at the world below me. It falls away in the wind rushing past my face. Tarsal is getting smaller and smaller below. He doesn't move, his eyes just watching me climb away from him.

Inside I hear a sweet voice call my name. It whispers to me until I understand the words, even though they're in another language and being spoken from another lifetime. There's something comforting and familiar about the voice, like I've heard it before, a million miles from here. It calms my fears and makes me feel stronger, like I could take on the world. It's a voice filled with love, destined only for me.

Then I understand.

It's my mother's voice, helping me through the ring, giving me her power and her abilities.

Somehow she locked her magic into this ring, leaving it for me to use. It's like she's here with me, offering words of wisdom so that I can do what I need to do. My heart soars as high as my wings. This is the greatest gift I could ever have been given; my mother has returned to me.

Maybe things will turn out okay after all.

I fly over the water, the moon dancing over the waves below, my heart dancing inside.

44

I t's a long trip home.

I stop to rest on small atolls and outcrops in the Atlantic Ocean, but I'm feeling tired and lonely long before I make it to American soil. Seth's disappearance has hit me hard, and I don't know how to fill the aching void he's left behind. Even the ring's magic pulsing inside me can't make me feel better about what's happened.

I'm struggling to figure out how I'm going to rescue my father on my own, and the pain in my broken forearm is making me feel woozy.

At first I don't know where to go, and I simply fly on over the landscape, aimlessly following the air currents. But eventually instinct makes me turn in the direction of Si's retreat. It's always felt like home to me, and the waterfall will help soothe my broken arm.

The Earthbound know about the retreat, but if they do come, I'll just fly away. One of the perks of being a dragon.

When I first see the house and training area in the distance, my throat clogs up like I've got a giant hairball stuck inside it. The last time I was here, Jeff was killed. I almost bank around and fly away right there.

It's only the pain in my forearm and thoughts of the healing powers of the waterfall that keep me moving forward.

I land outside the house and look around. It seems smaller than I remember. More empty...sadder.

A large reddish-brown patch on the driveway catches my eye. Dried blood has stained the concrete next to Seth's car, right where Jeff died. A shudder rolls across my scales. I'm frozen in place, unable to move my eyes away. I remember turning over his body, seeing the fresh blood coating his stupid Hawaiian shirt. It was designed to provoke me into a reaction, but it's probably what got him killed—he would have been an easy target.

My memories tumble on top of each other—seeing Si murdered, Seth getting shot, me suspecting him of leading our enemies to our sanctuary. It all seems so long ago, despite the rawness of the memories.

I shake out my scales and stomp off toward the waterfall. The familiar walkway calms me, but about halfway to the waterfall, I realize I'm too big as a dragon. I keep hitting my head, and I'm struggling to squeeze my body through the trees. I pause and think of my human shape. Immediately the magic flows through me, and my body starts to shift. The transformation is much less painful this time.

When the sparks disappear, I'm naked again. My clothes were ripped off me when I changed in Ireland, and I don't have any spares. Luckily I have other clothes here at the retreat, so my instincts to come here were right on that count, too.

The waterfall is exactly as I remember it. Water cascades over the rocks at the top, and falls noisily into the pool beside me. Its energy still captivates me, but now I understand the attraction.

I'm a water dragon. It all seems so obvious.

I jump in, luxuriating in the feeling of the cool, fresh water hitting my body. The water tingles along my skin, and is already working on healing my wound. My arm is numb, the pain somehow lessened from my time as a dragon, but the bone is still broken. I have a niggling fear that it might mend badly if I don't get someone to heal it properly.

The only problem is I don't know where to go or who to ask.

I don't think I'll be welcome in many supernatural homes, not now they know I'm a dragon. Everyone thinks dragons are terrible creatures who will do anything as long as it benefits themselves.

When I think about the two other dragons I've met recently, that perception seems pretty accurate.

But what about me? I'm not like that...am I?

Have I—just by transforming into my dragon form—started some kind of downward spiral into evil? Will I eventually become just like the others I've met?

Is it inevitable, becoming selfish? Mean? Violent?

Or will I still be me?

I don't know the answer to any of those questions, or even the more pressing question of how I'm going to rescue my father. I'm wounded, I don't have a plan, and I have fewer people helping me instead of more.

It seems like I'm doomed to failure.

A pulse of magic from the ring seems to argue that point. My mother's power flows through my veins, filling me with warmth and love, showing me I'm not completely alone.

I take a deep breath, gathering my resolve. I'm stronger

than this; Jeff and Si taught me better than to give up so easily. I close my eyes and consider my problems.

Look at it another way, as Jeff would say.

Can I use the ring's magic to save my father? I shake my head in the water, immediately opposed to that thought. I don't know enough about it, and after what happened last time I wore the ring, I'm not confident in my ability to control it.

I lift my hand, and hold up the ring in front of me. It looks so innocent; a small delicate gold band that fits perfectly on my finger, almost like it was made for me. Now that I know it was my mother's ring, my connection to it has grown even stronger.

But I remember the compulsion, and the way it took over my thinking. It created the destructive tidal wave almost without effort, without thinking.

Why would my mother create a ring that would do something like that?

What was my mother *really* like? Growing up, I always assumed she was a good person who died too young. The way my father talked about her at the SIG headquarters backed that up.

But if this is her ring, maybe that's not the case? Doubts rise to the surface, and I start to wonder...why did she *really* come out of hibernation? And did she steal another dragon's magic to hibernate in the first place?

She would have had to, according to Tarsal.

That thought makes me edgy and uncomfortable, as does everything I've learned about dragons since meeting Sergei and Tarsal.

They've managed to confuse me more than ever. One was crazy and the other selfish. Neither was a good ambassador for dragon-kind. Somehow it makes the argument for the Earthbound's slaughter of dragons a little stronger.

Were there no honorable dragons? No dragons who fought for the greater good, for their children, or their families?

I don't know the answer to that question. All I can do is hope that all dragons weren't like Tarsal and Sergei.

45

A rumble of hunger from my stomach disrupts the calming sounds of water and forest. I'm still floating face up in the waterfall pool, trying unsuccessfully to ignore my problems.

There'll probably still be food in the kitchen, so I swim to the side of the pool and climb out. My arm feels better after a long soak in the pool, although it still aches, and I can't do much more with it than allow it to hang at my side.

When I arrive back at the house, I cautiously open the front door, which is unlocked, and tip toe down the hallway to my bedroom. The air smells dusty and dry, and I'm pretty sure no one has been here in a while.

I find some comfortable trousers and a shirt and awkwardly drag them on one-handed, then head back to the kitchen. I find the first aid kit, and put together a sling for my arm, swearing as I discover just how difficult it is when you're on your own.

Then finally, I search the cupboards for something edible.

I hit the jackpot straight away—thankfully no one has looted Si's stores—and I'm soon cooking up a delicious pasta meal, and even doing okay at it, despite being one-handed.

It feels good to be home, and I let out a sigh of satisfaction as I sit down at the table, a large bowl of pasta and bottled tomato sauce on my plate. This is the first time I've felt even remotely safe since...well, since I came home and saw Jeff's dead body.

I spoon another mouthful of pasta into my mouth, trying to get rid of the image. I need to think about—

A noise outside grabs my attention and the proximity alarm in the kitchen starts to beep softly. I freeze. Surely it's not the Earthbound already?

But it has to be; they're the only other people who'd come here. I berate myself for assuming they'd leave this place alone. There must have been some kind of sensors left in place, or perhaps guards who were keeping watch from a distance.

Standing up, I creep around the kitchen table to peer out the window, trying to get a sense for who is out there. I frown. Whoever they are, they're well hidden, and that's a huge problem for me.

If I turn back into a dragon inside the house, I'll end up trapped in a space that's too small for me. I'm not in a fit state to fight, so I can't just head outside. My only real option at this point is a stealthy escape. And without visuals, there's no way to know numbers or where their blind spots might be. I'm going to have trouble finding a safe exit out of the house.

I grab my plate of pasta and the pot I used to make it, and hide them in the cupboard, just in case whoever is here doesn't know I'm inside the house. Then I flick the house alarm to active and sneak out of the kitchen, keeping low and away from the windows.

I head back to my room, swearing softly under my breath. I should have packed a bag and organized myself before cooking the food. Rookie mistake number one. As it is, I have to rapidly shove whatever I can find into the first bag I see, a small canvas tote I used for trips to the waterfall on hot days.

It doesn't have enough room for everything I want, but I fit in as much as I can. Next I head to Jeff's room, rummaging through his drawers for the key to the weapons store. It's under the house, well hidden and well protected.

It's the next best option, after getting the hell out of here. I don't know who the intruders are exactly, but if they're stupid, they might miss it.

If they're *not* stupid, they'll have me trapped in a cell under the house, unable to get out. But at least I'll have a truckload of weapons to play with.

It's not ideal, but I decide to take the chance. There's also a video monitor down there showing different views around the house. Hopefully I'll be able to put some eyes on whoever is out there.

The door is inside the linen cupboard, under the vacuum cleaner. I move the vacuum to one side and shut the door behind me. It's a tight space, but I'm small enough to manage it. Neither Jeff nor Si would have been, but we never planned to use it as a hiding place for ourselves.

I put the key into the small lock and then lift the trap-door. As I'm climbing down into the darkness, I have a moment of fear. Could this be a trap? Maybe the Earth-bound know about this hideaway? Perhaps I'm helping them trap me inside the house, making me an easy target.

But even as I hesitate, the alarm for the front door starts

beeping. I have no choice now, unless I want to fight someone with a broken arm. It's better to hide...but not by much.

I slide down the ladder and pull the trapdoor softly over me.

There's a short corridor and then the room opens out into a basement. Inside it's covered from floor to ceiling in weapons, from the martial arts ones like throwing stars, long and short fighting sticks, and nunchakus to grappling hooks, ropes, and other specialized equipment for climbing. Along another wall, there are different kinds of guns, from multiple small handguns to bigger automatic machinery. There's also gear like gloves, bulletproof vests, old-fashioned armor made of bamboo and chain mail, plus punching bags and mats that don't get used that often. In all, it's an impressive space.

I search the room, finding the weapons I think will be most useful to me. I shove rope, a couple of guns, and some of the throwing stars into my already overflowing bag. I briefly consider the leg and arm guards, but it would just make the change into a dragon harder, and I think that form will be more useful for me.

There's even a store of food down here. I grab some of the energy bars and put them into the bag, peeling back the wrapper on one of them and taking a bite.

Then I head to the monitors to see exactly who is upstairs.

The screens show a couple of dark forms, wearing black from head to toe. Swords cross on their backs, knives strapped at their feet and arms. I blink a few times, wondering if I'm seeing things. But no, they're Protectors in full gear.

But the next question that I don't know the answer to is: are they working for the Earthbound?

Just because Si and my other Protectors were sworn to help me, doesn't mean they all are. Lee's brother, Ben, was the one who gave me up to the Earthbound not so long ago.

It's my fault they lost five of their brethren, and for what? A lost dragon who might end up destroying the world? Now that it's common knowledge, I don't know what side anyone is on anymore.

It seems safer to assume I'm on my own.

I continue to watch the monitors, hoping that my hidey-hole stays hidden. There's no telling what they might know about this house. They search all the rooms, going quietly and carefully through each space. Finally, they meet in the living room and pull their head coverings off.

Taking a step back, I bump into a small table. Si is one of the faces revealed above me. For a moment, I hesitate. Is he still annoyed at me? What will his reaction be to me coming out of the cupboard? But he's been with me since I was a little kid. He's like a father to me. I can't do anything other than show my face and see what he says.

I climb the ladder, trying to make noise so I don't surprise them into attacking me. I open the door out into the hallway and find three large shadows standing over me, all in positions ready to attack.

"It's just me," I say grumpily to Si, who's standing at the left-hand side.

"Stand down, brothers. It's Mei."

The other two men relax their stances slightly, but their faces remain impassive. I stand up, holding my bag in my good hand and look at Si. "How are you?" I say, my voice shaking slightly.

He looks me over, his eyes stalling on my broken arm for a moment, and then he steps forward and envelops me in a hug. I'm tempted to cry inside his warm embrace.

It's good to have him back.

46

"**S**eth left you?" Si is sitting on the living room sofa with me. He's working on my arm, healing it as best he can.

I nod miserably. "I thought I was going to have to go in there by myself." I fumble with the knitted blanket that's usually folded over the back of the sofa, but is now under my arm, holding it in place.

Si shakes his head, looking up at me from his healing. "I might have been annoyed at you for forcing my hand, Mei, and even because you knocked me out, but I would never desert you. I was trying to find reinforcements. I thought Seth understood that."

It calms my nerves to hear him say that aloud. All those years, there was a tiny part of me that wondered what would happen to Si and Jeff if their bosses stopped paying them to look after me. Would they stick around?

Apparently the answer is yes, Si would.

And I'm pretty sure Jeff would have stuck around too. That tiny piece of my heart settles into place, and I smile at Si. "Thanks," I say. "I needed that."

"We need a plan if we're going to make this work. Could we get back in the same way you got out with Carrick?"

A sting of pain works its way up my arm and I wince. "Maybe," I say, breathing deeply. "It depends if they've found where he took me out. They seemed pretty sure of their ability to keep me inside the compound, so they've obviously got some kind of sophisticated technology running."

"But Carrick bypassed it?"

I nod again.

"Can we convince him to join us?"

I let out a breath. "I think he would be pretty reluctant to go back in there. Vincent held him captive for a long time."

"How long?"

"Years, I think."

"He would have been eager to get home." Si stops his ministrations and gazes out the window.

"Yes. And not so eager to go back."

"So it's just us?" He looks pensive a moment, then turns back to me and nods sharply. "Perhaps it's better to be a small team, able to get in and out without anyone noticing. We must plan our incursion into the compound with precision."

"Are you sure about this, Si?"

"Daniel is a friend of mine as well as your father. He helped me on numerous occasions. I want to get him out of there."

"My dad helped you?" I ask, surprised. Everyone seems to have secret backgrounds they haven't told me about.

Si hesitates. "He didn't always follow the SIG party line. He is much like Jeff in that way. Probably why they always got along."

"How are we going to do this?" I ask softly.

"I don't know. But we must." Si stands up and moves over to the kitchen. He pours himself a glass of milk from the container in the fridge. I investigate my arm, which is much better now that Si has helped with the healing.

There's shouting from outside, and I glance up. Si's two protector friends, Marco and Liam, are on guard outside, and don't seem the type to panic or yell unnecessarily.

From my spot on the sofa, I peer out the corner of the window, trying to get a good view. Overhead there's a dark shape blocking out the sun. The sun glints off gold and green scales as a large creature lands delicately in the driveway, and I put a hand up to shade my eyes.

It's Tarsal. He's found me.

Si turns to me, his eyebrows raised. "One of your new dragon friends?" he asks.

I nod. "The one who broke my arm." I glance down at the ring on my finger. I'll need the extra power it provides if I'm going to beat Tarsal again.

I felt Tarsal's presence as soon as we landed on the island where he was hiding, and I can feel him now. I'm sure the knowledge is mutual. He knows I'm here.

Standing carefully, I follow Si to the door. This is my fight; I won't allow the protectors to be harmed battling Tarsal. I can beat him again if I have to.

I think.

He's a much larger dragon, but I'm younger and fitter. Just as I'm stepping outside, another shape surges in to land next to Tarsal, causing a blast of hot air that whips my clothes and hair around my body.

This time it's a fiery creature that towers over us; blood-red and golden flames undulate across its body driven by an invisible magical wind, a giant beak snaps shut and unforgiving tawny eyes glare down at Marco and Liam. Midnight blue feathers intermingle with the flames in its long tail and at the crest on its head. Sparks drip from its wings, which are stretched out full to each side.

Liam and Marco stand their ground despite the two menacing intruders who have descended from the skies.

Then the fires settle, and the wind dies away. The wings are pulled in, and through the flames a figure emerges.

My heart lurches.

Seth is standing next to Tarsal, huge burning fire-wings coming off his back and his eyes glowing with the brightness of a bonfire.

My knees weaken and I almost fall. "Seth," I whisper, not sure what else to say. I knew he was a firebird, but I never really thought about it. This makes it all too real.

He deserted me back in Ireland, but he's back, and it looks like he's made the final change that Tarsal told us about. I hadn't even been sure it was the truth, given the way Tarsal toyed with us for his own gain.

I take a step toward Seth, almost forgetting about the threat Tarsal poses. Si hauls me back into the doorway. "Wait here. We don't know what's happening, or why they're here," he says.

I nod absently. He's right. "Tarsal tried to steal my magic," I say, without looking away from Seth. My shock at seeing Seth's new appearance is making me careless. It's at once beautiful and fearsome. He's got a clear flame aura around him now, like when it's a hot day and the heat rises up from the road. The dragon inside me is drawn to his fiery new presence.

Seth's talking urgently to the massive green and gold dragon, their voices too low for me to hear what they're saying. Did they arrive together? Or just at the same time?

I can't figure out what's happening. Adrenaline is

pumping through my body, making me edgy and uncertain. Am I about to battle a dragon for the second time? Or is Seth talking him out of it?

Seth says something more to Tarsal and then looks up. His eyes are a dark flame, and the outline of his wings shimmer behind him. He strides directly toward me, never taking his gaze from my face.

He comes up to me, his eyes blazing into mine. When he's a couple of feet away, he stops. "Mei," he says, his voice low and gravelly.

47

"Tarsal kidnapped me," he says. "He knocked me out and locked me in the shed."

I blink. They're not the words I was expecting. "What?"

"He thought he could overpower you more easily without me there."

"But..." I frown, looking over his shoulder to where Tarsal is waiting outside. "Why is he here now? How did you escape?"

Seth hesitates. "He was going to kill me. After you left, he was devastated. He opened the door all in a rage, set to do it... And then stopped. He said he saw something in my eyes, like I was prepared to fight to the death for you." His eyes are burning into mine.

My breath stops in my chest. "I thought you'd given up on me," I whisper.

He shakes his head. "I would never give up on you."

I put my hand out, touching the new aura near his arm with my fingertips. I feel a zing of energy. "What happened? Did you make the final change?"

"Tarsal took me to a volcano in Iceland. He said it was the only way for me to turn properly. He dropped me into the crater as he flew over." Seth pauses, then reaches up with one hand and cups my cheek. "I thought he'd changed his mind and that I was going to die without getting a chance to tell you how I feel about you," he whispers.

I gaze up into his face, tears gathering in my eyes.

"Don't cry," he whispers. "I don't like it when you cry." He wipes his thumb across my cheek, gentle against my skin.

I sniff and try to swallow back the tears. "How do you feel about me?" I ask, my voice rasping. I need him to say the words.

"I would do anything for you. I would never leave you."

"Me too." I reach up with one hand and pull him closer until our lips touch. Softly at first. Tentative. This kiss is different from the last time; it's a promise of things to come, of desires that we've kept pushed down as we tried to fulfil our mission.

His phoenix power is pulsing against mine, twisting together like they're meant to be one. My lips part and then we're kissing deeper, the sparks igniting into open flames. Seth's hands slip around my waist and I press myself against him, unable to get enough.

I surrender to the kiss, and he does the same. Time has disappeared and all I know is the feel of Seth's mouth against mine, his hands on my skin, and my arms curled around his neck. His flame aura licks at my body, almost like it's whispering promises of what it will be like when Seth and I—

A throat clears loudly and I flinch back. Si is standing right next to us, an amused expression on his face. My face flushes.

"As touching as all this is, we still have a dragon in the courtyard," he says with a wave toward Tarsal.

I pull back from Seth. "He says he's going to help?"

Seth nods. "I'm not sure we can trust him, but he did fly me to the volcano and then help me when I crawled out again. I couldn't make it all the way under my own steam, not from Iceland, so he's been helping me most of the way here too."

I let out a breath. "We need all the help we can get in the fight at the Earthbound compound. We'll just have to keep an eye on him." I glance over at Si. "I'll go talk to him. I want to hear what he has to say."

Si nods and gestures for me to go talk to Tarsal. "We'll be inside. I want to talk to Seth."

I narrow my eyes at them, but Si doesn't give anything away, and it's clear from Seth's expression that he doesn't know what it's about. Moving away from the door, I decide that I'm not going to let it worry me.

Tarsal, however, is a concern.

"Change into human form," I say fiercely when I'm standing in front of him. My arm still hurts with the echo of remembered pain.

He shakes his head from left to right, and then suddenly he's standing in front of me in human form. He's buck naked, tall and muscled, with his long blond hair artfully tousled. I grimace and turn toward the door to get him some clothes, but Seth is already there, handing me an old pair of cotton trousers from Si's collection. I smile at him gratefully.

Tarsal puts them on with a smothered grin, acknowledging that he's aware of his muscled beauty. But fresh from Seth's kiss, I'm immune to his charms—especially given that only a day ago he tried to kill me and Si has only just finished healing my arm.

"What are you doing here?"

"I've come to help," he says promptly. He glances at the ring on my finger.

"You don't want to help. You've come for the ring."

"No. At least not like that. I was thinking about the ring after you left, and I realized that it might be able to help you in your quest to defeat the Earthbound."

My brow wrinkles. "How?"

"The ring contains more than just the magic of the dragon who put it there. It contains their soul." He pauses. "I can feel it, right here," he says, putting his fist on his chest.

"So?" I already knew there was something more to this ring than simply magic.

"So I think you might be able to use it to bring down the spell web."

I take a step back, thinking fast. There's no way I'm going to destroy the spell web. "How will that help us?"

"The Earthbound won't be able to use their stolen magic to keep themselves in power. The spell web is everything that's bad about the Earthbound. How do you think they get the magic to destroy us?"

Shaking my head, I take another step backward. "I don't want to destroy the spell web. That's not what we're doing. We're saving my father."

"I thought you wanted to get rid of Vincent and destroy the Earthbound?"

"If I can," I admit reluctantly. "But the most important thing at the moment is to get my father out of there. Everything else can wait."

"To save your father and free yourself from the Earthbound, you must destroy the spell web. It's the only way."

Even in human form, I can almost feel my dragon scales

standing on end, just like Sergei's did when he was unhappy with me. "No. That's not true. We can use the spell web to our advantage. We can beat them at their own game." I pull the web around me like a blanket and consider sending enough energy along it to destroy Tarsal. He's talking about destroying the one thing in life that makes me feel safe. It's an extra sense that I rely on every day and it's saved me more than once. Why on earth would I destroy it?

"Not while they have the power of the spell web at their disposal too."

I lift one hand in an agitated motion. "Stop. Just stop. I'm not going to destroy the spell web. We're going to rescue my father and put a stop to Vincent if we can. That's all. If you're not okay with that, you can leave right now." I put my hands on my hips and glare at him, as if I can stare him into taking off again into the sky.

He shrugs. "I'm not leaving."

I let out a frustrated breath. "Why are you here, Tarsal? What could you possibly gain from being part of this?"

"I understand why you're angry at me. I'd be angry too. But you're right. I'm not living a full life. Dragons are supposed to roar. When I saw Seth, full of fire and brimstone, trying to defend himself and save you at the same time, I realized that he was more of a dragon than I was. I saw clearly what I'd been missing in my life."

"And what's that?"

"Something to believe in. To stand up for. To be passionate about."

I lift my eyebrows at him. This is unexpected. "I thought you were happy living your hibernation lifestyle?"

Tarsal shrugs. "I want to be like you, to have someone who would give their life for me."

I watch him carefully. Is he joking? Or is this for real? I don't know. "I don't trust you. You can stay, you can help us overcome the Earthbound—without destroying the spell web—but I'm going to be watching you. If you so much as look at anyone funny, I'm going to take you down."

Tarsal grins. "Of course. I wouldn't expect anything less."

48

Our plan is simple. Mainly because it has to be.

We don't know what we're going to find at the compound, or even precisely where to find my father. We have to be flexible about how we do it.

I'm flying back toward the compound, and wishing I could be anywhere else.

The wind is rushing along my scales, and the clouds are making visuals difficult. Seth is on my back—his flying isn't up to going long distances yet. Not far away, Tarsal is carrying the three protectors, his larger back able to fit more passengers. I'm hoping they'll stand more of a chance with three of them to fight him if he turns out to be against us.

We're going to fly in and land inside the compound wall, as discretely as possible. Then we're going to get in and out fast, seeing as few people as we can.

Simple.

Probably a little too vague.

I bank to the right, flying around a gathering of clouds that is blocking my way. We're almost at the compound, and I'm still not sure whether this is a good idea. I don't have any more special knowledge than I did before—at least nothing that's going to help with this mission.

Worst of all, it feels like we're flying into a trap.

Vincent wants a dragon to keep the spell web in place. I'm providing him with two. It'll be like a double shot of espresso to the spell web, which seems like a terrible idea.

But we can't just leave my father there. And where am I going to go? What am I going to do with my life if I don't face up to Vincent? I can't run my whole life. I can't always be hiding.

I glance over at Tarsal. He's flying close, his enormous wingspan dwarfing mine. For all my big words to him, I've been hiding my whole life too, running from the Earthbound like a scared rabbit. Standing up to them is a scary change of pace, and I'm not sure I'm ready.

Taking a deep breath, I force my nerves to settle. It's time to take action, to be on the offensive against whatever may come.

We're almost there. Seth's voice appears in my head, and I jerk, my wings tipping slightly to one side. I'm still not used to his new ability to communicate with me in dragon form. Now that he's a full phoenix, he's discovering new abilities all the time.

Below us is the barren landscape around the compound. In the distance is the big fence, and my heart lurches. This is the third time I've been here, but the first time that it's been under my own steam. I'm going in voluntarily.

It's about the right time to wonder if I'm crazy.

We land just inside the outer boundary. Both Tarsal and I turn back into our human form and pull on the clothes the others are carrying for us.

"Now what?" Tarsal asks, glancing around.

"Now we find my father. Get him out of here."

We run to the old shed where Carrick and I rested, and I wince, remembering how he took my injury.

Just as I'm peering around the corner, a large figure erupts from the shed. I jerk back, my heart thumping. They were expecting us. It's not part of the plan to be discovered so quickly.

There's a blur of movement as Tarsal attacks the intruder, leaping onto their back, and wrapping his arms around the person's neck. The intruder turns and I get a better look at his face. I rush in, trying to get myself between the two men.

"Stop! Tarsal! It's Carrick! He's on our side."

As I speak, Carrick shoves his elbow back into Tarsal's stomach, making the dragon cry out in pain, and leans forward, taking Tarsal off his feet.

I'm not sure who would win—both men are equally large. They ignore me at first, both unwilling to give up their position, but eventually Carrick releases his grip on Tarsal's arm, and Tarsal loosens his hold around Carrick's neck.

Both men are gasping for breath and bowed over next to each other. Tarsal glances up and glares at Carrick. "I thought you'd be dead, stone muncher," he says.

"I'm surprised you could drag yourself away from the mirror, lizard," Carrick says in reply.

"You know each other?" I say, surprised.

Carrick looks up at me. "It's a long story. But yes, we know each other."

I decide to let him get away with no explanation and give him a hug. "I'm so glad to see you. Your elders gave you permission to come?"

He shakes his head sadly. "No. I had to sneak away in the dark of night. There will be repercussions, but I couldn't leave you to fight alone."

Carrick glances around at our group. "I see you managed to find reinforcements."

I smile up at him and squeeze his arms where I'm holding on. "You know this compound better than anyone here. With you on our side, we have a chance of actually making this work."

Tarsal grunts from the far side of Carrick. "You were leading us on a suicide mission before he turned up?" he says.

"I just wasn't completely certain we'd be able to do it. Now I am."

I crouch down on the ground behind the shed and wave my hand to gather everyone close to me. "Change of plans. Tarsal and I will provide a distraction by going in straight at them in dragon form. Seth and Carrick will be more discrete and go find my father. Si and the protectors will plant the explosives where they can, and we'll detonate them as we leave, using the remotes." I nod toward Si, Liam, and Marco, who are dressed in black and carrying three bags full of explosives from the storage room under the house.

"We meet back here?" Seth asks, looking like he wants to disagree.

I nod. "We might have to improvise, depending on what we find inside. But the plan for now is to meet back here in forty minutes. That should be enough time to get in and out. Remember to keep your heads down and don't get caught," I say with a grin.

As Carrick gives Si directions for where to plant the explosives for best effect, I give Seth a hug. "Take care of yourself," I whisper into his ear, the warmth of his aura tickling my skin.

Seth and Carrick leave first. Watching them go, all I want to do is call them back, to tell them it's too dangerous. But I manage to hold my tongue. Si and the other protectors creep away next, heading in a different direction to Carrick and Seth.

I glance at Tarsal, who is watching me with great interest. "We're going to fight as dragons?" he says.

I nod. "We're not trying to win against them. We just want to distract them, keep them away from the areas where the others will be. We can do that in dragon form the easiest."

"Then let's go."

49

Sighing, I pull off my clothes again.

This is the one big downside of being a dragon. The constant on and off again of my human clothes. I'm going to invent some kind of dress that's easy to pull off and on. And a wearable pocket to put it in while I'm a dragon.

We both leap into the air at the same time, and I grin. He might be a pain in the butt, and I'm not sure I can trust him, but Tarsal is magnificent. Flying next to him makes me feel like a real dragon, strong and confident, ready to take on the world. Tarsal grins back at me, and then starts spinning through the air like a dart, heading toward the main buildings in the compound. I follow along, trying to mimic his graceful moves.

How are we going to get their attention? Tarsal asks.

I was thinking fire?

He nods and dives down closer to the building, letting loose a long stream of dragon fire. The concrete buildings don't light on fire, but the trees and wooden outdoor furniture lights up like it's bonfire night.

Right away, guards wearing black chest-armor start running out from inside the compound, their spell webs glowing. They're all supers, and seem to be drawing extra power from somewhere.

When they see two dragons hovering above their heads, several of them run back inside. A few brave souls stand their ground and start firing. They're only using handguns at the moment, and Tarsal assured me the bullets will just bounce off our scales with no more pain than a needle prick.

Tarsal comes around for a second run at the outside of the building, and his burst of dragon fire forces the guards back inside.

I dive down as well, sending flames along the other side of the same building. I don't have the same impressive lung power that Tarsal has, but my dragon flames are just as powerful as his.

We fly in and out over the main building, trying to stay out of range of the bullets as much as we can while doing the most damage.

The building is actually concrete, so harder to actually set fire to, but we're giving it a good shot. There are blackened burn marks all over the structures and across the ground and concrete paths outside. I fly over the garden where Carrick and I escaped and burn my way through the plants there, looking out for the gardener who let us go by and making sure I don't hit him.

So far, we've managed to avoid hurting anyone, and despite what Vincent has done to me, I'm glad. I don't want to be responsible for mass killings.

But when they wheel out a large automatic gun intended for us, I'm quick to join Tarsal in raining fire down on it and the guards standing around it. It's either us or them, and I know what I prefer.

Their charred forms fall to the ground as I swoop back up into the sky. It's the first time I've killed as a dragon, and it feels just as bad as it does when I'm in human form. There's a little bit of relief inside me at that realization.

On the far side of the building, I notice another group of guards surrounding a large mechanical contraption. It looks old and rusted in several places. But they're winding a large handle and cogs seem to be whirring along the side.

I don't understand what it could possibly be, but Tarsal lets out a dragon roar and dives for the machine. I follow behind him, trusting that he's got a reason for reacting like that.

I feel the tug on the spell web moments before the machine starts emitting a high-pitched whine. I see all the energy of the spell web around the machine being dragged into it via a large cone on one side. The whine gets higher and more painful, and I hold my front paws over my ears in an attempt to block it out. It doesn't work, and suddenly I'm falling out of the sky, unable to pump my wings, or save myself from falling.

Luckily, I'm close to the ground, but I land heavily, rolling along the grass a few yards. Beside me, Tarsal has fallen as well. He seems to be more affected by the whine than me, and he's moaning, his eyes fully closed.

Right before my eyes, he turns back into his human form, lying naked and vulnerable on the ground as dozens of armed and geared-up guards rush out from a nearby building, holding automatic rifles pointed strait at us.

I feel the change happen for me moments later, and suddenly I'm lying there naked as well. And not only is my dragon form is gone, but my magic, too. I can't see the spell web around me, and that core of power that I've always taken for granted has disappeared. I feel empty, a shell of what I've always been. It hurts so badly, I want to cry out.

Instead I bite my lip and hold it in.

Something clicks in the back of my mind. This must be the machine that Sergei was talking about, the one the Earthbound used against the dragons all those years ago.

I should have known better than to assume Vincent didn't have it. I can't believe I thought he wouldn't have all this planned out. Of course he did.

Our mission is over before it even got started.

I look around and see Vincent standing next to the machine, staring at Tarsal, a smug expression on his face.

He just got everything he ever wanted.

50

When hands reach down to grab me, I fight back.

There's no question in my mind—I'm going to make this difficult for them.

No matter that I'm naked. No matter that they've stolen my magic. No matter that Tarsal is groaning in pain next to me.

I punch the guard in front of me and then throw an elbow into the face of the guard behind me. Their chest armor means I have to be precise about where I aim. I roll to my feet and snarl at the two guards in front of me. I launch a series of kicks and punches at them, designed to make them pull back away from me.

The high-pitched whining is making me sick, and I wobble slightly as I'm about to make another kick. Something hits me from behind, and I fall forward into the dirt again. Multiple hands grab me, pulling my hands up behind my back and forcing my legs into a bend. Plastic bindings are zipped onto my hands and ankles, and I'm bound securely, just like that.

One of the men moves forward, as if to pick me up.

"Wait. I want to see her face. Look her in the eyes," Vincent says from behind me.

My heart is beating fast and I'm trembling, but I'm not going to let him see how scared I am. When he pulls my head up by my hair, I sneer at him. "Still getting other people to do your dirty work, Vincent?" I say.

He smiles, ever the gracious host. "Enjoy the last moments of your life as a dragon, my dear, because it's all about to come to a terrible, painful end."

I struggle against the hands that are keeping me secure, trying to ignore his self-satisfied expression.

Vincent continues as if he's having a lovely conversation: "That whining sound you hear—none of us can hear it by the way, but we can all see what it's doing to you—is a little something our ancestors invented to help destroy the dragons. It works wonderfully well, don't you think?" His arrogant expression is the last thing I see before he drops my hair and my head falls back down again. I seem to be having trouble holding it up while the whining noise infiltrates every corner of my body.

He pauses in front of Tarsal. "I really must thank you. You've brought me a much greater prize than I could ever have expected. A male dragon, still in his prime."

I glance over at Tarsal. He hasn't even fought them. They're tying him up just as roughly as they did me, but he's sitting with his head hanging, his long hair covering his face.

Come on, Tarsal. This isn't over yet.

He glances over at me and shakes his head. His eyes are bleak with the expectation of death. And something more. Suspicion. Does he think I did this on purpose?

We fight until the last moment. The others will help us. We're not in this alone.

He looks down again and doesn't look at me as we're picked up and carried by multiple men, all dressed in protective gear.

I try to pay attention to where they're taking us, but I can't. My focus is shot, and all I can see is blurry figures walking alongside me and Tarsal. I feel bad about mixing Tarsal up in this. He was right; he would have been better off staying on his island and going back into hibernation. Maybe I should have just given him my mother's ring and let him go.

My mother's ring.

I finger the ring to make sure it's still there. The hard metal is cold against my skin and I let out a sigh of relief.

Hope flares inside my stomach. Maybe I can use the extra power in the ring to get us out of this.

It's not long before we're dumped on the ground in the middle of the same great hall where Vincent first introduced himself to me. A blanket is draped over my shoulders.

I glance over at Tarsal—he's not getting the same nice treatment. He's obviously seen as the greater threat.

Vincent walks over to Tarsal and pats his lowered head. "This one will power up the spell web for so much longer than I had been expecting."

I struggle for a moment; the temptation to attack, to break free is so strong, I'm sure I'm going to be able to do it.

"Don't bother," Vincent says without looking in my direction. "I've found a few useful tricks in the old Earth-bound books. No one has read them for a long time, not since the last dragons were supposed to have died. No need, right? But I went back through them. I found some forgotten texts that tell how the Earthbound of old defeated the dragons."

He wanders over to me. "As long as the machine is sending out that noise, it negates your strength. I found it buried deep in one of our dungeons. It's the original, you know. The actual one they used against the dragons in the final battle. The one where the last of the dragons"—he glances over at Tarsal—"bar the most cowardly, lost to the Earthbound."

There's a noise behind us and a guard comes through the door. Clothes are dumped at our feet.

"Undo their bindings," says Vincent, waving a hand at the clothes. "Please, dress yourself."

My plastic ties are cut, and I scramble to pull on the cotton trousers and shirt that Vincent has provided. My movements are awkward and off-balance; the whining makes me feel like I've got vertigo. Tarsal doesn't move as quickly as I do; he seems far more affected by the noise, but eventually we're both dressed.

"What now?" I ask, determined to stay in control, despite my spinning head.

"Bind them again," Vincent says to the guards behind us. My hands are grabbed roughly and held behind my back as they put new plastic ties around my wrists. My head is spinning so badly, I can't do a thing to stop them.

"I wasn't sure the machine would work, but look at you both." Vincent smiles and gestures to us. "It's almost too easy."

"What's it doing to us?" I ask, trying to keep him talking. The longer he talks, the more time there is for Carrick and Seth to find us.

"The machine emits a noise on a frequency that disrupts a dragon's magic. Does something to their spell web, suffocates their magic and their ability to find their dragon form. You become a puny human, sick and vomiting, lying naked on the ground."

"So that's how your ancestors killed the dragons? Not in great battles like the ones on your walls? By killing them as they lay on the ground, unable to move?" I can't help the sneer that spreads across my face. So much for the grand imagery of battles won through valor and honor on their walls.

"The dragons needed to be killed. It doesn't matter how it was done. They *saved* lives."

Beside me, Tarsal coughs and I see blood on his lips. He seems far more affected by the machine than I am.

"Not now, surely? There are only two of us. It's not like we can do any damage."

"I'm protecting the future. If I let you live, generations from now, when dragons are again fighting among themselves and causing destruction on Earth, my children's children will swear on my name.

"Even more than that, however, is the need to protect the spell web. It is weakening, and using your magic to power it up again is the only way to save it."

I shake my head. "Do you even know if that's true? Have you even tried anything else?"

"It's my duty to kill dragons and protect the spell web. When I can do both those things in one go, it means I'm fulfilling my duty to the world. There is no downside."

Footsteps sound behind me. "Sir, we have them."

"Excellent. Bring the dragons. We do this right now."

As hands grab my arms again, I glance around me. "Who do you have?"

"You didn't think I would be so naive as to assume that your little diversion was all there was to it?" says Vincent.

"I've been waiting for days for you and your friends to attempt this attack. Plenty of time to plan."

My eyes go wild for a moment, panic taking over my whole body. They have the others? We knew they'd be expecting us, but I'd hoped the arrogance that Vincent always displayed would make them overconfident. Instead it just made *me* overconfident.

My head hangs down like Tarsal's.

I've failed them all.

51

They drag us down into the bowels of the compound, through stone tunnels and down stairs until we reach a steel door with bars on a small window.

Vincent unlocks it and gestures to two of the guards behind us. "Get Walker and the others. I want them all to witness this."

I catch a glimpse of my father being led out of the room, followed by Carrick and Seth. All three look worse for wear, bruises and cuts the obvious leftovers from their capture.

Seth's eyes are glowing red, and he looks at me intently as if he's making sure I'm okay. I don't think what he sees reassures him at all. I wish I could reassure him, but I can't even manage to talk into his head, my head is so woozy.

We're dragged ahead of them along a dark corridor, until we come to an enormous pair of old oak doors, carved with intricate patterns.

Vincent steps forward, and with a reverent air, pushes open the doors. We're dragged inside, and the doors are shut with a deafening boom.

Inside is a cavernous room, lit entirely with the glowing-red grid lines of the spell web. I've never seen anything like it. This room is so full of power, it's got its own spell web covering.

At the far end of the room there's a large slowly spinning globe suspended in the air. Lights glow all over it, and it's lit up like a strange, round Christmas tree. I'm mesmerized by the immense power I can feel emanating from it. The desire to be closer to the sphere slows me down as we enter the room.

"Is that...?" I hesitate. "Is that the spell web?" My skin tingles. The whole room is lit up, but the globe is at the epicenter of it all.

"From here, we can see every single supernatural in the world," Vincent says proudly. "This is the center of the invocation that the original Earthbound used to create the spell web and defeat the dragons. From here it flows outward, covering the whole of the supernatural population. As you can see, there are dark patches on the spell web that no longer glow." Vincent gestures toward the sphere, and I see what he's talking about. Darkened pieces in the web, like little patches of decay.

I don't know what to say, I can only stare. I don't think Vincent is seeing the same thing as me. The small dark patches are far outweighed by the vast areas of sparkling light that skitter across the surface, creating waves of power in a kaleidoscope of colors.

The spell web globe is more than I was expecting; I just want to put my hand on it, perhaps absorb a little of the shimmering magic flowing over its surface. The fascination I'm experiencing feels like an amplified version of my connection to the rest of the spell web.

He turns back to me. "But now I'm going to use it to

capture your dragon magic and make it strong again."

The globe is spinning gently on its axis, the glow of thousands of supernaturals lighting up the room. The ring on my finger heats up, and I curl my hands into fists. I don't think Vincent understands just how powerful the magic in this room is.

At the back of the chamber, away from the globe, Amos, Liling, and the Director are waiting for us. Down one side of the room are other strange mechanical devices and a long table with leather straps on it.

"It's amazing how many people are willing to watch the death of a dragon or two," Vincent says softly near my ear.

"You're okay with this, all of you?" I say, looking at Amos and Liling.

Amos glowers; he's angry with me. It must have been like salt on a wound when I escaped with Carrick. He was probably blamed for it by his over-zealous father. But Liling looks pale, like she's here because she has to be, not because she wants to be.

The guards lead my father and Carrick over to the other side of the room and make them sit on the wooden bench seats waiting there. As he's led past me, Seth tries to pull his arms free from the two guards holding him, his eyes fierce. One of the guards pushes his arm up his back until he bends forward. The other knees him in the stomach. Seth gasps out a breath and stops struggling.

They drag him over to sit next to Carrick and my father. I can only watch helplessly, my own guards keeping me close. Their spell webs glow brightly, Seth's most of all. It seems like everyone's power is amped up from being this close to the center of the spell web.

There are more armed guards stationed along the wall, which makes me think Vincent isn't quite as confident as he's pretending to be. The fact that they don't seem to have found Si and his protectors gives me hope as well.

I gaze around the room trying to assess everyone based on their spell web—

Sudden elation fills my chest. The spell web. I can see it in this room. Somehow their machine doesn't work down here.

It's not over, Tarsal. We can get out of this.

Can't you just give up? This is it. We're done.

No. I won't let Vincent win. He wants our power for himself, despite his high talk of protecting people.

You can't win. We're powerless down here.

Do you hear the whine anymore?

He lifts his head.

It's stopped. They can't hear it, so they've no way of knowing if it's still working. I pause, listening. An idea occurs to me. *Perhaps the others have turned it off?*

Tarsal nods slightly. *I can move again.*

So can I. But we need the right moment.

Tarsal blinks and looks over at me.

"Liling, how does it feel to know they would be doing the same thing to you if you'd turned out to be the dragon?" I say loudly. "The Director is buddies with Vincent. Do you think he would have saved you?" I watch her face and see her trying not to be affected by what I'm saying. But it's the truth. She would have been right where I am if she'd been the dragon.

"It's a good cause," she whispers. The Director glances down at her, frowning.

"But it's not a good cause," I say, keeping my eyes on her face. "This is just about Vincent trying to grab power. He isn't really trying to save the spell web."

The Director puts a hand on Liling's shoulder. "Don't listen to her. She's a liar."

Liling stands up, brushing his hand away from her shoulder. "But what would have happened if I *had* been the dragon? Would you have really given me up to Vincent? To certain death?"

She's obviously expecting more from the Director than he's going to give. I can see it in his eyes, although he tries to reassure her. "Of course not. You're much more valuable than her."

Liling frowns. "Why? What makes me better than Mei?"

"She's... She's not..." The Director can't find the words that will convince her.

I struggle against my bindings, to show her how vulnerable I am. "I don't toe the party line. I'm not going to let them do something horrific to me, just because they want to," I say. I can feel the bindings loosening, but I pretend to give up in frustration.

"You have no say in the matter, I'm afraid," says Vincent from across the room, where he's setting up the table with leather straps across it.

Liling takes a step forward. "This isn't right. You can't just kill them like this."

Vincent gestures with his head to Liling, and two guards immediately step up to her, holding her arms.

"As I said, you have no say in the matter, my dear. None of you do. This is going to happen, and there's nothing you can do to stop it."

Without the whining noise in my head, I can look along the spell web, trying to find a way to use it against Vincent. The bright glowing orb at the front of the room is moving and shuddering, the grid dancing across the surface.I'm not sure how the power works in this room. I don't know if I can manipulate it the way I always have.

If I make a move and it doesn't work, we'll have lost our advantage. I have to be slow and careful. We'll only get one chance.

"Right, let's get started," says Vincent. "I think I'm going to practice on Mei, just to be sure."

52

Two guards grab my arms.

This is it, I have to make a move. I surge up, breaking the last of the bonds around my hands.

Pulling power from my mother's ring, I force energy out along the spell web, knocking out the two guards and breaking the bonds around my legs. Beside me, Tarsal is also fighting the guards who held us captive only moments before.

We're the only ones who were tied up; they must have thought they could handle the others. But as soon as Tarsal and I start fighting, my father, Seth, and Carrick surge to their feet and enter the fray.

The room is too small to transform into a dragon, so we have to fight in our human form. I can see that it's hampering Tarsal, but he fights like a madman, throwing swinging punches at the guards who are trying to subdue him. He's big enough that it's intimidating, however he does it.

On the other hand, I look small and innocuous. If I'd ever gone to high school, I might have been voted least likely to intimidate in my yearbook. But Jeff taught me how to use that to my advantage.

Two guards approach me warily, looking at the unconscious men already surrounding me. My super sensitive hearing picks up someone trying to ambush me from behind, and I throw out a powerful back kick into their stomach. I hear an "oomph" as I make contact and push them backward.

The two guards in front of me have used my moment of distraction to surge forward, but I was prepared for them as well.

I kick out at the man on the left, aiming for his knee. It doesn't hit in the right place and doesn't buckle in the way I was hoping, but it slows him down, leaving me a second or two to block the other guard's attack and punch him in the neck. He grunts in pain, and tries back away.

But I grasp the arm I just blocked and pull him close, grabbing him around the neck.

It's a dangerous move, considering the difference in our sizes—he's much bigger than me—but I use the spell web to disable him and he collapses to the floor.

The spell web. It's the only way to stop Vincent. You're going to have to bring down the spell web.

Tarsal's voice in my head distracts me for a moment, and I glance over to where he's fighting three guards at once.

My immediate reaction is to shake my head. *No. I don't even know how I would do that.*

You have the power in your ability to manipulate it, and the ring on your finger.

What are you talking about?

A series of images push themselves into my head as Tarsal shows me what he means. He really has been thinking about this. The idea makes me tremble, even as the second guard comes in to attack. I grab his arm and twist it back behind him. When someone starts shooting, I turn and use him as a shield. He grunts as a bullet hits his chest, but his bulletproof armor keeps him alive.

I search the room full of grappling people for the shooter. No one else has taken out their guns, probably because, in a made scramble like this, there's no guarantee who'll be hit.

Amos is crouched in one corner, down behind the chairs. His head pokes out, and he points his gun again, this time aiming for Tarsal. I hear Vincent yelling at him from the other corner, but the words are indecipherable in the noise of the fight.

Tarsal! Watch out behind you. He's using a gun.

Tarsal turns, pulling a guard in front of him like I did. The bullets hit the man's chest and then his leg. The guard screams in agony, and Tarsal drops him and grabs another guard who's been circling him, looking for the right opening to attack.

Punching my guard in the face and then twisting him to the ground, I race toward Amos. He's trying to hit Tarsal, and it's hampering the big dragon's ability to fight.

We're going to lose if we're not careful. More guards are piling into the room, a sea of black armor-plated guards trying to control our uprising. Just as I reach Amos, he lets off one final shot, and I hear Tarsal grunt in pain a second later. I don't turn, I'm too focused on knocking Amos out so he can't shoot anyone.

Tarsal will be fine, he's a dragon.

Amos backs away from me, his fear written clearly on his face. It's so different to the soft looks he used to give me that I almost sneer at him. So much for his undying love. As soon as I was confirmed as a dragon, he could only see that.

I reach out to grab him, and he belatedly holds up his handgun, pointing it at my chest.

"I'll do it. I'll shoot," he says.

"I thought your father wanted us alive, so he could be the one to kill us and take our power?" I say.

Amos hesitates, glancing over to where his father is hiding in the far corner beside his machinery.

I use his hesitation to leap forward, knocking the gun to one side and punching him in the kidneys before elbowing him in the side of the face. I grab his gun and use it to throw one last hit to his head, knocking him out.

Turning, I leap back into the battle. There are more guards now, but Seth and Carrick are dispatching them with ease in one corner, and my father is fighting like a demon by the door, not letting anyone else come in.

I can't see Tarsal, but a guard races up to me in full attack mode, so I don't have time to do anything but concentrate on him. He lands a good hit to my side, and I grunt, but I'm back to full dragon strength now, and it hurts me less than it might have.

I block his next attack and land a punch to his side. I hear someone moaning nearby, but I can't see who it is. Punching out with the heel of my hand, I hit his nose, breaking it. Blood pours out his nostrils, and I slam my foot down on the side of his knee. I hear the sound of his kneecap popping out, and he falls to the floor, screaming.

I step around him and look for the next guard to take on. But instead of a guard, I see Tarsal lying on the ground, holding his stomach, blood pouring out of a bullet wound. I race over, kneeling down beside him. His eyes open as he feels me approach.

"Hold still. I'll try to heal it." I put my hands over the

wound, trying to stem the blood flow. I grab the spell web around him, and use it to push healing magic into him.

He just looks up at me, his golden eyes dimmed. "No, stop it. Too late. That machine...was too much. I'm...too weak. I'm not going...to survive. Take my powers...shut down the spell web."

I shake my head. "No. Absolutely not. There's no way I'm doing that. I can heal you." Despite everything he's done, tears well in my eyes. Tarsal voluntarily came with us on this mission. I wasn't sure I could trust him, but he's proven himself.

He's also one of only two dragons I've ever met—I don't want to lose him. Especially seeing as the other one is stark, raving mad.

Tarsal grabs my hand tightly. "You...must. The spell web... was choking us. Dragons aren't...meant to be bound. Don't let them...win again."

53

He's weakening right in front of my eyes. I concentrate on sending healing energy along the spell web into his body.

But instead of receiving my healing magic, he pushes his own magic back into me along the spell web. More than just his magic. His soul.

It fills me up, warm and golden, like a waterfall of fairy dust pulsing into my body. It doesn't hurt, but it feels strange, uncomfortable, like I've got too much inside me. It feels like it wants to burst out from inside me, but I don't know how or if I even want it to do that.

Tarsal gives me a grim half smile, and then slumps backward, his hand going limp in mine.

His eyes stare up into nothing, and it feels like I'm being broken in two. He's gone and his magic is now inside me.

Don't let the Earthbound win.

His last words bring me back to reality, and I glance around the room.

The fighting has slowed; there are no more guards

fighting in the room. My father is standing by the door, a gun pointed down the hallway.

Vincent is still crouched down in one corner next to his table; Liling, a sluggish-looking Amos, and the director are huddled in the other while Carrick stands menacingly over them.

Seth is advancing on Vincent.

"Be careful, Seth. He's got a few new tricks up his sleeves," I say.

Seth nods, but doesn't take his eyes off Vincent.

Vincent stands slowly, his hands behind his back. "You've changed, agent. There's something different about you now." He puts his head to one side. "Has your little dragon girlfriend been sharing her power with you?"

"Put your hands in the air," says Seth. He's holding a handgun in both hands and it's pointed directly at Vincent's chest.

"You won't win," Vincent says. "You're not strong enough. You don't deserve to win."

I surge to my feet and stride over to where Seth is standing. "This is over, right now."

Vincent shakes his head. "I'm afraid not, Mei. I haven't even started." He swings his arm around and aims a strange long-nosed weapon at my chest. Vincent pulls the trigger and a wide stream of clear liquid bursts from the nozzle. It looks like water, except white wisps of fog curl up from it.

Seth surges in front of me, pushing me backwards, and takes the hit from Vincent. The fluid strikes his body, and white gas seethes off his skin.

I'm so used to Seth being impervious because of his phoenix blood, that at first I don't see how it could possibly hurt him. But then he cries out, a strangled noise that I feel deep in my bones. His skin turns the color of stone and he's literally frozen in place.

His eyes dart to mine in panic, and I can see the strain in his face, his body shaking with effort as he tries to move, but can't. I reach forward, and some of the liquid falls onto the skin on my wrist. It burns like nothing I've ever experienced. Agony sears up my arms, and all I can do is howl.

Seth is trapped in burning ice.

His eyes glow with burning flames and his phoenix wings slowly extend from his back, air and fire fighting with whatever Vincent has done to him. But instead of being able to change fully into his phoenix form, cracks cut through his skin, fissures running across his body as though an earthquake is splitting him in pieces.

His body tips forward, unbalanced by the movement. I leap forward, my arms extended to catch him.

But I'm too slow.

Seth's frozen body hits the ground and shatters into a million pieces. The noise is so loud it hurts my ears. Frozen particles scatter across the floor.

I land heavily next to where he was standing. Little frozen shards pierce my skin, and tiny beads of blood emerge on my hands and arms.

Seth! I shout the word, but there's nothing, no mind to accept my frenzied plea.

Desperately, I gather the frozen pieces of flesh together, trying to find every one of the tiny shards. He needs to be able to reform. Isn't that what phoenixes do? I need to keep him together, so he won't die.

But there are too many pieces. They're too scattered. His whole body has shattered into so many tiny fragments that I can't imagine ever being able to find them all.

This can't be happening. Seth can't die.

My heart contracts, then it splinters apart just like Seth's body. A howl of pain cuts the air, and it's my voice.

"What did you do to him?" I scream at Vincent.

"You didn't think I'd let you come back without protection?" A drop of sweat runs down the side of Vincent's face. "That was liquid nitrogen. I'll do the same to you if you come any closer." His eyes dart from left to right as if he knows he's never going to escape me now.

I growl, and pull myself to my feet, brushing little pieces of Seth's body off me. I gag, and manage to keep the bile from rising too far up my throat. My legs shake, and I stagger. There are strange noises coming out my mouth; animal sounds of pain and loss.

Seth can't be gone. He *can't* be. But somehow he is.

The bile rises in my throat at the same time as power surges through me like a raging fire. "You're going to wish you were never born," I growl, the words half strangled as my dragon shape starts to form.

I'm going to kill him right here.

54

Vincent stands with his liquid nitrogen gun aimed at my chest.

My transformation into a dragon is probably the fastest I've ever managed, but I don't care. I'm focused on bringing death to the man who killed Seth. My body is scrunched up against the roof of the chamber, and I can hardly move. But I'm riding a tidal wave of rage and grief, and it doesn't matter. I breathe flames at Vincent, long and hot, straight at his chest.

Instead of burning to a crisp, he manages to slither under the table away from my flames. I'm too big to turn, so I swipe with my tail, trying to stun him.

"Mei! Stop that," Carrick yells from the end of the room. "You're going to hurt one of *us*."

Carrick's voice breaks through my rage-fueled reactions and helps me think. If I don't watch out, Vincent will escape. For Seth's sake, I'm not going to let that happen.

I transform back into human form and turn, only to find Vincent with his ice-thrower standing directly behind me. Instead of aiming it at me, he's got my father in his sights.

"I'll kill your father if you don't stand down."

Putting my hands out palms up, I try to think quickly. "I'm not moving," I grind out. If I could be sure I would kill him before he took a shot with his gun, I would flame him where he stands.

Instead I try to push out with the spell web, aiming to knock him out like I did to his guards, but it's like hitting a magical brick wall. He's got some kind of magic in place that's keeping him protected.

He smirks at me, obviously able to feel my attempt.

My eyes dart around the room. Tarsal's body is on the floor near me; Seth's remains are scattered over the unconscious forms of several guards. Carrick and my father are standing in a frozen tableau, waiting for me to act.

"You're going to stand to one side and let me leave," says Vincent, his eyes darting between my father and me. "I'm going to take your father with me as insurance. If you do anything stupid, your father will end up in tiny pieces, just like your friend."

Rage and grief bubble up from deep inside me, confusing my thoughts once again. But one thing is clear. "Take me instead of my father," I say. "I'm the one you want."

Vincent shakes his head. "I'll be back for you. But right now, I'm leaving this room in one piece and there's nothing you can do about it."

Smoke puffs out of my nostrils, the first time my dragon-self has ever been so present in my human form. I'm desperate to transform and blast a throatful of dragon fire at Vincent, burning him where he stands. But I hesitate, thinking of Seth's fractured body. I don't want that to happen to my father because I took too long to change.

"Okay, take my father," I say. "But I'm going to hunt you

down and get him back." I'm not planning to let Vincent leave this room, but he doesn't need to know that.

Vincent's face lights up in triumph, and he gestures for my father to move forward. Damien hesitates and glances at me. He's no more willing to be in Vincent's power than I am.

Out of the corner of my eye, I see the glowing spell web globe flickering against the light. I know one way to destroy everything Vincent has been working toward and upset the plans of the Earthbound.

Tarsal's magic flows through my body, alongside the power of the ring, and it teases me with his last words. He was certain that destroying the spell web was the only possible way to be free of Vincent and the Earthbound forever.

I hesitate, but the idea of getting even with Vincent is too strong, too compelling. I know I'm not thinking clearly, but I don't care. All I can see is Seth's eyes as he gazed at me, knowing he was about to die.

I want Vincent to die knowing his precious spell web is gone forever, and that it was his fault.

I push some of my magic out along the spell web grid, testing my strength. I hesitate, not sure whether I can actually go through with it. It's like I'm contemplating cutting off my arm. But then I see tiny shards of Seth's body scattered over the ground and I harden my resolve. Vincent has to be stopped. Without the spell web, he'll be nothing more than a pariah among his people.

Taking a deep breath, I send a surge of power along the grid directly toward the spinning globe at the front of the room. I push all my magic, plus everything I have from Tarsal, and my mother's ring. It's like an arrow, directly aimed at the center of the shimmering ball. The globe blazes brightly, like it's overloaded with magic. Its radiance becomes so vivid, I have to turn my gaze away.

"What are you doing? No!" Vincent yells.

But it's too late. The bulk of my magic has hit the globe, and it's melting, sparks flying into the air. Vincent drops his ice gun and runs to the globe, holding his hands up to the surface as if he can hold it all together. He cries out in pain and pulls back, blisters on his palms.

As I watch, the lines on the sphere start vanishing, and I can literally feel the connections dying right in front of me. Tears drip down my face, and I tremble as I watch its relentless deterioration, sparks flying and magic fizzing from the outside.

The sphere starts getting hotter and hotter at the center, until it suddenly explodes, shards of light and magic flying everywhere. I don't duck out of the way, and something hits me in the arm and side. Pain pushes itself up my body and I glance down. A glowing white shard of glass is stuck into the side of my stomach.

Even as I look down at the wound I find it hard to care. I'm too empty to go on.

I fall to my knees. It doesn't matter. Seth is gone. The spell web is gone. Tarsal is dead. Nothing will ever be the same again. I've done what I can; the world will have to figure itself out without me.

I'm on my side on the floor when I see Carrick punch Vincent in the face, knocking him off his feet. Blood splatters against the wall, and I watch it drip slowly downward. My father rushes to my side, reaching up to place a hand on the side of my face. The ring on my finger is burning my skin, and I moan in pain.

"It's going to be okay, Mei. Just hold on," says my father, holding my hand. "We'll find Si. He'll heal you."

Carrick comes to stand behind my father. He takes off his jacket and places it over my naked body. "We have to get out of here. I think the globe is making this whole place unstable. I'll carry her."

"I'm coming with you." Liling steps into view.

There are voices behind her, arguing, but Liling shakes her head.

"Tarsal. You have to bring Tarsal," I whisper, my voice hoarse.

Liling and my father glance at each other. "I don't think—"

"Do it," I say, my voice rising on a wave of power. There's no way we can take Seth with us, but I'm not leaving Tarsal here to be picked over by Vincent's minions.

My father goes over to the body of the Irish dragon, and Liling sighs and follows him.

As my vision starts to go, Carrick picks me up in his arms. "Don't you dare take this wound," I say to him.

"I—"

"Promise me," I say fiercely. "Too many people have died for me. I can't take any more."

"I promise," he whispers softly.

As I close my eyes, I picture Seth's face, telling me that he loves me.

55

W hen I come to again, I'm being jostled against Carrick's chest as he runs down a hallway.

He's doing something to me, keeping me calm and soothing my shot nerves. But he hasn't taken the wound, and for that I'm grateful.

I don't think he'd survive this injury.

I don't think *I'm* going to survive this injury. But I'm not sure I care.

At some point, we catch up with Si, who grabs my hand and pushes some of his magic into me. I feel a surge and then somehow lighter. But something is missing; I'm off balance. I look out along the spell web...and realize it's not there anymore.

Panic flares inside me, and I whimper. It's like a dark, musty blanket has been thrown over my body, blocking my usual senses. I don't know how to live without the spell web to help me understand the world. I stare with wide eyes at Si as he runs alongside Carrick.

"Use your own magic, Mei," Si says. "You have enough of your own to help the healing process."

I touch the ring on my finger and wonder how to use the magic for healing. Even as I think it, a swirling light comes out from the ring and along my body. It bathes me in a strange glow, and my head starts to clear.

"Do you think..." I try again, the words stuck in my throat. "Do you think Seth could have survived? Because he's a phoenix?"

I see Carrick share a loaded glance with Si. He takes a breath and the sound sighs against my body. "I don't think so, Mei. There were too many pieces. I'm sorry."

It's like I'm losing Seth all over again. My breath comes in small gasps and pain burns up my throat. I realize some small part of me was hoping that his ability to rise from the fire could save him.

We keep running, but don't meet anyone willing to take us on. My father is ahead of Carrick, running alongside Marco, who is helping him carry Tarsal's body. Liling is in front, leading us out of the compound. Si sticks close to my side, but doesn't offer any more healing.

We reach the outside wall and I open my eyes. "How are we going to get out? I can't fly."

"I have a pickup truck parked not far away," says Carrick.

When we get through the fence and into the truck, Carrick rummages around in the back and finds an old pair of cargo pants for me. They're miles too big, and I almost faint from the pain of pulling them on, but at least I have something covering me. Then Carrick lays me carefully down across his lap in the back seat. Si climbs in next to him, and the other protectors clamber onto the cargo bed with Tarsal's body.

Liling and my father are in the front.

My father turns his head and leans an arm over the seat, looking back at me. "How is she, Si?"

I stare down at the large glass shard still sticking into my skin.

Si looks down at it too. "I'm going to have to pull it out," he says quietly. "It's going to hurt."

I nod and squeeze my eyes shut.

Carrick moves underneath me as Si kneels next to my body. I feel a sharp tug and then nothing for a few seconds. Then a blinding pain bursts across my body and I scream.

The ring on my finger heats up to boiling point and magic glows across my body. I have the magic of two dragons inside me, and it's all focused on healing the gaping wound in my side.

It feels like hours before I can think again. I'm shivering and a cold sweat covers my body. The truck is moving as my father drives us away from the compound.

We haven't been driving for much more than an hour when we arrive at a town along the road.

I gaze blearily out the window at the street; it's strangely lit up for this time of night. People are wandering the footpaths in groups, and many of them have guns and other weapons.

"What's going on?" Liling asks from the front seat.

My father looks grimly around us, his eyes dark. "The spell web is down. The humans are realizing who they're sharing the world with, and they don't like it." A woman screams in the distance, and his hands clench on the wheel.

"So soon?" I whisper. "It only just came down."

"Supernaturals have been hiding in plain sight all this time, mingling with the humans. Between one blink of the eye and the next, they've been made visible." My father doesn't take his eyes off the road. The lights turn red at the intersection ahead of us, and he brings the pickup to a stop. "Fear is a powerful emotion."

"We have to help them," says Si, his eyes focused on a group of five men striding down the opposite side of the street toward us, rifles held at the ready.

A man turns a corner onto the street just ahead of the armed group. They break into a run, shouting and cursing. Gunshots ring out in the night and little puffs of dust swirl behind their victim as the shots go wide. He has the glowing green eyes and shaggy hair of a wolf shifter. In the back, Marco yells and gestures at him, and he turns. We watch as he sprints across the road toward our truck, his strong legs carrying him faster than any human. Marco and Liam lean forward with their arms outstretched, ready to drag him onto the truck bed. My father guns the engine, preparing to speed off.

A single shot rings out, and I jerk against Carrick. Almost immediately a bloodstain appears on the middle of the wolf's shirt. He looks down in surprise, stumbles, and then falls to the ground.

Blood pools around his body.

My father accelerates away from the intersection, tires squealing. His face is pale in the reflection of the street lamps. "We can't help anyone else. Not yet. We have to get Mei to safety." Behind us, the triumphant shouts of the men fill the night.

Silence fills the truck.

I watch the streetlights pass by out the window until we're back on the open road and I can see only stars and inky darkness.

A tear leaks out of the corner of my eye as I lie there, watching the sky and wishing I could turn back time.

You made it to the end...

What's going to happen next?

How is Mei going to survive without Seth? (And is he *really* dead?)

What will the humans do now they can see the supernaturals? (Hint: nothing good...)

Don't worry, Mei's journey isn't over yet... The third installment is waiting for you at your favorite retailer...

Read on for an excerpt...

The time has come to stand up and fight.

Fighting Dragon Excerpt

I follow Liling at a run, her longer strides eating up the ground faster than I can match.

We reach the war room just as the cameras flick to an image of Vincent walking up to a podium. Voiceovers announce excitedly that the Earthbound leader will be revealing a breakthrough in the ongoing war against the supernaturals.

There's a muttering through the room at the mention of a war—from our perspective, there doesn't need to be any conflict at all. But fear has done a great job of whipping the humans into a frenzy.

"Thank you all for coming today," says Vincent as soon as he's behind the podium. His face looks more haggard than I remember, and his hair has gone completely white. His blue eyes stare straight into the camera like he can see me directly, and I shiver.

I still have nightmares about my last confrontation with him, where he's looming over me like a scary cartoon figure, laughing maniacally, long spindly fingers stretched out in my direction.

If I'm honest, I'm terrified of him.

"I have an announcement that I believe the world's populations will be very pleased to hear." Vincent pauses for effect, and I can almost feel audiences the world over leaning forward.

"Since the destruction of the spell web by the notorious dragon-shifter criminal, Mei Walker, we have experienced a period of sustained violence and brutality like never before in our history."

"Only because the humans keep attacking us," I mutter, stung by his description of me.

"We have been studying the old texts from my Earth-bound ancestors and have rediscovered much that was lost to us."

I'm trembling now, remembering the machine that immobilized Tarsal. This is starting to sound like my worst nightmare.

I give myself a small pinch on my arm, just in case. It hurts, especially given the goose bumps that are still running along my skin. I rub my hands up and down over my arms, trying to warm myself up, but the chill is coming from somewhere deep inside me. My father moves into place just behind where I'm standing, although he doesn't actually put out a hand to touch me. It's comforting none-theless.

Onscreen, Vincent gives a small half smile. "Most importantly, we have discovered a way to reinstate the spell web that kept the supernaturals in line before it was so maliciously destroyed. We know how we can put these horrific creatures back under the powerful control that kept us safe for three hundred years."

He pauses, and the area in front of him flares with voices as the waiting journalists fire questions at him. He holds up his hands, indicating he has something more to say. His face is serious, but I can see him trying to hide his God-awful smirk from the world.

"Not only that, we know how to make it stronger. We have found a way to extract even more supernatural magic, so they will be weaker and never be able to harm humans again."

The room around me erupts, and many of the supernaturals who are part of my father's resistance stand and start gesticulating at the television. Most supers are just getting used to living without the spell web and have adjusted to the extra magic flowing around our bodies.

But Vincent isn't finished.

He pauses as the journalists again bombard him with questions, their voices raised like dogs baying to be fed. Then he gestures for silence. "I can take us back to the safety of the spell web, where we will control the supernatural abominations so they can't give in to their baser natures.

"I can save the world. But there's a problem we must work together to solve. We need a certain kind of magic. A type of power like no other."

Again, Vincent pauses for effect.

But I know what's coming. Vincent is nothing if not predictable. "He wants a dragon," I whisper. Beside me, Zane glances in my direction, his eyebrows lifted.

Up on the screen, Vincent's eyes again turn toward the television camera, and it's like he's staring straight at me. The urge to take a step backward is overwhelming, but I manage to hold my place. "I need a dragon. A live dragon, who will provide me with the magic we need to protect the world.

"I can save us all, but we must capture one of the beasts to do it."

END OF EXCERPT

If you enjoyed this excerpt, head to your favorite retailer to buy *Fighting Dragon*.

Hi! My name is Trudi Jaye, and I've got a secret.

A secret society, that is.

Especially designed for people like you who love reading my books, the Trudi Jaye Secret Society is a place filled with magic and laughter, and most of all... free stories.

Everyone who joins the society is given access to an ancient tome full of the stories, novellas, bonus epilogues, and deleted scenes from all the different Trudi Jaye series.

Called **The Shadow Archives,** you can access it by heading to my website and joining the secret society...

Join my Secret Society today... if you dare!

www.trudijayewrites.com/shadow-archives

Other Books by Trudi Jaye

Dragon Rising Series
Lost Dragon (Prequel Novella available via the Trudi Jaye
Secret Society)
Hidden Dragon
Searching Dragon
Fighting Dragon
Cursed Dragon
Warrior Dragon (coming soon)

Demon Hunter in Hiding Series
Dreams & Demons (Prequel Novella available via the Trudi
Jaye Secret Society)
Secrets & Demons
Agents & Demons
Magic & Demons
Dragons & Demons
Spells & Demons

Elemental Witch Series (With Tania Hutley)
The Trouble with Magic
The Problem with Witches
The Danger with Demons

Firecaller Series
Salt (Prequel Novella available via the Trudi Jaye Secret
Society)
Subtle Knife (Prequel Novella available via the Trudi Jaye
Secret Society)
Fire Mage
Royal Mage (coming soon)

Dark Carnival Series

The First Ever Wish (Prequel Novella available via the Trudi Jaye Secret Society)

If Magic Were Wishes

The Gift

Magic for Lost Souls (available via the Trudi Jaye Secret Society)

High Flyer

Hidden Magic

The Shadow Prophecy

Hi! I'm Trudi Jaye and I'm the author of this book.

I'm from New Zealand, where I currently live on a beautiful rural property surrounded by horses and cows (not mine!) with my lovely husband and my cheeky tween daughter.

I've been writing since I was a kid, and for ten years I worked as a magazine writer and editor, on topics ranging from hardware and electronics to holidays, recipes and university-level research projects.

Now I write novels full time.

I enjoy yoga, although I'm not very bendy, and karate, although I don't like the idea of hitting anyone.

Find out more about me by heading to www.trudijayewrites.com